P9-EEI-685

3 1833 02703 6216

FICTION
DENTON, JAMIE ANN.
THE SECRET CHILD

Enrollment Form

☐ *Yes!* I WANT TO BE A *Privileged Woman*.
Enclosed is one *PAGES & PRIVILEGES*™ Proof of
Purchase from any Harlequin or Silhouette book currently for
sale in stores (Proofs of Purchase are found on the back pages
of books) and the store cash register receipt. Please enroll me
in *PAGES & PRIVILEGES*™. Send my Welcome Kit and FREE
Gifts -- and activate my FREE benefits -- immediately.

More great gifts and benefits to come.

NAME (please print)

_____

ADDRESS   APT. NO

_____

CITY   STATE   ZIP/POSTAL CODE

PROOF OF PURCHASE ONLY

**NO CLUB!
NO COMMITMENT!**
*Just one purchase brings
you great Free Gifts and
Benefits!*

Please allow 6-8 weeks for delivery. Quantities are limited. We reserve the right to
substitute items. Enroll before October 31, 1995 and receive one full year of benefits.

Name of store where this book was purchased_____

Date of purchase_____

Type of store:

☐ Bookstore   ☐ Supermarket   ☐ Drugstore
☐ Dept. or discount store (e.g. K-Mart or Walmart)
☐ Other (specify)_____

Which Harlequin or Silhouette series do you usually read?

_____

Complete and mail with one Proof of Purchase and store receipt to:
U.S.: *PAGES & PRIVILEGES*™, P.O. Box 1960, Danbury, CT 06813-1960
Canada: *PAGES & PRIVILEGES*™, 49-6A The Donway West, P.O. 813,
North York, ON M3C 2E8

HS-PP6B

▼ DETACH HERE AND MAIL TODAY! ▼

Marni pulled into the driveway, relieved to be home

Jenna came bounding out of the house, the screen door banging behind her. The light from the porch cast a hazy yellow glow over the small veranda and spilled onto a fraction of the manicured lawn. A large German shepherd rounded the corner, trampling the dormant rose garden, and barked.

"Arlo, shush. It's only Mom," Jenna scolded the dog.

"Sorry I'm late," Marni said, stepping from the car. "It was one of those days." She still couldn't get over the fact that Rebecca had insisted she tell Cole about Jenna. The idea bordered on insanity. She put her arm around her daughter and they entered the house. As they headed toward the master bedroom, the phone rang, and Marni said, "Will you get that, sweetie? I don't want to talk to anyone tonight unless it's urgent."

Jenna darted past Marni into the bedroom and picked up the cordless phone. "Hello? Uh, she's not here right now. Can I take a message? Okay, and what's your name?" She paused. "Say that again?"

Jenna frowned, and a cold knot formed in the pit of Marni's stomach. Jenna's voice suddenly sounded miles away. "Cole Ballinger? *My father?*"

ABOUT THE AUTHOR

Until the day she rolled her first blank sheet of paper into her typewriter, Jamie Ann Denton had always imagined she'd go to law school. But by the end of that first page, she knew for certain that writing would be her chosen profession. Now she's a published romance novelist with her award-winning first book, *The Secret Child*.

Jamie Ann married her high school sweetheart nearly two decades ago, and together they have three teenage sons, who, she says, still "teeter on the edge of adorable from time to time." When she's not writing, she's reading or exploring North Dakota, where she and her family now make their home. Being a Southern California native, she truly enjoys the wide-open and untamed landscapes.

Jamie Ann Denton

THE SECRET CHILD

Harlequin Books

TORONTO • NEW YORK • LONDON
AMSTERDAM • PARIS • SYDNEY • HAMBURG
STOCKHOLM • ATHENS • TOKYO • MILAN
MADRID • WARSAW • BUDAPEST • AUCKLAND

ISBN 0-373-70663-4

THE SECRET CHILD

Copyright © 1995 by Jamie Ann Denton.

For Tony
For two decades of love and encouragement,
patience and understanding
and not having me committed when I
argue with my characters

and Janelle Denison
For having the wisdom to look inside
and the generosity to highlight
the positive
And for not paying attention in
history class

CHAPTER ONE

MARNI RODGERS TURNED to face the reporters. They were out in full force today. Bright lights from television cameras reflected off the heavy wood interior of the courtroom. The august forum had been transformed into a media circus. Dozens of reporters thrust microphones into her face as cameras clicked all around her, and Marni knew her photo would be splashed across the pages of newspapers throughout the nation. Her conviction of the serial killer had seen to that.

Grabbing her dilapidated briefcase from the table, she moved forward, trying to ignore the shouted questions.

"Ms. Rodgers, will the state be seeking the death penalty?"

"Yes, we will."

"Marni, will the D.A. be assigning you to 'death row' now?"

She recognized the voice of Mack Henley, a field reporter from the *Times,* and grinned, dropping her professional demeanor for a split second. Death row was a term the local press gave to A.D.A.s who routinely prosecuted special-circumstance cases. "You'll have to ask District Attorney Dorlan, Mack."

"What about a political career, Marni?"

She almost laughed. These guys were amazing. One high-profile case and the media had her running for pub-

lic office. She recognized the reporter from one of the local news shows. "No comment."

April Burnell stepped to the front of the crowd and
thrust a microphone in front of her. "How does it feel,
Ms. Rodgers?"

Marni had dealt with April before and didn't particularly like her style. The woman had the tact of a bulldozer. "How does what feel, Ms. Burnell?" Marni asked,
unable to keep the sarcasm out of her voice.

"To be responsible for sending James Kendell to his
death?"

Marni took a deep breath before answering. "The penalty phase of the trial doesn't start for another two
weeks."

"But aren't you seeking the death penalty?"

"I'm doing my job, Ms. Burnell. The job *you,* a tax-
payer, are paying me to perform. Tell me, how do you feel
when you do your job well?" Marni shouldered her way
past April and reached for the door.

The family of one of the victims came into the hall-
way, and the surge of reporters changed course, heading
toward their new target like vultures intent on the remains of a two-day-old carcass. Relieved, Marni veered
away from the throng and headed toward the elevators.
Her escape went unnoticed.

The elevator doors opened on the ground floor and
Marni headed toward the exit. She pushed through the
glass doors of the courthouse into the bright, unseason-
ably warm January sunshine, her steps hurried. As she
neared the concrete steps, she glanced at her watch.
Jenna, her twelve-year-old daughter, would be home from
school in a few minutes. Marni couldn't wait to tell her the
case was finally over. She smiled for the second time since

hearing the jury had finally reached a verdict, a decision that had taken three weeks.

Marni stepped forward and bumped into what she immediately thought of as a brick wall in an Armani suit. Her attaché slipped from her fingers and the faulty latch clicked open. Papers tumbled out and skittered to the ground.

"I'm sorry," she said, bending to pick up the papers before they scattered away in the light breeze. "I wasn't paying attention."

The brick wall didn't say anything, but bent over to help. After the mess had been picked up, he extended his hand to give her the forms.

Marni shoved them back into the briefcase. The scent of his cologne reached her nostrils. Polo. She inhaled deeply, then lifted her gaze to get a look at the guy who smelled so good. Her mouth fell open in shock.

Cole Ballinger.

Her Cole.

Jenna's father. *Oh, God!*

Recognition and then surprise flickered in his polished jade eyes. His lips curved into a disarming smile. "Marni. It's been a long time." His voice was velvet-edged and strong.

Marni didn't know what to say. Yes, it had been a long time. Thirteen years, and if he wanted to get technical about the whole thing, she'd give him weeks and days, too. Oh, yes, a long time indeed since she'd accepted Cole's father's offer and left Elk Falls. Too long, since Cole had married someone else while Marni carried his child. A child he knew nothing about.

Time had been good to him. His neatly trimmed sable hair had no signs of gray. More devastatingly handsome than she remembered, he showed new strength and maturity. But, she reminded herself, he'd only been twenty then, tall and gangly. He'd filled out quite nicely if the way his broad shoulders fit the Armani suit was any indication.

His name echoed through her mind. "Cole," she whispered as he took her elbow and helped her to her feet. In an instant, Marni was eighteen again. Memories of the summer they'd shared in Kansas before she left for California assaulted her suddenly fragile composure.

"What brings you to Los Angeles?" She struggled to maintain an even, conciliatory tone. Dear God, he hadn't found out about Jenna, had he?

An odd expression crossed Cole's features, one Marni couldn't define. "Ballinger Electronics is being sued," he told her.

A slight surge of relief shot through her. She nodded, unsure what to say to him. A thrum of tension filled the air. Her composure slipped again under his watchful eyes, and she shifted her feet. "Are you in town long?" she asked tensely.

An older gentleman stepped forward to stand next to Cole and glanced pointedly at his watch.

"Gordon Bentley, this is Marni Rodgers. We're old friends," Cole said casually. Too casually.

We were more than old friends, she wanted to say, but kept silent. No sense dredging up the past. No good would come of it.

"Gordon's my attorney," he told her.

Marni extended her hand to the lawyer. "Pleased to meet you." She hoped neither of them noticed the shakiness of her voice.

She welcomed the man's intrusion and shook his hand, thankful for the reprieve. Cole had left a burning imprint on her soul and one look at him, one simple touch, was

enough to scorch her still. How could he be so dangerous
to her sanity and her heart after all these years? He's *not*,
she told herself. *It's only the shock of seeing him again.*

Gordon interrupted her thoughts. "I'll meet you inside, Cole. Miss Rodgers, it was a pleasure." Marni nodded and watched him disappear into the courthouse. She
hadn't even noticed the man's initial approach. But Cole
had always had that affect on her. His nearness could
cause her to forget the world existed. But not any longer.
Not after the way he'd hurt her when he married Elizabeth Wakefield. Regardless of Marni's bargain with the
devil, she knew she'd been young and foolish and wrong.
Horribly wrong. Thirteen years of loneliness had taught
her just how mistaken she'd been in accepting Carson
Ballinger's offer.

"I should be going." Her senses were under siege. She
had to get away from him. He'd given her a shock and she
needed time to recover.

Cole glanced at his watch. She couldn't help noticing
how large his hands were. Manicured, yet strong. "Look,
I've got to get inside. Would you meet me for a drink
later?"

Marni forced herself to settle down. The blood pounding in her ears deafened her. "It's not a good idea."

"One drink, Marni. Surely you can fit an *old friend*
into your busy schedule?" He studied her with an intensity she found unnerving.

"Cole, really, I—" Her thoughts trailed off when he
gave her that lopsided grin she'd always loved so much.
The light winter breeze ruffled his dark hair, and for a
split instant they were kids again. Young, innocent and
free of Carson's influence.

"One drink." He was obviously determined. Cole could
be relentless when he set his mind on something.

"I'm sorry." Marni moved to step around him, anxious to be away before she gave in to him.

"Marni." He sounded almost desperate. When he laid a hand on her arm to prevent her escape, a twinge of excitement raced through her. What was wrong with her? She hadn't seen Cole in years. It was ridiculous to react this way.

Marni chewed her lower lip. If she had that drink, maybe she could find out what he knew about Jenna, if anything. Besides, what harm could one drink with Cole Ballinger do? She was a grown woman, not a kid with stars in her eyes and dreams of happily ever after. The Ballinger wealth couldn't hurt her anymore. Cole was no longer a part of her life. Seriously doubting her powers of reason, she agreed. "Okay. One drink. Muldoon's at five-thirty. It's on the corner of Sixth and Spring."

Before she could change her mind, she pulled away from him and ran down the concrete steps of the courthouse. She didn't stop until she reached her car. Unlocking the door, she slipped in behind the wheel of the Honda Prelude and tossed her attaché on the passenger seat. The lock unhitched and Marni glared at the old briefcase. "I'm buying a new one. Tomorrow."

WITH COLE OCCUPYING her thoughts, Marni drove across town to her office. He hadn't told her how long he'd be in town. Was he only here as a witness or would he be attending the trial on a daily basis? She'd have to find out which judge was hearing his case. Marni had always made a point of having a good rapport with all the judges' clerks, and now it was about to pay off. She could easily ask for the estimated length of the trial without raising suspicion. With as much time as she spent at the courts, she supposed running into Cole would be inevitable, but the thought of seeing him on a daily basis was almost more than she could bear.

She guided the car into her assigned parking slot and killed the engine. Leaning back in the seat, she closed her eyes and rubbed the throbbing ache in her temples. Why had she agreed to meet him for a drink? *Stupid, Marni. Real stupid.* She'd have to call Jenna and let her know she'd be late.

The thought of Jenna got her moving. She collected her things, making certain the latch to her briefcase was secured.

A group of attorneys and secretaries stood waiting in the lobby when she entered the dingy county offices. A resounding cheer went up when she closed the door behind her. Marni couldn't help but laugh. She'd worked hard to win the Kendell case, and now, because of her, one less killer roamed the streets of Los Angeles. And no matter how corny *that* sounded, the thrill of prosecuting such an important case was heady. Still, she'd better keep her feet on the ground. There were other dangers in her life now.

Her secretary, Peg, stood to the side of the group, holding a dozen latex helium balloons secured with colorful curly ribbons. Someone popped open a bottle of champagne and shoved a glass in her hand. Before Marni realized it, she was regaling her colleagues with the finer points of the murder trial.

Her boss, Walter Dorlan, approached. "You're the lead story on tonight's news."

Marni smiled. "Mack Henley wants to know if I'm being assigned to death row."

Walter may have been an active prosecutor at one time, but now politics were his mainstay. His term as D.A. would be over in another year, and rumors were already circulating that he was seeking the governor's office. Walter grinned, his pale blue eyes twinkling. "Sure, if the butterflies you get waiting for the juries to come in don't kill you first."

Marni's teasing tone evaporated. "Walter, are you serious?"

The D.A. took a sip of champagne, then nodded. "I've been thinking about it. No one's taken over on a permanent basis since Jackson left. You could handle the responsibility for a while."

"I don't know what to say." And she didn't. Despite her euphoria over winning the case, did she *really* want to send people to their deaths, no matter what she'd told April Burnell? She pushed the unwanted thought aside.

"Don't say anything, Marni. Just do your job."

"Rodgers!" someone called. "Telephone."

Marni excused herself from Walter and the group. They didn't need her to continue the celebration. Drinking and raising hell were two things attorneys did extremely well.

Marni took the call in her office. She plopped down in the squeaky leather chair and cradled the receiver between her ear and shoulder. "Marni Rodgers," she said absently as she looked at the stack of mail on her desk. Her secretary sorted her mail into separate folders according to importance. Even junk mail had its own file.

"Mom?"

"Jenna. Hi, sweetie. What's up?" Marni opened the folder for junk mail and emptied the contents in the trash bin under her desk.

"I saw you on the news!" Jenna's exuberance vibrated through the telephone.

Marni could picture Jenna standing in their cozy kitchen, her jade green eyes sparkling with excitement. Her thick, waist-length sable hair, so like her father's, would be pulled back into a ponytail. Marni would kill for hair like Jenna's. Her own blond hair hung in unruly curls just past her shoulders. She usually kept it pulled away from her face in a tight French braid.

"Everyone's gonna be talking about you tomorrow. My mother the celebrity. I'll be famous."

Marni laughed. "No, Jenna, I'm not a celebrity and I doubt you'll be famous just because I was on the five o'clock news."

"Well, Denise Lambert already called and her mom said you're a famous lawyer now."

Marni rolled her eyes and looked at her watch. She was supposed to meet Cole in fifteen minutes. "I'm gonna be a little late. I have a . . . meeting. Still ready for pizza?"

Jenna's laughter made Marni smile. "Pizza? Mom, you deserve a night on the town for what you did today. Do you have a date?"

Marni opened the folder entitled For Your Signature and ignored the hopeful note in Jenna's voice. "No, I don't have a date."

"You need a man, Mom."

Marni couldn't believe her ears. "Jenna!"

"Denise's mom thinks you do. She says you work too hard and if you don't get out more, you'll—"

"Jenna, that's enough."

Jenna sighed heavily, her exasperation registering clearly.

"You wanna order in or go out for pizza?" asked Marni, anxious to steer the topic away from her lack of male companionship. She'd had offers, plenty of them, but the truth was, she just wasn't interested. She'd convinced herself her career and Jenna were all that mattered. Especially since she had paid such a high price for both.

Marni could practically feel her daughter's shrug. "Doesn't matter."

"Why don't we decide when I get home? Around seven, okay?" She signed her name to a letter without proofreading it. She didn't need to; Peg's efficiency spoke for itself.

"Sure, Mom. Oh, the phone's beeping, I've got another call coming in. It's probably Denise again."

"Sweetie?" Marni said before her daughter could hang up on her. "I love you."

"Yeah, me, too, Mom. I'll see ya tonight."

An indefinable fear settled over Marni. If she told Jenna her father was in town, she would insist on seeing him. When Jenna had asked the identity of her father, Marni had told her daughter as much as her young mind could understand at the time. She had been careful not to color her daughter's feelings in any way.

What had happened between Cole and Marni had been special, at least on her part. How she'd loved Cole, and she'd thought he'd returned that love. But Marni hadn't been gone two months when Cole married Elizabeth Wakefield, a woman of his own social class. Even though Marni had ended their relationship without explanation, she still experienced an unreasonable stab of jealousy every time she thought of Cole with Elizabeth.

Marni replaced the receiver, finished signing the rest of the correspondence, then put the remaining folders in her briefcase. "I'm really gonna get a new one tomorrow," she promised herself.

She flicked off the light and closed the door to her office, then dropped the folder with the signed correspondence on Peg's desk. She picked up her messages, stuffed them into her jacket pocket and headed toward the door.

The crowd had thinned somewhat, and Marni escaped without too much trouble.

Entering the parking garage with her keys in hand, Marni headed for her car. She opened the door and slipped inside.

Muldoon's.

Cole.

The drive would take her about twenty minutes in downtown traffic. Glancing at her watch, Marni realized she was already late. Maybe if she was lucky, he'd have already left and she'd never have to see him again. She tossed the briefcase onto the passenger seat, and the latch flipped open again. The old leather case had been a gift from her mother, and if she hadn't been so attached to it, she never would have run into Cole.

Marni sighed, glaring at the briefcase. She had an uneasy feeling that fate had just intervened.

FATE HAD DEFINITELY smiled on Cole Ballinger today. He arrived at Muldoon's thirty minutes before he was supposed to meet Marni and secured a table in the back of the downtown pub. Happy hour would be in full swing before long, and he wanted to ensure they had a relatively quiet place to talk.

The day he arrived in Los Angeles, he'd seen Marni on the nightly news. He couldn't believe his eyes. Marni—*his* Marni—was prosecuting an extremely high-profile serial killer. He'd immediately gotten the number to the D.A.'s office from the information operator. But every time he picked up the phone to call he replaced the receiver before he could punch in her number. Too much time had passed. After all these years, she certainly had to have a life of her own—a point she'd made perfectly clear when she'd told him she never wanted to see him again. No explanation, no justification. Simply goodbye. The next day she'd been gone, almost as if she'd never existed in the first place.

She was even more beautiful than he remembered. She'd matured, naturally, and although the image she projected in her navy blue suit spoke of a fashionable professional, her conservative attire could not completely hide her sensuality. Yet cool was the word that came to Cole's mind when he thought about her. She had a don't-touch-me look, and he wondered why. Had someone hurt her? What had happened to change the soft, warm young woman he'd loved? Hell, he still wanted to know why she'd left him. He'd played their parting scene over and over in his mind and still couldn't come up with a plausible reason for her actions.

Cole ordered a light beer and nursed it while he waited. He couldn't help wondering if she would show up or not. She'd been anxious to get away from him. He thought he'd seen fear in her eyes, and again he questioned her reasons. Why would she fear him? Cole decided there was only one way to find out.

Nearly an hour later, he spotted her at the front entrance. He stood, impatient for her to see him. He waved, caught her attention and watched her cross the crowded pub with the natural grace of a dancer. There was an easy confidence about her Cole didn't remember from their youth. In the dim light of the bar, she appeared ethereal. He caught himself wishing she'd worn her hair down, bouncing around her face. Did it still shimmer like a wheat field swaying in a gentle breeze? Her delicate features hinted at a patrician background. No one would suspect she was a fatherless girl from a rundown trailer park on the wrong side of town.

"You're late," he told her tersely, hiding his relief that she'd really come.

She cast him a quick, nervous glance, nodded, then scooted into the booth. The skirt of her navy blue suit hitched up, showing him a goodly portion of her legs. Cole admired the long shapely limbs for a moment before signaling for the waitress. Sliding into the booth opposite her, he asked, "What'll you have?"

She kept her gaze averted from his, and he wondered if she was truly afraid, after all. The notion was ridiculous.

"Whatever you're having is fine."

"Beer?" When she nodded, he chuckled. "A woman after my own heart." The waitress glanced his way and Cole motioned for two beers.

"I heard your name on the radio while driving here. Congratulations." Pride had surged through him when the newscaster reported the conviction of James Kendell and the part Marni played in bringing him to justice.

She shrugged her slim shoulders as if the event was a common occurrence. "I'm sure I'm on the six o'clock news right now, too." Her voice held a detachment he found unnerving. She used to look at him with such adoration and he silently berated himself for wanting to see that look in her eyes again. Marni had always been bubbly, a happy-go-lucky type. Time had changed her, hardened her. He wondered if it was because of her job.

Cole dropped a bill on the table when the waitress delivered two bottles of beer and a bowl of warmed peanuts, along with a glass for Marni. "Did you get a conviction on all the charges against this guy?" He hoped to bring her out of wherever she was hiding. Maybe talking about her victory today would do the trick.

She glanced his way. Her eyes darted back and forth, refusing to hold his gaze for longer than a second or two.

"I was able to get him for the kidnapping and murder for five of the six victims."

Cole leaned back into the dark green Naugahyde. "Why only five?"

She looked at him and he saw the intelligence in her eyes. The coffee-colored orbs were sharp and assessing, as if she sized up everything and everyone within seconds. A habit, he assumed, she'd developed since becoming an attorney.

"The fourth victim may have been a copycat and we had no hard evidence." She absently fingered the bowl of peanuts. "I should still be able to convince the jury to go for the death penalty."

"Good. Kendell is a real scumbag." Taking a sip of beer, he watched her transformation. Within minutes, she was talking animatedly, gesturing to make her points. Still, a detachment in her demeanor irritated him. He'd seen that look before, the day she told him to get lost.

She laughed lightly at one of his remarks. Cole liked the soft, melodious tones drifting over him.

"Doesn't it get to you, though?" he asked, becoming serious again. "You see the very worst side of humanity every day." He didn't care if they were discussing the exchange rate in China—at least she was talking to him.

She sighed. "You get used to it." Marni took a sip of beer, then glanced away. She stared at the cheap, framed print behind him as if it were the most fascinating work of art she'd ever seen. "So, are you in town long?"

"I moved here about six months ago," he answered lazily, and waited for her reaction.

She looked back at him abruptly. "Why?"

Cole frowned at the alarm in her gaze. The yellow flecks in her eyes turned to gold, signaling the intensity of her reaction. "I've taken over the software division of Ballinger Electronics."

She took a deep breath as if to calm herself. "Oh. I read about the lawsuit. You're being sued for copyright infringement, aren't you?"

Cole nodded, disappointed she preferred to keep their conversation on an impersonal level. "An overzealous employee duplicated a program and sold it as ours."

Marni's brow creased. "Why don't you just settle?"

Cole lifted the beer bottle in his hand and took a quick drink before answering. "We've tried, but the guy who developed the program wants blood."

A hint of a smile touched her lips. "You're fighting a losing battle, Cole. Juries don't take too kindly to the big guys stealing from the little guys."

"We haven't gone to trial. We only arbitrated today," he told her. "I didn't ask you here to talk law, Marni. How have you been?"

The smile disappeared, and Cole could almost see the protective barrier she drew around herself again. "Fine. I've got a good job, a nice little house by the beach. I couldn't be happier."

That wasn't what he wanted to know. "Married?"

"No." She answered too quickly, as if the subject was off limits. Cole let it drop, for the time being.

He brought the conversation back to business. When she talked about her work, she didn't seem so damned nervous. "You been with the D.A.'s office long?"

"Six years." She lifted the glass of beer to her mouth.

Cole watched with interest as her lips settled on the rim. The first stirring of desire pulsed through him, settling in his belly. He attempted to douse the provocative thoughts with another shot of beer and failed.

Marni regarded Cole carefully. He'd acquired a polished veneer over the years. Even from across the table he looked powerful. And the man had a definite monopoly on virility, whether he realized it or not. Cole was pure male, and he affected her more than she cared to admit.

An uncomfortable silence stretched between them, and Marni didn't know how to break it. She was a successful lawyer, fast on her feet and able to shift tactics without missing a beat. Speaking to juries and judges nearly every day, she'd rarely been at a loss for words, but she stared mutely as Cole lifted his beer bottle to his lips. She averted her eyes and concentrated on the beer label, willing the memories of Cole to go away. Absently she fingered the label and began to peel it off the amber bottle.

"How's your mother?" he asked her.

She sighed. "We—I lost my mother a few years ago."

Cole caught her slip and could only wonder about it. Who was *us?* She'd said she wasn't married. Could it be an *ex*-husband?

"What about your family?" she returned politely.

Cole shrugged. "My sister married Don Turner and claims to be miserable because he works all the time. Daily shopping consoles her. She has two great kids, though."

A small smile touched her lips. "Janelle has kids?"

"I know. Janelle hated kids until she had her own. Two adorable little girls."

"And your parents?"

Cole noticed the barely laced sarcasm in her voice. "Mom and Dad will never change. Dad's talking about retirement now, and Mom complains about the lack of male grandchildren to carry on the Ballinger name." He saw an odd light flicker briefly in Marni's eyes before she glanced at her watch, and he wondered if she had a date. A surge of jealousy he didn't understand vibrated through him. He spoke without thinking. "I've missed you, Marni."

"How's your wife, Cole?" Her voice was hard, cold.

He creased his brow in surprise. "How did you know about Elizabeth?"

The hardness in her voice was reflected in her eyes. "Your father told me. I wasn't gone more than two months before you were on your honeymoon."

His irritation returned at her accusatory tone. "Hey, you dumped me, remember? Besides, Elizabeth was a mistake."

Her short bark of laughter held no humor. "Was it?"

"Marni, it's a long story—"

"And I'm sorry, but I don't have time to listen to it now. I have to be somewhere." The coldness of her voice clawed at his heart with icy fingers.

Marni attempted to slide from the booth, but Cole reached out to stop her. His hand settled over hers. Her soft, smooth skin evoked memories of the night they'd made love by the lake. Candlelight from the glass globe on the table flickered, and for a moment Cole thought of Marni's skin shimmering in the moonlit night. His eyes held hers. "Don't go, Marni."

"I have to." She spoke calmly, without emotion, but the heat burning in her eyes told him she was just as affected as he was by the simple touch.

"Elizabeth tricked me into marriage," he said, unsure why he felt compelled to explain. He owed her nothing. "She said she was pregnant and then conveniently 'lost' the baby a few weeks after the wedding."

"Elizabeth was pregnant?" Her voice was a choked whisper. "You slept with her while we were together?"

Cole watched as the blood drained from her face. Pain, fierce and tangible, flared in her gaze. A heaviness settled in his chest when she looked away.

"No," he said. "Not then." Guilt he didn't understand washed over him. He'd gotten drunk in an attempt to drown his anger when Marni had broken up with him with no explanation. "Why did you give me the brushoff?" he asked, turning the tables.

"How is Elizabeth?" she countered.

Cole didn't miss the censure in her voice, or the fact that once again she'd evaded his question. "Elizabeth and I divorced more than ten years ago. Last I heard, she was living in Europe."

She lifted her gaze to his, anguish evident in her deep brown eyes. He wished he was privy to her thoughts. God only knew what went on in Marni Rodgers's mind.

"I have to go," she said hastily. "I have an early day in court tomorrow."

"How about dinner? You need to eat." Cole was reluctant to let her get away from him. He told himself it was because he wanted the past resolved, not because he wanted to delay her departure.

"I'm not hungry," she said. She truly doubted she'd be able to eat a thing after the blow Cole had just dealt her. He'd married Elizabeth because she *said* she was pregnant. Marni ached with the same inner pain she'd experienced when she'd first learned he'd married Elizabeth. When had Cole made love to Elizabeth? How long had she been in California before he turned to someone else? A week? Ten days? Not much longer if he'd married Elizabeth within two months of her departure from Kansas.

"Come on, Marni. I haven't seen you in nearly thirteen years and you can't even spare a few hours to have dinner with me?" His voice was soft and coaxing. Reaching across the table, he covered her small hand with his large one.

Marni pulled her hand free. "It won't work, Cole."

"I'm not asking you for a lifetime, Marni. Only dinner."

"I can't," she said firmly. Why couldn't he just leave her alone?

He threw up his hands. "Okay, okay, don't get upset."

Marni's sigh of relief was short-lived.

"I'd like to see you again." He spoke with a huskiness that unnerved her.

"Dammit, Cole," she snapped in irritation. "I can't see you. It's out of the question."

"Why?"

Marni looked at his face. His gentle eyes belied the demand of his tone. "Can't you just accept it? I don't want to see you." Her voice shook with emotion. "I thought we had this conversation thirteen years ago."

"We did, but you're still lying," he stated matter-of-factly.

With a confidence she didn't feel, she rejected his words as nonsense. She was over Cole. He meant nothing to her any longer.

Liar! her inner voice shouted.

"I have to go," she said again, scooting out from behind the table.

Cole frowned at her and slid out of his seat. "I'll walk you to your car," he said, dropping a couple of bills on the table. When they reached the entrance of the restaurant, he moved in front of her and held the door. She cast a quick glance at him, but his face was somber and she couldn't tell what he was thinking.

"Where are you parked?"

"In the back. The white Prelude." They walked together in silence in the crisp evening air.

"There." She pointed when the sleek car came into view.

Marni retrieved her keys from her purse and disengaged the car alarm. A high-toned bleep pierced the silence between them.

"How about dinner tomorrow?" he asked.

Marni sighed heavily. "No." She could just see Cole pulling up in front of her beach house and Jenna bounding down the steps to greet him. Pain twisted Marni's heart as she fantasized about father and daughter together as they should have been. Images of Jenna in a high chair at eighteen months, her green eyes and sable hair so like Cole's, while a battle of wills ensued over a jar of strained carrots. Cole teaching Jenna how to ride a bicycle or helping Jenna understand the theory behind multiplication tables. Dreams, only dreams, of a life not meant to be. Memories Marni and Jenna had been cheated of because of her self-doubt and her concern about her mother's failing health. Carson Ballinger had played on her insecurities and financial problems expertly, finally convincing Marni he was right. She wasn't good enough for Cole.

"You're not married, right?" Cole asked her again, his voice pulling her back to the present. Back to the harsh reality of the truth.

"No, Cole. I'm not married."

"Involved with someone?"

For an instant, Marni thought about lying to him. "No."

"Then have dinner with me." The look he gave her told her he wasn't going to give up until he got his way.

"I can't," she repeated emphatically.

He opened the car door for her. "I'll pick you up at your office at five tomorrow."

"Please don't do this to me, Cole," Marni whispered.

"Not unless you give me a good reason why not."

Marni could give him not one, but *two,* great reasons—his father and Jenna—she thought bitterly.

"I'm waiting." Cole's voice was husky, the expression in his eyes unreadable.

He radiated a vitality that still drew her, and if she wasn't careful, she could easily get caught up in his potent sexual magnetism again. She was already fighting the tingling in the pit of her stomach. "Then you'll have a long wait," she said, determined not to give in to her physical reaction to Cole. She looked at him then, wishing she could call the words back. Faint lines of pain were etched around his eyes. She recalled that look from the balmy summer night when she'd ended their relationship.

Tell me why, Marni. You aren't making any sense. I'm waiting.

Then you'll have a long wait.

"I have to go," she said, choked with emotion. She slipped behind the wheel before she made a complete fool of herself. Cole's hand on the car door prevented her from closing it.

"I'll call you tomorrow," he said, a hard glint of determination in his eyes.

Marni shook her head in exasperation. "Why, Cole? Why is this so damned important to you? I wasn't so important thirteen years ago when you married Elizabeth Wakefield, was I?" She didn't care if she sounded jealous, or even that she had no right to be angry with him.

"You were the one who walked out, remember?" The harsh tone of his voice made her wince all the same.

Marni yanked the door out of his grasp and slammed it shut. Slipping the key into the ignition, she gunned the car to life. She promptly found Reverse and pulled out of the parking slot.

The car easily slipped into first gear, and Marni stepped on the gas. When she reached the driveway, she glanced in the rearview mirror and searched for Cole. The darkness prevented her from seeing his expression, but she had a pretty good idea he wasn't too happy at the moment. The Cole Ballinger she knew wasn't accustomed to being turned down and she seriously doubted he'd changed over the years.

CHAPTER TWO

"JENNA!" MARNI CALLED from the kitchen. "We're going to be late."

After rinsing her coffee cup, she pulled back the white lace curtains over the sink. She cracked open the window, allowing the early morning sea breeze to waft into the cozy blue-and-white kitchen, and thought about Cole.

The shock of seeing him, talking to him, touching him, brought back every precious memory she'd kept close to her heart over the years. Unfortunately, pain followed close behind. Marni wondered if Cole had really loved her as he'd claimed. How could he have when he turned to Elizabeth so quickly? Carson predicted Cole would tire of her sooner or later. Seemed that Carson had been right.

A part of her, a very selfish part, wanted to see Cole again. Regardless of how foolish the idea, she knew to allow him into her life again would only be a mistake. A disastrous one. How long would it be before he learned the truth?

"Mom!"

Marni turned to see Jenna standing in the doorway, her arms crossed over her chest, impatience evident in her sea green eyes. "What were you thinking about?"

Marni mentally shook herself. "Nothing in particular."

"I called you a dozen times and you just kept staring out the window."

Marni gave a nervous laugh. "A dozen, indeed. Are you ready?"

"I have to get my books." Jenna turned to leave, then stopped. "Oh. You left these in the dining room." She held the message slips Marni had stuffed into her pocket on her way out of the office last night, and laid them on the white tiled countertop before scampering off.

Marni read the messages. One was from the public defender on the Kendell case, two others were from defense attorneys on minor offenses she was handling, and there was one from Cole. Her hand shook. The message was only a reminder to meet him at Muldoon's. He must have called her office right after they ran into each other on the courthouse steps. Marni crumpled the pink slip and tossed it into the trash bin under the sink. What if Jenna had seen the message? She was not a dull-witted child; she knew her father's name. What were the chances of another Cole Ballinger calling? She resolved to be more attentive in the future.

After dropping Jenna off at the junior high school, Marni drove straight to the courthouse. Fridays were devoted to felony arraignments. When she entered the courtroom, the prisoners had already been led into the jury box. Marni perused the prisoners as she took her seat at the prosecutor's table. Three men and one woman in chains. The remainder were more than likely arrested on drug offenses.

Marni glanced at the defense table to see who she'd be opposing. She saw a couple of young public defenders and sized them up quickly. They'd provide no problem. She recognized a few criminal attorneys and her friend and former classmate, Rebecca Parks, a family law attorney. Probably representing a deadbeat dad, she surmised.

The bailiff directed the court to order. After the judge was seated, he called the first case. The chained woman glared hard at Marni and stood.

Marni quickly located and scanned the file. She stood to address Judge Bickerman. "The state requests the defendant be held over for a bail hearing, Your Honor."

Rebecca stepped forward, her rich, straight black hair pulled away from her face in a tight knot at her nape. Sharp blue eyes assessed Marni, their friendship forgotten for the moment. "The defendant has no record of any prior convictions."

"None in this state," Marni said before turning her attention back to the bench. "Your Honor, we've just received word from Tulsa, Oklahoma, of an outstanding bench warrant. The defendant has a history of failing to appear."

The judge, a hulk of a man with a thick patch of gray hair, shuffled through the paperwork in front of him. "I see no record of this in the court's file, Ms. Rodgers."

Marni held up a piece of paper.

"Hand it to the bailiff," the judge instructed, an inflection of boredom in his tone.

Rebecca sent Marni a baleful glare. "I request a copy, Your Honor."

The judge reviewed the arrest warrant, ignoring the request. "A hearing to establish bail will be heard Monday at two o'clock." He stared hard at Rebecca. "Do you have any further objections, Ms. Parks?"

Rebecca lowered her eyes. "None, Your Honor."

Marni cringed inwardly at the judge's harsh tone. Poor Rebecca. She didn't deserve such treatment, but Judge Bickerman obviously hadn't forgotten Rebecca had represented *Mrs.* Bickerman in their divorce three years ago.

When the last prisoner was led from the courtroom, Marni gathered the armload of files together, then turned toward the low swinging door separating the attorneys from the audience. Rebecca Parks held the door for her.

"I'll see you get a copy of the bench warrant." Marni smiled at her friend. "What are you doing here today?"

"The firm's criminal attorney is on vacation." Rebecca grimaced. "Free for lunch?" Their earlier courtroom demeanor dissolved as they slipped into a familiar and easy friendship.

They walked side by side out of the courtroom. Marni looked up and down the corridor. She half expected to see Cole, but she was relieved to find he wasn't there. He continued to occupy her thoughts; she knew he wouldn't let up until he got his way. "I'd love to, but I haven't even been to the office yet," she explained. "How's next week?"

Rebecca shifted the bulk of files in her arms and pressed the button for the elevator. "Hectic. I'm stuck with criminal arraignments on top of my regular caseload. How about dinner next week? You and Jenna can come over and I'll cook."

"Actually, I do need to see you," she said turning serious.

"Sure. Problem?"

Marni shook her head. "Not yet. I just need some legal advice." She glanced above at the bank of elevators and watched the flashing lights behind the floor numbers, ignoring Rebecca's questioning blue eyes.

A low-toned ping signaled the arrival of the elevator car. The center door slid open and Marni gasped. Cole stepped out dressed in khaki slacks and a navy blazer. The whiteness of his shirt emphasized his golden tan and the color of his eyes. A blue paisley tie completed the picture of a well-dressed man.

Recovering quickly from her shock, she stiffened both her spine and her resolve not to let him into her life again, no matter how much he affected her. "What are you doing here?" she asked. Her tone was harsher than she'd intended, if the perplexed expression on Rebecca's classically beautiful face was any indication.

Cole graced her with one of his disarming smiles, the corners of his eyes crinkling. "I came to take you to lunch."

Marni sighed. "Cole, I can't."

"Are we going to have that old argument again?" He turned his attention to Rebecca. "She needs to eat, right?"

Rebecca eyed Cole appreciatively. "Absolutely. Now I understand why you turned *me* down."

The silky purr of Rebecca's voice made Marni bristle. No one could claim her friend wasn't a smart woman, but at this moment, she was simply a woman who appreciated a handsome man. And that man was Cole Ballinger.

"I didn't know he was—" Marni began as Rebecca stepped through the open doors of the elevator.

"Don't worry about it." Rebecca gave a deep, throaty chuckle. "I'll talk to you later," she called as the door slid closed.

Marni was left alone with Cole.

He reached for the files in her arm. "Can I take those?"

"No." Marni pushed the button to signal for another car. "I have to get to the office." She kept her eyes on the lights above the elevators. "I have a busy day."

The smile on his face disappeared, only to be replaced by a tensing of his jaw. "There are a few questions I want answered."

Now, what was that supposed to mean? Fear gripped her, but she shook the sensation away. "Cole, please. Leave me alone." She concentrated on the indicators. Two more floors and she'd be free of Cole.

"Why?" he demanded.

"I have a lot to do this afternoon." *If I don't look at him, he'll go away.*

"You can't be all that busy."

Marni's shoulders sagged. So much for mind over matter. "I am. Now, please, just go away. It's been great seeing you, but really, I just don't have the time."

When the elevator finally arrived, Marni stepped inside, trying desperately to ignore him. She punched the button for the garage and prayed the door would close before Cole could step through the portal.

Her guardian angel must have been on a coffee break, because Cole sauntered into the lift and stood close beside her. Her shoulder rested against his upper arm in the crowded car. Marni could feel the muscles bunch beneath the fabric of his blazer. His cologne mingled with his masculine scent, tickling her senses. God, he smelled good. Marni's pulse quickened as she cast him a sideways glance. He smiled down at her, but the look in his eyes said something she wasn't ready to analyze.

The doors opened on the third floor, and a few people pushed their way forward. Cole rested his hands on her shoulders in a possessive gesture and stepped behind her. His fingers lightly brushed the side of her neck, and Marni closed her eyes against her increased awareness of him.

The doors closed and Cole released her, moving again to her side. She could sense his eyes on her but willed herself not to look in his direction. She had to find a way to escape him. She couldn't have Cole following her to her office. She rarely dated, and if Cole came waltzing into the D.A.'s office, surely people would talk. Lawyers were the worst when it came to gossip. Maybe if she had lunch with him he'd be satisfied and not bother her again. Besides, he'd tracked her down to the courthouse, he could just as easily discover where she worked—or lived. Then he'd be sure to find out about Jenna, and Marni refused to even think about the possible ramifications.

They reached the garage and Marni stepped out of the elevator, Cole on her heels. "All right. I'll have lunch with you, but I have to be back in the office this afternoon."

Cole said nothing but followed her to her car. She opened the trunk to place the files and briefcase inside. Alarm sparked through her. A box full of clothes Jenna had outgrown sat in the center of the trunk. Marni had planned to drop them off at the Salvation Army but hadn't gotten around to it. She struggled to fight back rising hysteria. Practically throwing the files in the trunk, she bent to pick up the briefcase, but Cole held it in his hands. Before she could stop him, he set the case in the trunk. He'd barely moved out of harm's way when she slammed the lid closed, praying he hadn't seen the contents of the open box.

"Where do you want to eat?" She spoke quickly, hoping Cole wouldn't detect her nervousness.

"I'll drive," he told her. He placed his hand on the small of her back and steered her away from her car before she could argue.

Seated within the confines of Cole's sleek black Jaguar, Marni was surrounded by the scent of new leather. She concentrated on the country song flowing through the elaborate sound system. At least they still had the same taste in music, she mused, wondering when Cole had stopped listening to the heavier rock music of their younger days.

"Where are we going?" she asked, noting they were leaving the downtown area.

"A little place I found. I think you'll like it," he told her while he guided the Jag onto the freeway on ramp.

About twenty minutes later, Cole pulled into a hamburger stand. Waitresses dressed in short spandex skirts and T-shirts a size too small roller-skated around the cars. Cole pulled into one of the parking slots, killed the engine and rolled down the window.

"This is it?" Marni asked incredulously, unfastening her seat belt. She wasn't certain what she'd expected. A dark restaurant, maybe. Candlelight, perhaps. Certainly not a drive-in with carhops.

Cole shrugged, his expression noncommittal. "I thought you'd like it." He unfastened his own safety belt, then turned the key in the ignition so they could listen to the stereo as they ate.

A perky brunette skated up to the driver's side. "What'll ya have?"

"Two cheeseburgers, two fries and two root beer floats," he said, and looked at Marni for approval.

She nodded slowly as realization struck her. The first time Cole had taken her out they'd gone to the local drive-in restaurant in Elk Falls. Now, in his attempt to re-create their first date, Cole had even duplicated the menu. She couldn't believe he remembered. Marni couldn't even remember when she'd last indulged in a root beer float, but she remembered other things, like the time she believed Cole loved her.

The waitress skated away and Marni reached out to him, placing her hand on his arm. When he looked at her, she said, "You were right. I do like it." The soft expression in his eyes told her he was pleased.

"I wasn't sure you'd remember." His voice was low and seductive.

Marni removed her hand, uncomfortable with the sudden intimacy. Cole was close, too close, and she had to be careful. She had Jenna to think of, and she couldn't afford to lose her heart to Cole again. The price of loving him was simply too high to pay and had cost her dearly already.

Cole watched her retreat inside herself, and frowned. For an instant she'd let her defenses down, but now the veil covering her emotions fell back into place. He wanted to shout in frustration. The questions that had plagued him for years needed answers, yet he found he was strangely reluctant to learn the truth. What if she had never experienced the same strong emotional pull he had all those years ago? Cole took a deep breath, then let it out slowly. He turned to face her, his arm resting on the seat inches from her hair. The jacket of her peach suit cast a soft hue against her skin. "You still like football?" Cole wanted to shake himself for being such a coward, for not asking what he really wanted to know.

A slow smile lit her face. "Football and classic movies. That's me."

Cole couldn't help laughing. "You're the only woman I know who understands the offensive patterns of the Chiefs, then cries no matter how many times she sees *Old Yeller*."

He enjoyed the sparkle in her eyes. The yellow flecks appeared to shimmer with a blend of humor and indignation. She lifted a delicate brow. "One has nothing to do with the other. Besides, I thought it terribly unjust when they had to shoot the poor dog."

"If I remember correctly, you even cried during the chariot races in that Heston movie."

"I did not." Her voice lacked conviction.

"Still a sucker for animals." He shook his head. "You'll never change, Marni."

"Oh, I've changed."

The laughter left her voice, and he wondered what had changed her. Had she met someone after leaving Elk Falls? No matter how painful, Cole had to know the truth. Things should have been so different for them. "Why did you leave Kansas so abruptly?"

"Let's not get into this. It was a long time ago. *We* were a long time ago." She kept her eyes on the waitresses gliding back and forth, toting trays above their heads.

Cole drew his brows together. "Just answer my question."

"What does it matter? I left town and you married Elizabeth."

Cole froze at the coldness in her tone. He didn't know what to say, but he had to know the truth. "I only want to know why. I thought we had something special."

Marni sighed and turned to face him. She noted the stubborn lift of his chin but couldn't understand why he didn't just drop the subject. The past was behind them. "It's not important."

His tenacious expression was replaced by a brief flash of anger. "I think it's damned important." His voice was hard. "One day we were planning our future together, and the next, you were gone."

The harshness of his tone surprised her. Marni rested her head against the seat and closed her eyes. "Oh, God." Maybe, just maybe, she *had* meant something to Cole. She wanted to weep for the years she'd been cheated out of sharing his life, of the years Jenna had been cheated. At the time, she'd thought she was doing the right thing by ending their relationship. Now she wasn't so sure.

Perhaps they had both suffered needlessly. "I thought you would lose interest in me because I didn't fit into your world." Tears blinded her eyes and choked her voice.

Cole reached across the front seat and gathered her into his arms. "Ah, Marni."

She slid easily into his embrace and enjoyed the strength of his strong hands massaging her back in a slow, sensual caress. Laying her head against his chest, she drew comfort from the even, steady rhythm of his heart.

He tilted her head back until she was looking into his eyes, and her heartbeat skyrocketed. Slowly he lowered his lips, brushing them gently against hers in a feather-light touch. A dam had broken, destroying every ounce of sanity she possessed. He teased her mouth open and Marni welcomed the sensual invasion. Her senses came alive, spiraling in a wave of heat, and she returned his kiss, not at all shocked at her own eager response to his slow, drugging seduction.

When he pulled away to look at her, the emerald fire of his eyes matched the inferno inside her. Then his mouth slanted over hers and she fully understood the hunger they shared. A need denied to them for too many years.

Cole demanded and Marni responded. He took and she gave. Gave herself up to the passion enveloping them. She clung to Cole as if to a lifeline. Blood pounded in her ears as jolt after jolt of wild sensation rocketed through her.

An eternity later, he pulled his mouth from hers and slid his lips along her cheek, kissing her jaw, nibbling on the lobe of her ear, then moving on to her temple. Sanity slowly returned, and with it the realization of what she was doing—succumbing to a man who would break her heart when he learned the truth. That Carson had paid her off. She pushed against Cole in an attempt to right herself, but he held her tight.

She pulled back and looked into his eyes. Emotion choked her at the tenderness in his gaze.

He brought his hand up and cupped her cheek. "I've missed you, Marni."

"Don't." She couldn't bear the gentleness of his voice, the way he held her in his arms. Pulling out of his embrace, she returned to her side of the car.

"Marni?" Cole's soft voice drifted over her. He reached out and caressed her cheek.

Marni closed her eyes to ward off the pain in her chest. "What good will it do? Too much time has passed, Cole." Her voice was barely above a whisper. She opened her eyes and moved further away from him. She couldn't think when he was so near.

Their waitress rolled toward them, a tray laden with their order balanced against her shoulder. Cole paid her after she placed the tray on the driver's-side window. The carhop skated away, and Cole stared straight ahead.

Marni took the opportunity to examine him closely. His finely chiseled profile spoke of power and strength; firm and sensual lips set below a straight, aristocratic nose. She thought again of how much he affected her. Deep in thought, his left arm slung over the steering wheel, he chewed absently on the inside of his lower lip—a habit he hadn't lost over the years.

"I never heard from you after you broke things off between us. I'd hoped you'd change your mind, but then you left town without even so much as a goodbye." His low voice startled her and Marni had trouble hearing him. She leaned over and snapped off the radio, silence settling over them like a thick fog rolling in off the sea.

"I went a little crazy after you left. No one knew where to find you. It was as if you'd disappeared off the face of the earth. Almost as if you'd never existed to begin with."

Marni chose her words carefully. "I never knew."

Cole emitted a short bark of laughter. He scrubbed his hand over his face and sighed heavily. "At first I worried, then I got mad. I thought you'd met someone else and didn't have the decency to tell me about it."

"There was no one." Marni couldn't help the pleading note in her voice. She'd never have hurt him that way. Never. When she'd told him she loved him, she'd meant it.

"Not long afterward I went to a party with some friends and proceeded to get smashed. I was going to track you down and find out what was going on. I don't remember a whole lot except the next morning Elizabeth was in bed with me." Cole shook his head as if to clear away a few remaining cobwebs. "I was sick over what I'd done at first. To my mind, I'd cheated on you, but then I figured *you* dumped *me,* so what the hell.

"Three weeks later, Elizabeth told me she was pregnant and it was mine. I slept with her, so I took responsibility for my actions. She said she didn't want to get an abortion. Claimed she didn't believe in them."

Marni didn't understand the derision in his voice but kept silent, not wanting to interrupt him.

"When I told my father I'd gotten her pregnant, he insisted I do the right thing and marry her. Two months after we married, Elizabeth 'lost' the baby."

Something in Cole's eyes told Marni a different story. "You don't think she was pregnant?" she asked.

"Sweetheart, I *know* she wasn't pregnant."

Pain twisted Marni's heart. Elizabeth had tricked him into marriage by claiming she was pregnant with his child. The irony of the situation hit her full force. Elizabeth's lies were Marni's truth. She even had a beautiful twelve-year-old daughter to prove her claim. "How did you know?"

"She told me when we divorced." Cole took a deep breath. "Elizabeth *did* get pregnant two years later, but she had an abortion. She did it to get back at me."

"I don't understand." Marni's throat ached with unshed tears. She didn't understand how anyone could do such a thing.

"Our marriage was not an easy one. We fought constantly. After she supposedly lost the baby, I slept in the guest room and we rarely talked. I was angry. I blamed Elizabeth because I was so miserable. I admit, I was a real jerk, and I did sleep with her occasionally. The last time I shared her bed, she accused me of not loving her and I couldn't deny it. She never forgave me. When she discovered she was pregnant, she got rid of it, then bragged to me about what she'd done. God, she took so much pleasure in robbing me of my child."

Marni didn't want to feel sorry for him but she couldn't help herself. Tears of pain rolled down her cheeks, not only for Cole, but for herself and Jenna and for the child he'd lost because of his ex-wife's vengeance. Cole's father and Elizabeth Wakefield had made sure that they'd all suffered.

Cole smacked the steering wheel. "Dammit, I might not have loved Elizabeth, but I wanted my child. Elizabeth denied me the chance to be a father."

Marni eyed him cautiously. She'd seen Cole angry the night she ended their relationship, but his reaction to his ex-wife's betrayal frightened her. "What if Elizabeth had had the baby? Would you still have divorced her?"

"I'm sure we would have divorced eventually. We didn't love each other, Marni. We were completely unsuitable. We both wanted different things out of life. Elizabeth's idea of family night was an evening of dining and dancing at the country club. For me it would be spending a quiet evening at home with my wife and kids.''

Marni's heart twisted painfully and dread climbed up her spine. "But what would you have done about the child?''

"Taken responsibility for it. What else?''

He spoke with such conviction Marni nearly shivered. What was he trying to say? She had to know. "Do you mean financially?'' Marni held her breath waiting for Cole to answer.

"No, I would have insisted on having an active role in my son or daughter's life. I would have sued for joint custody. Full custody if she hadn't really wanted a child.'' Cole gripped the steering wheel as he spoke. His dark brows slanted in harsh lines over his eyes. "The point is moot, though. She didn't give me a choice.''

Marni found it difficult to swallow and impossible to breathe. *Full custody*. She knew she could never let Cole know about Jenna. Elizabeth had aborted his baby, but Marni had his child—an adorable, precocious twelve-year-old, and he didn't even know about her.

Cole reached across the expanse of the car and caressed her cheek tenderly. "Marni, what's wrong? You look scared to death.''

She moved away from him and whispered, "Don't,'' her voice strained with tension.

"Why? I think—I *know*—you still care about me.'' His brows drew together fiercely, yet there was no anger in his voice. Only a gentleness that pierced her heart.

"It won't work.'' She didn't know how to make him understand. As much as she loved him, even after all this time, she could not allow him back into her life. If she told him about Jenna, he would hold her little secret against her. Even worse, with the power his father wielded, Cole could try to take Jenna away from her. No, telling Cole the truth was out of the question.

"Why?" he asked again, more forcefully.

"Cole, what we had was a long time ago. People change." But she was lying. She loved him as fiercely now as she had thirteen years ago, and every day of her life she saw a reminder of her love for him. Their daughter.

Cole didn't say anything, he just continued to stare at her, then a slow smile touched his lips. "Yes, it has been a long time. Too long."

Marni had no idea what he was thinking, but she knew Cole wasn't about to give up. He'd never been one to accept defeat, and while the thought of Cole's pursuit frightened her, it also gave her a slight surge of female satisfaction. A ridiculous reaction under the circumstances.

AFTER COLE DROPPED her off at her car, Marni drove straight to the Salvation Army to deliver the clothes in the trunk, then stopped at a luggage shop on Wilshire to pick up a new briefcase. She should have bought a new one months ago. If she had, she wouldn't be a jumble of nerves right now.

Her resolve not to tell Cole about Jenna increased. Besides, she reasoned, how would she tell him? She supposed she could give him the letter she'd sent him when Jenna was born. The letter had been returned—unopened—by Carson, no doubt. But at least he hadn't read the contents, so he didn't know about Jenna. Nevertheless, she'd made an attempt to do the right thing, regardless of her deal with his father.

She deposited the new briefcase in the trunk of the car, then drove the few blocks to her office, trying not to think of Cole. Yes, she decided, her life would be much less complicated if she stayed away from Cole Ballinger. Her response to his kisses was far too troubling.

Marni arrived at her office by midafternoon to find a frantic Peg fielding telephone calls. "Where have you been?" her secretary asked in an exasperated tone.

"I had an unexpected lunch date." A stab of guilt pierced Marni. She should have called to check in.

"Someone tall, dark and handsome?" Peg sounded hopeful, and Marni winced.

"What's up?" she asked, determined not to discuss her "lunch date" with her secretary.

"This arrived just before noon." Peg picked up a bound manuscript, then tossed it back on the desk to emphasize her displeasure.

Marni reached for the document, and her heart sank to her feet. An appellate brief from Kendell's attorney. "Have you read it?"

"With a ham sandwich and a Coke."

What Marni liked most about Peg was her ability to get involved with the cases. Peg knew almost as much as Marni did when it came to the files assigned to them.

She nodded toward her office and Peg followed, grabbing her dictation pad. Marni slipped out of her jacket and hung it on the coatrack in the corner, then adjusted the cuffs of her blouse. Light streamed into the small office through the venetian blinds, and she closed them to help cool the office. The air conditioning in the old county building worked with as much efficiency as an unrestored vintage automobile and was probably just as ancient.

"On what grounds is the defense appealing?" Marni crossed the gray industrial carpeting to her desk. Peg closed the door.

"Judicial error." Peg's outrage was apparent in her pale blue eyes. She adjusted her wire-rimmed glasses over her small, upturned nose, and pushed a lock of nondescript brown hair out of her face.

"Judicial error? Gladstone runs his courtroom by the book." Marni sat behind the desk in the squeaky leather chair.

"I highlighted the important sections for you," explained Peg, lowering herself into the chair across from Marni's desk. She held her pen over the stenographic pad, ready to take down her employer's every word.

Marni took a minute to review the brief, particularly the sections Peg had highlighted. The more she read, the angrier she became. The defense was claiming that Gladstone should never have admitted the testimony of Kendell's cell mate, who, they alleged, had been coerced. The brief went on to claim that the witness had been promised a reduction in his sentence if he agreed to testify.

"I can't believe this. Who took the witness's statement?"

Peg flipped through her notepad and produced the names of two policemen.

"I'll need to talk to Dorlan. Does he know about this?"

"Not yet. He's out of town until Monday."

"Damn. Let his secretary know I have to talk to him if he calls in. And try to get hold of the officers," Marni said. "I want to see them first thing Monday morning."

Peg jotted notes on her pad. "Sure thing."

"Better yet, give them my home phone number and have them call me over the weekend if necessary. We've got to prepare a response, and I want to have it filed by Tuesday afternoon."

"Do you need me to stay late tonight?"

Marni shook her head. "No. I'll get as much done this weekend as possible and have it to you by noon Monday. Will that give you enough time?"

Peg nodded. "Don't worry, Marni. We'll win this round, too."

The phone rang and Marni jumped on it. "Marni Rodgers. Hold on," she said tersely, still upset over the appellate brief. Cradling the receiver against her shoulder, she said to Peg, "Order the transcript. I need any argument between counsel regarding the witness and his subsequent testimony."

Peg stood and adjusted her glasses again. "It's taken care of. The court reporter promised we'd have it before five. Do you want me to take it home and index it?"

Marni appreciated Peg's offer but couldn't ask her secretary to work on a weekend. Peg had a family of her own to take care of. "I'll handle it. Oh, Peg. Call Jenna for me and tell her I'll be late, would you?"

Peg nodded, and slipped out of the office after dropping a stack of messages onto Marni's desk.

Marni turned her attention back to the telephone. "I'm sorry. Hello?"

"Do you have plans for dinner?" Cole's deep, resonant voice responded.

The room tilted and Marni clasped a hand to her throat. Had he been listening? *Oh, God. No!*

"I have to work." Her voice quaked with emotion, but at least the room righted itself again.

"You sound angry."

"You're damn right I'm angry." Angry and scared, she thought. *Call Jenna for me and tell her I'll be late.* Please God, she silently prayed.

"Something I said?" His voice was soothing, and Marni's pulse slowed a fraction. She wasn't angry at him, only at her own carelessness.

"The defense filed a brief on the Kendell case," she said, trying to concentrate on the conversation.

"Sounds bad."

"It is."

"Care to talk about it?"

Marni found herself responding to his gentle coaxing, and before she realized it, she was telling him all about the defendant's contentions of coercion of a material witness, explaining that if the appellate court overturned the trial court's ruling, Kendell would have to be retried without the testimony of the witness. And if that happened, the prosecution's case could be weakened. "What's even worse is that the defense knows our strategy. It'll be like starting from scratch, and this case was tough enough the first time round."

Cole leaned back in the soft executive chair of his office overlooking Century City. He smiled as he listened to Marni relate the legal issues involved in the murder trial. When she talked about her work, there were no barriers. "Is it true?" he asked.

"I don't know. I have to talk to the officers who took his statement. If they promised him anything, we could be in big trouble."

A light tapping sound drifted over the phone lines. He pictured her drumming the tip of her pen on the desk, deep in concentration as she planned her counterattack. "Could Kendell be freed?"

"Not unless a new trial proves him innocent."

"But if the press paints a picture of impropriety on the D.A.'s part—"

"Exactly," she said. "I'll be fighting an uphill battle. April Burnell will tear the state to shreds, and who knows how many other members of the press will join ranks with her."

He didn't miss the despair in her voice and wished he could do something to help her. "How important is this witness?"

"Very," she stated emphatically. "He testified that Kendell told him in intimate detail how he murdered those girls."

Cole stood and looked out the twentieth-story window at the heavy traffic below the elegant offices of Ballinger Electronics as Marni finished her account of the importance of the witness testimony. "I wish I could help," he told her.

"Me, too." Her voice softened.

Cole smiled into the phone. He was reluctant to let her get away from him again. Grasping for something to say to keep her talking, he asked, "Who's Jenna?"

CHAPTER THREE

MARNI COULD FEEL the blood drain from her face at his question. Her stomach churned from shock. "Who?" she managed to choke out, surprised she could utter the simple word.

"Jenna."

She swallowed with difficulty. "Who?" Cole probably thought he was talking to an owl. An unintelligent owl.

"You asked Peg to tell her you'd be late. Is she a friend of yours?"

Marni tried to ignore the humming in her ears and stirred uneasily in her chair. "Oh, yes, yes. We did have plans for dinner, but well, you know." She closed her eyes and prayed. Prayed he'd accept her feeble explanation and drop this line of questioning.

"Marni, are you all right?" The concern in his tone only increased her wariness.

"Fine," she said with forced brightness. Her hands shook uncontrollably. "I'm just thinking about all the work I have to do."

"Hmmm. So I guess you'll be working through the weekend now." He spoke tentatively, as if he hoped she might be free, after all.

"Yes, I will. I really have to go." Marni tried to lower her tone an octave. She took a deep breath and willed her hands to stop shaking. The limbs refused to cooperate.

"I'll call you next week, then."

"Sure. Bye, Cole." He'd sounded disappointed, but she practically flung the receiver back onto the cradle before he could ask her anything else about Jenna.

Marni leaned back in the worn burgundy chair and stared at the phone, concentrating on resuming a normal breathing pattern. What was she going to do? He couldn't keep calling her or following her to the courthouse! Marni glanced at the framed school photo of Jenna on her desk. If he came to her office and saw the photo...Marni refused to think about it. She couldn't or she'd go crazy.

The door to her office opened and Rebecca Parks stepped in. "I was in the neighborhood and thought I'd stop by."

"Really? Come to get a copy of the warrant?" Marni didn't believe her friend for a minute. She'd come here for one reason, and it had nothing to do with law. Rebecca wanted to know about Cole.

She smiled sheepishly. "Obvious, huh?"

"Uh-huh." Marni nodded, still shaken by her near disaster with Cole.

Rebecca lowered herself into the chair across from Marni's desk. "Can you blame me for being curious? Who is he?" Her blue eyes sparkled with anticipation.

"Who?" Marni seriously doubted her ability to converse logically. If all she uttered were inane animal sounds, her career would be over.

Rebecca sighed heavily. "The hunk, Marni."

"An old friend." *Full custody.* The dreadful words reverberated through Marni's mind.

"Ha! You don't expect me to believe that, do you?" Rebecca drummed her fingers impatiently on the coarse fabric of the chair. "Give up, Rodgers."

Marni stood abruptly, crossing the room to the bookshelves. She stared at the titles, unable to concentrate. An uncomfortable silence filled the room, and Marni could feel Rebecca's eyes on her.

"Who is he? Really." Her friend spoke quietly, her demeanor serious.

Marni slipped a law book from the shelf and continued to peruse the other titles. "I told you, an old friend. We grew up together."

"High school sweethearts?" Rebecca teased.

"Something like that," Marni mumbled, fingering one of the books filled with precedent-setting case law.

Rebecca issued a deep, throaty chuckle. "Where's he been all your life?"

Rebecca's pumps hit the floor with a thud, a sure indication her friend wasn't leaving until she got the information she wanted.

Marni pulled another book from the shelf and rested it against her hip. "Married."

Rebecca sighed dramatically. "Why are all the gorgeous ones taken?"

"He's not. He married someone else two months after I moved to California, but they divorced." Marni pulled two more books from the shelves and returned to her desk, still not looking at Rebecca.

"Someone else?" Rebecca asked in a silky voice. "Marni. Who *is* this guy?"

Marni let out a long, audible sigh. Now Rebecca would have to know everything. She would need her friend's legal expertise if Cole found out about Jenna. "I really hate to burden you with my problems."

"Sweetie, if you can't talk to me, who can you talk to? Jenna? I know the kid's bright, but she doesn't have much experience in the male gender department."

"Heavens, no." What an interesting conversation *that* would be, Marni mused.

Rebecca remained quiet. Marni glanced at her friend and nearly shuddered at the thoughtful look on her face. Pulling one of the law books from the pile on her desk, Marni flipped through the pages trying to locate the case law she needed to prepare her opposing brief.

"It's *him,* isn't it."

Marni's shoulders sagged. Her friend hadn't become a successful attorney because she was dumb.

Rebecca leaned forward in the chair, her blue eyes piercing. "He's the guy who got you pregnant and then skipped out, isn't he."

"He didn't skip out," Marni corrected her. "I just never told him about Jenna."

"Well, he didn't give you a chance if he got married two months after you split."

The sarcasm in Rebecca's voice made Marni wince. She sent Rebecca what she hoped was a glare. "Would you please stop!" Marni snapped the book closed in irritation. "Cole Ballinger is not one to run from his responsibilities."

A startled gasp escaped Rebecca. "Cole Ballinger? Ballinger Electronics' Cole Ballinger? Marni, you dog. Do you know who he is?"

Marni rolled her eyes. "Jenna's father?"

Rebecca ignored Marni's bad humor. "No, I mean financially. There was a big article on Ballinger Electronics in *Time* or *Newsweek* a month or so ago. He's a rich guy."

"Gee, I must have missed a little detail." Marni couldn't help the mockery of her tone. When it came to Cole, she knew just about everything there was to know.

"They were thinking of closing shop on their software division, and then Daddy gave it to Sonny Boy to play with. Boom. Six months later they're showing a huge profit margin. From what I understand, this isn't the first division Golden Boy's turned around.''

"Good. Maybe he'll go away and save another division of Daddy's company and leave me alone." If only she could be so lucky.

Rebecca became serious again. "You're not going to tell him about Jenna, are you?"

Marni stood and walked to the window. She opened the venetian blinds and gazed out at the setting sun casting a deep orange hue over the skyline. "No, and he's not going to find out, either." Turning back to face Rebecca, she leaned against the windowsill.

"He's bound to if he keeps coming around. And I get the impression this guy won't give up until he gets what he wants. Looks to me to be the determined type." Rebecca looked pointedly at the framed photograph of Jenna on Marni's desk. "Is that what you wanted to talk to me about?"

Marni nodded.

Rebecca leaned back in the chair again. "Well, the initial consultation is free, kiddo. I think it's time you told me everything."

Marni stepped away from the window and reached into her desk to retrieve a legal pad. She tossed it to Rebecca. "I don't know where to start."

Rebecca suddenly became every inch the lawyer. "The beginning is always a good place."

Marni punched the Do Not Disturb button on her telephone, then came around to stand in front of the desk. "Do you need to know the first time I ever saw him?" She couldn't help the smile tugging at the corners of her mouth. Propping her hip against the desk, a vivid recollection struck her of the first time she'd ever laid eyes on Cole Ballinger. A heavy sigh escaped her.

"If that's where it begins, then go for it." Rebecca's voice was soft and coaxing. She leaned back in the chair again and waited for Marni to speak.

"He was a football hero. Captain of the wrestling team. You name it, Cole did it. A rich kid with everything going for him. Good looks, charm, a hot car and Elizabeth Wakefield on his arm. After he graduated from high school, he attended the university in Lawrence. Life was pretty lonely after he left town."

"But he had a girlfriend? I don't understand."

"I had a such a crush on Cole, it wouldn't have mattered if he'd had ten girls shackled to his leg! He never noticed me until he returned to Elk Falls two years later. He came back to see his sister, Janelle, graduate. I finally got up the nerve to talk to him and the next day he called and asked me out." Marni sat on the edge of her desk. "God, I was in heaven. Cole Ballinger asked *me* out on a date."

She glanced at Rebecca. "I worked that summer in a law office as a receptionist, trying to save up enough money for college so I could get my paralegal certificate. My mother's health was getting worse and we couldn't afford much. It was up to me to pay my own way. I worked all day, but my evenings were spent with Cole. We did everything together. I was young and foolish, and I believed it when he told me he loved me."

Rebecca chuckled. "A man will tell you anything when he's got a hard..."

"I know, I know." Marni grimaced.

"What happened to this Wakefield woman?"

Marni shrugged. "Cole said they'd split up."

Rebecca shook her head. "So you made love to the guy, came here, then found out you were pregnant."

"I called, but I spoke to his father. Carson told me his son was on his honeymoon."

Rebecca lifted a brow at Marni's barely controlled sarcasm. "With Wakefield?"

Marni nodded, a stab of pain wrenching her heart. Pain at what she'd lost, at what she could never have. "Cole told me today Elizabeth claimed to be pregnant, but she really wasn't."

"So he slept with Elizabeth right after you left. What a jerk!"

Marni detected the heat in Rebecca's words, and despite the gravity of the situation, she found herself defending Cole. "It wasn't like that. If it were, this wouldn't be so difficult."

"I don't understand."

"Cole's father never liked me. My mother was a waitress, my father skipped out when I was two. I wasn't socially connected. All the usual stereotype clichés about a poor kid from the wrong side of town fit, and Carson Ballinger didn't think I was good enough for his son. Carson offered to pay for my education and take care of my mom's medical expenses if I stopped seeing Cole. He played on my insecurities and used my mom's diabetes as ammunition. I'd never fit into Cole's crowd. I had no education, no breeding, as he put it. He convinced me Cole would eventually tire of making excuses for my lack of social connections and my ignorance of his way of life. He made me believe I'd only become an embarrassment to Cole."

A hard glint came into Rebecca's eyes. "And you accepted that?"

"Oh, yeah. I even took him up on his offer and told Cole the next day it was over between us. Mom and I came to L.A., and I applied to USC."

Rebecca sniffed in derision. "Did Sonny Boy lie to you when he said Wakefield was out of the picture?"

"No, he didn't. When he didn't hear from me again, he was angry. He passed out drunk at a party one night, and when he woke up, Elizabeth was in bed with him. She told Cole when they divorced she hadn't really been pregnant at all."

"What a witch!"

Marni ignored her friend's outburst. "Today, when he explained what happened, he told me Elizabeth got pregnant two years later. She aborted it and he divorced her. I asked him what he would have done if Elizabeth had had the baby. He was so angry, Rebecca. Really angry."

"Can't say I blame him."

Marni closed her eyes, remembering his harsh expression when he told her what Elizabeth had done. She opened her eyes and clasped her hands in front of her. "He said he would have sued her for custody—maybe even full custody."

"Ah, I'm beginning to understand. Still, you're not married to him. Why the worry? You're the one with all the rights here, kiddo. You can sue him for support. Thirteen years' worth of it. A nice little nest egg if you ask me."

"You don't understand. Cole's whole point is that Elizabeth didn't give him a choice. She robbed him of the opportunity to be a father."

"Marni, I think you're worrying for nothing. Besides, *Roe v. Wade* is about a woman's choice, not a man's, and has absolutely nothing to do with your situation."

"You didn't see his face."

"Still, what his ex-wife did has nothing to do with you and Jenna."

Marni couldn't accept Rebecca's logic. "I think it does. Don't you see? I didn't give him a choice, either. I even took money from his father."

"Well, Cole didn't give *you* much of a choice from what I've heard. He married someone else while you carried his child!"

"But I didn't tell him."

"That's beside the point. The money part—that's between Cole and Daddy. It's not a legal problem for you. I don't think Sonny Boy'll have a leg to stand on if he does attempt to sue you for custody. You're a great mother, Marni. He'll have to petition for paternity first, then you can get him for child support. We can tie that little process up in the system for a long time." Rebecca smiled, a slow, catlike grin. "But without proving paternity first, he doesn't stand a chance of gaining so much as visitation rights, so that little scenario will never have to be played out."

"Rebecca, Cole is named as Jenna's father on her birth certificate." Marni spoke softly, dreading the lawyer's response.

"Tell me you're kidding." The incredulity in Rebecca's voice only increased Marni's trepidation.

Marni shook her head silently.

"Oh, Marni." Rebecca looked as if she'd just lost her best friend.

"I never thought I'd see him again," she reasoned, "but I still wanted Jenna to know who her father was. She *is* a Ballinger whether or not she lives with her father."

Rebecca gave Marni a hard stare. "Does Jenna have his name?"

Marni couldn't answer.

"Is Jenna's name Ballinger?" she repeated.

Marni looked at her hands, clenched in her lap. She'd fully understood the implications of her actions when she put Cole's name on Jenna's birth certificate. Now she wished she hadn't been so hopeful and foolhardy. "Yes." The word came out in a choked whisper.

Marni couldn't bear to face Rebecca. The thought of seeing the look on her friend's face was simply too much for her to take right now. Marni knew she'd been a fool; she didn't need to see it mirrored in Rebecca's eyes.

The phone on Peg's desk rang, but Marni knew her secretary wouldn't be interrupting them; the red light on Peg's phone indicated Marni was not to be disturbed. The air-conditioning system hummed, then sputtered, then resumed its low purr. The clock on the wall ticked, reminding her of a bomb in an old B-movie.

After an eternity, Rebecca finally spoke. "Marni, I hate to tell you this, but I think you should tell him about Jenna."

Marni sprang from the desk, as if shot from a cannon. "No."

"Listen to me," Rebecca pleaded.

"No." Marni paced the confines of the office like a caged tiger. The sensation of being trapped frightened her almost as much as Cole's learning the truth. "It's out of the question. I won't let him take Jenna away from me."

Rebecca tossed the legal pad down on Marni's desk with a resounding slap. "Dammit, Marni. Would you listen? Sit down."

Marni plopped into the chair next to Rebecca and crossed her arms over her chest in a defensive gesture. "Okay, I'm listening."

"You wanted my legal advice, and I say tell him. If he finds out on his own, he's going to be angry. If he's angry, he'll probably retaliate. How would you feel if the situation were reversed? Tell him, Marni. Explain to him what you just told me. He's bound to understand.''

''No.'' Marni tapped her foot irritably.

''You're not using your head.'' Rebecca's exasperation was obvious.

Marni stared hard at her friend and, now, lawyer. ''I can't tell him.''

''Oh, for heaven's sake. Would you tell me why?''

''Because I'm not going to give him a chance to take Jenna away from me.'' Marni cringed at the desperation in her voice. God, how she hated this. She hated feeling vulnerable.

Rebecca spoke in a soft voice. ''I don't think he can or will.''

''I won't give him a chance. I can't, Rebecca. Carson has made a career out of buying people. Who's to say he couldn't purchase himself a judge? And how would Jenna feel if she was ripped from her home to live God knows where with a man she doesn't even know? Am I supposed to stand by and allow her to be subjected to Carson Ballinger's narrow-minded attitudes? He'd hate Jenna as much as he hated me. I won't do that to her.''

''Marni, he isn't some forties mobster with judges and politicians in his pocket.''

''You don't know him.''

''You're not being fair.''

''I don't have to be fair,'' Marni answered childishly. ''I'm protecting Jenna.''

Rebecca looked at her intently. ''Are you? Or are you protecting yourself?''

Marni had no response.

COLE SET ASIDE THE REPORT he'd been unable to concentrate on and pushed himself away from the oversized chrome-and-glass desk. Stepping over to the window, he stared out at the evening traffic below and thought about Marni. He wanted to see her again. Now. Tonight. He tried to forget the heat of the kiss they'd shared at the drive-in restaurant, but he couldn't. The memory only served to cause a slow burn in the pit of his stomach. He still needed to know why she'd left Elk Falls—and him.

She'd said he would have lost interest in her because she didn't fit into his world, but that didn't make sense. The Marni he'd known would have confronted her problems head on. He'd seen fear in her eyes today, and he couldn't begin to understand why. The only thing he *did* know was he didn't want to wait until Monday to be with her again. She must have some free time before then.

Cole reached for the telephone and dialed her office. On the second ring, Marni's secretary picked up the phone.

"Ms. Rodgers's office. This is Peg."

Cole could hear the smile in Peg's voice. "Peg, this is Cole Ballinger. Is Marni available?"

"She's gone for the day. Can I take a message?" Cole detected a hopeful note in Peg's voice. If Peg was on his side, then maybe he'd pull this little stunt off without a hitch. He could only hope.

"No, that's okay. I'll see her tonight." A stab of guilt assailed him for lying, but he ignored it. He was determined to see Marni again before the weekend was over.

"I'm leaving in a minute, but if she phones in, I'll tell her you called."

"Thanks, Peg." Cole hung up and counted to one hundred. He picked up the phone and redialed the number.

After the third ring, Cole began to think Peg had already left. The woman must have bolted from her desk.

She picked up on the fourth ring.

"Ms. Rodgers's office."

Cole smiled. "Peg, this is Cole Ballinger again. I'm sorry to bother you, but I can't seem to find Marni's number. She gave it to me today, but I seem to have lost it."

"I should really ask Marni first." Cole noted the hesitation in Peg's voice.

What the hell, he thought. No sense stopping now. "I was supposed to pick her up about eight-thirty and I need to let her know I'll be late," he improvised.

Peg was quiet and Cole waited. He could almost imagine her weighing the consequences of releasing Marni's home number.

"Have you got a pen?" Peg finally asked.

Cole jotted the number on a scratch pad, thanked Peg and hung up the phone before his luck changed. That had been too easy. He wrote the number on his Rolodex, then placed the slip of paper in his wallet. Dear, sweet Peg. She deserved a raise for her cooperation, or at least a bouquet.

The drive across town took him twenty minutes in Friday evening traffic. He let himself into his quiet, ultra-modern apartment, checked his answering machine for messages, then took a cool shower.

Dressed in a worn pair of Levi's and a University of Kansas sweatshirt, he glanced at the clock on the bedside table. Six-twenty. Marni had said she lived by the beach. But which beach? Southern California was one long coastline. She could live anywhere from Malibu to Newport. Cole decided she'd be home in an hour, either way. He snapped on the television on his way to the kitchen, made himself a sandwich, grabbed a Coke from the fridge and went back into the living room to wait.

The phone rang and Cole reached for it. "Hello?"

"How's the software end of things, son?" Carson Ballinger's baritone voice sounded affable.

"Fine," Cole answered, surprised to be hearing from him.

"Your mother's been complaining you haven't called her."

"I've been busy." Cole wondered what his father really wanted.

"I'm flying out next week. I'll be arriving on Wednesday."

"Coming to check up on me?" Cole wanted nothing more than to tell his father to stop breathing down his neck, but wisdom prevailed. For now, Carson Ballinger still called the shots, but Cole was becoming increasingly weary of living in his father's shadow.

"Just routine. Wouldn't be doing my job if I didn't make the rounds occasionally." Carson chuckled.

"Well, it's nice to hear from you, Dad, but I've got an appointment. I have to run."

"Can I tell your mother you've got a date?"

"You could say that," Cole answered, not yet willing to divulge the fact Marni might become part of his life again. She didn't seem too willing, but Cole hoped like hell he could change her mind.

"Anyone we know? That vice president of marketing is a nice young lady. Her father owns the Masters Hardware chain."

"Really." Cole didn't care if her father was president of the United States. Hanna Masters was an attractive and intelligent woman, but she reminded him too much of

Elizabeth. Definitely not the kind of woman he wanted to become involved with.

"I ran into an old friend yesterday," he offered, hoping to steer his father away from the subject of Hanna Masters's financial attributes.

"Who is she?"

Cole ran a hand through his hair in an agitated gesture. No sense putting it off. "Marni Rodgers. She went to school with Janelle."

"Oh, yes. Her mother was ill. No father, either, if I remember correctly."

"That's her," Cole answered.

Silence.

"How is she?" Carson finally asked.

Cole wondered about the caution in his father's voice. "She's an assistant D.A. here in Los Angeles." A surge of pride filled him. She'd accomplished her dream to become an attorney. He'd never imagined her as a prosecutor, though. To him, Marni was more of an environmental type. Save the whales, or the kangaroo rat, or some other endangered species.

"I see. You're not planning to see her again, are you?"

"I've thought about it." Who was he kidding? She was all he'd thought about for the past twenty-four hours.

"That's not a good idea."

"Oh?" Cole ignored the warning note in Carson's voice.

"She has no background, son. Her mother was a waitress, for goodness' sake. She's all wrong for you."

"And Elizabeth was right for me?" Cole thought again about his father's reaction when Cole had told him Elizabeth was pregnant. He'd expected a tirade, a stern lecture on how he'd disappointed the family, but his father had been strangely elated. Not for the first time, Cole wondered why.

"At least Elizabeth had breeding," Carson shot at him.

"Breeding? What about a heart? Compassion? Sincerity? Those are the qualities I look for in a person."

"I only want what's best for you, son. I don't want you to get hurt. Marni turned her back on you once before. Thank goodness you had Elizabeth."

"I have to go," Cole said, not wanting to argue with his father—at least not over the telephone. He'd known for a while now it was time for him to step away from Ballinger Electronics. After successfully turning two faltering divisions into profit-making entities, Cole knew he was ready. More than ready. If anything, the move might improve his relationship with his father.

"All right, son. I'll see you next week."

Cole replaced the receiver and glanced at the clock again, putting the conversation with his father behind him. He'd deal with Carson next week.

MARNI PULLED INTO the driveway of the white beach house twenty minutes after seven. Fortunately the transcript of the Kendell trial had arrived early, and Marni managed to escape the office sooner than she'd expected, leaving Peg to field any last-minute telephone calls. With the Kendell appeal and Cole's appearance in her life, she needed time to catch her breath. Somehow she had to handle both calamities, but she didn't have the faintest idea how.

Jenna came bounding out of the house, the screen door banging behind her. The light from the porch cast a hazy yellow glow over the small veranda and spilled onto a fraction of the manicured lawn. A large German shepherd rounded the house, trampling through the dormant rose garden, and barked, wagging his tail at Jenna.

"Arlo, shush. It's only Mom," Jenna scolded the dog. The point was lost on the large animal, who barked again in reply.

"Sorry I'm late," Marni said, stepping from the car. "It was one of those days."

"Denise called. She wants to know if I can go skiing with her tomorrow."

Marni stepped through the gate and put her arm around her daughter. A flood of protectiveness and love rushed through her. She was reluctant to let Jenna out of her sight but quickly quashed her foolishness. "I don't see why not. I've got a lot of work to do this weekend, anyway. Have you eaten?"

"Yeah. I was hungry so I warmed up the leftover pizza. I saved you some." Jenna opened the front door and Arlo trotted into the house.

Marni didn't think she could eat a bite. Not after her conversation with Rebecca. She couldn't get over the fact that her friend had insisted she tell Cole about Jenna. The notion bordered on insanity.

"Oh, there's an old movie on cable tonight," Jenna said, dropping onto the sofa.

Arlo wandered into the kitchen. Probably to search the floor for crumbs. Marni couldn't seem to keep the junk food out of her daughter or her dog.

"Which one?"

"*Oklahoma.*" Jenna shared Marni's love for old movies, particularly old musicals. Marni had taken her to a Rodgers and Hammerstein film festival in Venice, and Jenna had become as hooked as Marni.

Marni smiled at her daughter. "Let me get out of this monkey suit." She crossed the beige carpeting and headed toward the master bedroom. The phone rang, and Marni said, "Will you get that, sweetie. I don't want to talk to anyone tonight, unless it's urgent."

Jenna darted past Marni into the bedroom and picked up the cordless phone. "Hello?

"Uh, she's not here right now. Can I take a message?" Jenna mouthed the words "It's a man" to Marni and grinned broadly.

Marni rolled her eyes at her daughter and kicked off her pumps. Probably one of the policemen who'd taken the witness's statement. Well, Marni could call him back tomorrow after she had reviewed the transcript. Tonight more than anything, she wanted to spend time with her daughter.

"What's the number?" Jenna jotted down the number while Marni stepped into the walk-in closet to change her clothes, pulling off her jacket along the way.

"Okay, and what's your name?" Jenna asked.

She smiled at her daughter's attempt at professionalism and hung the suit on a hanger and unbuttoned her silk blouse, tossing it in the basket of clothes destined for the dry cleaners.

"Say that again?" Jenna asked cautiously.

Marni discarded her slip, camisole and stockings, then slipped into the navy blue sweats she pulled from a drawer and tugged a matching hooded sweatshirt over her head. She quickly loosened the tight French braid and shook her hair before scrubbing her fingers over her scalp.

"Cole Ballinger?"

Marni's heart stopped beating as she gripped the built-in dresser for support. She began to shake. She gasped, trying to suck air into her lungs as the small room swam before her eyes. A cold knot formed in the pit of her stomach.

Jenna's voice sounded miles away. "Cole Ballinger? My father?"

CHAPTER FOUR

"THIS IS SO COOL," Jenna said.

Move, dammit! Marni couldn't get her body to cooperate with the commands issued by her brain. Too late to sever the connection between father and daughter. Her secret could no longer be hidden from Cole. He knew the truth.

"Me? I'm Jenna. Marni's daughter."

Marni got moving, but not fast enough.

"I'll be thirteen in May."

Jenna responded to her father's questions openly. Through the years Marni had tried to teach her daughter honesty was all-important, telling her that the omission of facts was the same as deceit. She'd never imagined herself a hypocrite until now.

She bolted out of the walk-in closet and practically tore the phone out of Jenna's hands, ignoring the startled look on her daughter's face. Pushing the button to disconnect the phone nearly proved impossible, her hands were shaking so badly.

"Mom!" Jenna wailed, a fierce frown creasing her brow. "What are you doing? You hung up on him!"

Marni ignored Jenna's indignation and began to pace. "I know." She had to think of a plan. There had to be a way out of this rapidly growing nightmare.

"Why did you do that?" Jenna repeated.

Marni knew she was behaving like a first-class idiot, but she couldn't help herself. Panic did that to a person.

The phone rang again, she turned to look at her daughter. She pressed the button with her thumb and lifted the phone to her ear. "Hello?"

"Marni? What the hell is going on?" Cole sounded angry. More than angry.

Marni pushed the Disconnect button again. *My world is falling apart!*

"Mom!" Jenna cried.

Marni sat down on the bed and stared at the phone. The darn thing rang again. She pushed the button to answer, then promptly disconnected the caller, unable to face the dreadful fact that Cole had finally learned the truth. She wondered if she should feel guilty, yet the only emotion she felt was cold, stark fear. Fear of what Cole would do next.

"Mom? What are you doing?" Jenna asked again. She stood in front of Marni, hands placed on her slightly rounded hips. "Mom?" Her voice was soft, questioning, and Marni didn't know how to begin to explain her fears to Jenna. How could she tell her daughter she could lose her? That the father of a man she didn't even know had the power to take her away? That the cozy life they shared might never be the same again?

"Mom, why did he call here?"

She should unplug the phone. No, she thought, better to keep it off the hook. She couldn't turn off the ringers on the other two extensions in case of an emergency.

"Mom? Are you all right?" Jenna said, her tone even and controlled and much too grown-up. Her eyes held unanswerable questions, and Marni wished she could be anywhere in the world right now except this bedroom, facing her daughter's inquisitive gaze.

A high-pitched tone emanated from the phone, and Marni reached across the bed and covered it with a pillow.

"Why did he call, Mom?" Jenna asked again.

Marni took a deep breath and grabbed Jenna's hand, guiding the girl to the bed to sit beside her. She struggled for the right words to explain to her daughter what they could be facing in the not-too-distant future. "Jenna, until a few minutes ago, your father didn't know about you."

"I know." Bright green eyes looked at Marni. A slight smile, almost as crooked as Cole's, was on Jenna's lips. "I guess I gave him a shock, huh?"

Despite the possible frailty of their future together, Marni chuckled. "I'm sure you did." She pictured Cole, frustrated because he couldn't get through, questions pounding through his mind. How could she avoid him until Monday? She needed time. Time to bolster her waning courage before she faced Cole's wrath.

She began to wonder if perhaps Rebecca had been right. Maybe she should have told Cole before he learned the truth. But when? How? None of that mattered now. He knew and he was angry. Marni supposed she really couldn't blame him; if she was in his shoes right now, she'd be downright furious.

"Why did he call?" Jenna asked for the third time.

Arlo sauntered into the bedroom and nudged Marni's hand, begging for attention. She absently scratched the dog behind the ear. "I ran into him yesterday."

"You saw him?" Jenna shot off the bed. "You saw him and you didn't tell me?" Confusion threaded through her young voice.

"Jenna, I..."

"Why didn't you tell me?" the girl demanded, her arms bouncing off her sides in agitation.

"Jenna, calm down."

"When can I see him? I want to meet him. He knows about me now, so there's no reason why I can't."

"Jenna, you don't understand. It's complicated."

"Then explain it to me." Jenna plopped on the bed and stretched out across the bedspread. Resting on her elbow, she placed her head in her palm and looked pointedly at Marni, waiting for her to begin. Arlo hopped up on the bed beside her and laid his large head on her hip, as if he, too, were waiting for an explanation. The dog moaned and closed his eyes while Jenna rubbed his dark muzzle.

Marni's voice choked with emotion. "I didn't mean for any of this to happen," she managed to say.

Regaining her composure, she tried to be as honest as possible, describing to Jenna as best she could what Cole had related to her about his disastrous marriage to Elizabeth Wakefield and his feelings about their child. "Now do you understand? If I told him about you, I was afraid he'd try to sue me for partial custody, sweetheart."

Jenna remained quiet and thoughtful while she digested the information Marni imparted about her father. "But do you know for sure? Would he really do that to us?"

The worry in her daughter's voice tugged at Marni's heart. "I didn't want to take the chance." Now that he knew about Jenna, anything was possible. Imagining the worst, Marni closed her eyes, but her fears for her daughter refused to be quelled. As did her fear of Carson. He'd paid her to stay out of his son's life, and she was certain he'd see he got his money's worth.

Jenna sat up and scooted close to Marni, wrapping her arms around her mother's neck. "I love you, Mom. I wouldn't ever leave you."

Marni hugged her daughter close, tears burning the backs of her eyes at the heartfelt confession. "I love you, too, Jenna."

Jenna released her hold on Marni and sat back on her heels. "What are we gonna do?"

Falling back on the bed, Marni laid her arm over her eyes. Her head ached, and the light from the bedside table stung her eyes. "I'm not sure yet. I've got to think about this for a while."

"I guess I shouldn't go with Denise now, huh?"

Marni lifted her arm to stare at her daughter. If Jenna really wanted to go skiing with the Lamberts, then she should go. Maybe getting away for the day would be good for her. Jenna was too young to be saddled with this sort of a dilemma. "You go ahead. I still have to work this weekend, and I need time to think this thing with your father through before Monday. I have a feeling he'll be waiting in my office when I get there."

"I wish you'd let me meet him," Jenna said in a wistful tone.

Marni sighed and stood up. She tried to smile, but the result was more of a grimace. "I'm sure he'll want to meet you, too." In fact, if she knew Cole as well as she thought she did, he would *demand* to see his daughter.

Jenna reached over Arlo to the pillow covering the phone. "I've gotta call Denise and tell her I can go."

"Just make sure you take the phone off the hook again when you're done," Marni told her.

Jenna nodded, then called Arlo before heading toward the door. "You still wanna watch the movie?" she asked, sounding hopeful.

Marni had no intention of denying her daughter anything tonight. Anything except seeing her father. "Sure. Just give me a few minutes, okay?"

"Okay, Mom." Jenna smiled brightly. As if the entire situation threatening their lives no longer held importance, she bounded out of the room, Arlo at her heels. In a matter of seconds the pair would be ensconced on the old sofa in the den, the phone glued to Jenna's ear as she chatted with Denise, no doubt informing her friend of the exciting turn of events.

Marni entered the bathroom and filled the sink with cold water. The wonder of youth, she thought while splashing the icy water on her face. If only she could share the same resilience as her daughter. But Marni was a realist and knew she had no choice but to face her problem with Cole. For a fleeting moment she thought of packing Jenna up in the car and driving away, destination unknown. When they found a place they liked, they could stop. Marni could wait tables if she had to, just to keep Jenna with her. But life wasn't quite so simple.

She drained the water out of the sink and flipped off the light. Walking over to the night table, she opened the drawer and sat down on the floral bedspread. Marni reached beneath an array of silk scarves until she found what she was looking for.

The cheap gold frame was cracked and peeled and nearly as old as the photographs behind the protective glass. Marni looked at the four small snapshots of herself and Cole. The pictures had been taken in a photo booth a few days before she'd left for California. She ran her hand over the glass, outlining Cole's firm jaw, tracing her finger over his full lower lip. Precious memories of a short time in her life when she'd been truly happy.

Regardless of her reasons for ending her relationship with Cole, no matter what her motivation for coming to California, Marni knew in her heart her adorable, precocious daughter was a product of the love she had once shared with Cole. A love that would now turn to hatred, since she, like Elizabeth, had denied him the choice of being a father.

COLE GLANCED AT THE CLOCK on the VCR and downed the remains of the whiskey, the soda he'd opened earlier neglected in favor of something stronger. He tried Marni's number again only to receive the irritating buzz indicating the line was busy. She'd taken the phone off the hook.

He had a daughter. And she'd be a teenager in less than six months. When he wasn't cursing Marni, he wondered what the girl looked like. Did she have her mother's huge brown eyes? Was she a blonde or a brunette, or a combination of the two? He wondered if she was tall and coltish or petite and slender like Marni. Did she hate math or was she a whiz at science? Cole had too many unanswered questions. Especially why hadn't he been told about her.

Pacing the confines of his living room, he wavered between anger and disbelief. Marni had completed her education, attended graduate school, secured a promising career as a district attorney and raised a child. How had she done it? Her mother had been ill and couldn't have been much help. Why hadn't she told him about the baby?

His anger resurfaced and he picked up the phone again. She'd probably unplugged the damn thing. He heard three rings and then a click.

"Hello?" The sound of Jenna's soft voice filtered through the telephone lines and Cole found himself at a loss for words. He didn't know what to say to her.

"Hello?" she asked again, whispering. "Is this you?"

The kid was smart. "Hi, Jenna."

"I'm glad you called. Mom's in the bedroom, so I can talk for a minute. She thinks I'm on the phone with Denise Lambert. I'd like to meet you."

"I'd like to meet you, too." Cole couldn't help but smile.

"Are you mad at my mom?" she asked him warily.

Cole didn't know how to answer. He didn't want to lie to his own kid. "I have some questions for her," he hedged, not wanting to frighten the girl. None of the blame could be laid at Jenna's feet.

"That's a good idea," Jenna stated matter-of-factly, sounding much wiser than her age.

"You don't suppose she'd want to talk to me now, do you?"

Jenna giggled. "If she even knew I was talking to you, she'd hang up the phone again."

"How is your mom?" He felt a little guilty pumping Jenna, but he couldn't help himself.

"She's kinda scared."

Cole didn't doubt it for a minute. As angry as he was right now, Marni should be scared to death. "Jenna? Would you give me your address?"

"I guess I could. I mean, it's not like you're a total stranger, right?"

Cole chuckled. He couldn't wait to meet his daughter.

"It's 623 Magnolia Circle, Malibu. Do you need directions?" she asked.

"No. I'll find it."

"I won't tell Mom you called. It would only upset her again."

"You shouldn't lie to your mother, Jenna," he scolded her gently, feeling very parental. The sensation was new to him. He'd always wanted a family, a large family, but the opportunity had never come his way. Until now.

"If she doesn't ask me, then I don't have to say anything. Besides, you guys need to talk. Are you coming over now?"

"I'm on my way."

They said their goodbyes and Cole looked the address up on the map. The drive should take him thirty minutes, twenty if he pushed it a little. Then he'd meet his daughter face-to-face *and* have a long talk with Marni. Tonight, she'd answer all his questions. Tonight, she wouldn't be able to escape him.

MARNI ENTERED the cedar-paneled den to find Jenna lying on the blue plaid love seat, the cordless phone sitting on the pine cocktail table. Arlo lay in a heap of fur in front of the cold hearth, snoring softly. She placed kindling in the fireplace, added logs, then set the wood to burn.

"Did you call Denise?" Marni asked, moving to the matching sofa.

"Yeah. They're picking me up at six in the morning. Mr. Lambert wants to beat the traffic up to Big Bear. Are you sure you don't want me to stay home with you?" Jenna asked cautiously.

The girl who had run from the bedroom with such enthusiasm nearly thirty minutes ago had been replaced by a pensive young lady. Marni decided the change was natural enough, considering the evening's events. "No. You go on ahead. Maybe by the time you get home, I'll have figured something out. You have fun, and don't worry about anything.''

"Mom? Can I meet him?"

"I think that's inevitable, don't you?"

Jenna smiled sheepishly, "Yeah, I guess so." She turned her attention back toward the television and immediately became engrossed in the movie starring Gordon MacRae and Shirley Jones. She chewed absently on the inside of her lower lip. Another trait she'd inherited from her father.

Marni sighed and curled up on the long sofa, her slippered feet tucked beneath her, and tried to keep her attention on the musical. Her powers of concentration were shot. Her thoughts continually returned to Cole and their upcoming confrontation. She had the entire weekend before she had to face him, but the thought offered her little comfort. As much as she tried, she couldn't compose the right words to explain why she'd kept Jenna's existence to herself all these years. After her two failed attempts to tell him, she'd never bothered again. Now she had to deal with the consequences of her actions.

Arlo lifted his head and emitted a low growl, seconds before the doorbell sounded. The huge dog lumbered through the house toward the unfortunate soul who had dared to disturb his nap.

Marni jumped. Her nerves were shattered. Cole didn't know where she lived, she reminded herself. Otherwise he would have been here nearly an hour ago. Still, a feeling of dread coursed through her. She glanced at Jenna, whose eyes were glued to the television.

The bell sounded again and Marni stood. "I'll get it," she mumbled, and headed toward the living room to the front door, wondering who would be stopping by at this hour. Someone from the office who hadn't been able to reach her? She felt a pang of guilt.

Arlo waited at the door, looking back at Marni as if she were taking entirely too long. She patted the dog on the head, flipped on the porch light and peered through the tiny peephole. Her heart, or what was left of it, fell to her feet.

Cole.

Cole was here.

A front door and three rooms separated father from daughter. Three states wouldn't have been enough.

She rested her head against the wooden door and concentrated on resuming a steady heartbeat. This couldn't be happening. None of this was real. She would wake up any second now in her bed and life would be normal again. *Okay,* she thought, and drew in a deep breath. *Maybe I'm being just a little too melodramatic. I can deal with this.*

She looked through the peephole again and sighed heavily. Cole really was standing on her porch. How had he found out where she lived?

"Open the door, Marni." He didn't sound angry, only determined.

She hesitated.

"Dammit, open the door!" Now he sounded angry.

Surprised she still had the capacity to function, she unlocked the door and swung it open. Cole stepped through the portal, not bothering to wait for an invitation. "Why didn't you tell me?" he demanded, striding past her into the tiled entryway, stopping short at the sight of Arlo. "Does he bite?" he asked, keeping his gaze on the dog.

She wished Arlo was the biting type, but the huge shepherd was more likely to lick an adversary into submission. Only his size and deep bark were a deterrent to would-be trespassers. "No. He won't even chase cats."

Arlo glanced at Cole, then lay down at his feet with a groan.

Cole turned to face her, his large hands thrust firmly on jeans-clad hips. He wore no jacket, only a white University of Kansas sweatshirt.

"Come in."

Cole ignored her sarcasm and repeated his question. "Why didn't you tell me I had a daughter?"

"Cole, I really don't think—"

"No, you obviously didn't think." He threw the words at her like stones. "I have a kid. She's twelve years old and I only learned about her ninety minutes ago." He'd told himself on the drive to Malibu he wouldn't lose his cool. There were things he wanted to discuss with Marni, and if he lost his tightly reined temper, they'd end up arguing and nothing would be resolved.

She bit her lip and looked away. "Please, Cole."

He glared at her, crossing his arms over his chest. "Please, what?"

She looked at him again and Cole saw the pleading expression in her eyes. Large eyes, dark and luminous, gazed at him in confusion.

"Calm down," Marni said. "I can't think straight anymore."

Marni stepped around him, and Cole followed her into an elegantly furnished living room. Slowly, she sat in one of two rose-colored chairs positioned opposite a floral sofa of soft muted shades of blue, mauve and cream. She ran a shaky hand through her unruly blond curls, looking no older than the eighteen-year-old girl he'd once thought he loved. His heart tightened in his chest with the memory.

He took a steadying breath and tried to control his emotions. Moving to the sofa, he sat and faced Marni. Aiming for a semblance of calm, he spoke carefully. "What is there to think about? I want to know why you didn't bother to tell me I had a daughter."

If maturity had done anything for Cole, it had improved his ability to wait out his opponent, to assess a situation, to strike when an attack was least expected. He'd wait all night if that's what it took to get Marni to answer his questions. And this was one time he wouldn't let her skirt around the subject.

He stared at her, but she only looked straight ahead at a vase filled with exotic silk flowers resting on the low oval table between them. "I tried. You were on your honeymoon by the time I realized I was pregnant." Her words came out in a choked whisper and tears brimmed in her eyes.

He fought the urge to wipe away the lone tear that escaped, his earlier anger evaporating. A part of him longed to take her in his arms and hold her tight against him to ease her pain.

He pictured Marni, young, pregnant and probably very frightened. To think she had gone through such an ordeal virtually alone tugged at emotions buried deep inside him. Yet how could he want to hold her, offer her comfort, when she'd turned her back on the love he'd given her so long ago? "You still should have told me," he said gruffly.

"What did you want me to do?" Her voice held a sarcastic bite. "Should I have found out where you and Elizabeth were staying and phoned you there? Better yet, I could have come in person. Wouldn't that have been fun?"

Cole bristled. He wanted to comprehend her reasons for not telling him about Jenna, but at the same time he couldn't understand why she wouldn't reveal something so important. The birth of a child was not the kind of news one kept to oneself. Before he could put his thoughts into words, a flash of movement caught his attention. Turning, he saw her. His daughter. Emotions he couldn't name overwhelmed him.

"Mom? Are you okay?" Jenna's voice held a note of concern that tugged at Cole's heart.

Marni's shoulders sagged for a moment as if in defeat. When she glanced his way, panic flashed in her soulful eyes. She stood and went to the girl, pulling her into a tight hug. "I'm fine, sweetie." Her voice was whisper-soft.

He tried to breathe but found the simple task difficult. Nearly as tall as Marni, Jenna would likely soon be taller than her mother by a few inches. Her eyes were closed and he wanted her to open them, anxious to get a good look at the girl he'd fathered thirteen years ago.

Jenna stepped out of Marni's embrace and Cole stood, watching his daughter. He didn't know how long they faced each other, but time seemed to stop. The glass-domed clock on one of the cherrywood side tables ticked in unison with the beat of his heart.

"Jenna, this is Cole Ballinger."

He heard the resignation in Marni's voice, but Cole could only stare at the coltish figure of his daughter. He knew without a doubt the young girl returning his gaze with open curiosity would one day be a beautiful young woman. His daughter. His heart overflowed with pride.

He stole a quick glance at Marni. The tears that had threatened earlier fell freely down her cheeks. With a shiver of recollection he remembered another time he'd seen her cry. The day she'd told him she never wanted to see him again. He still wanted to know why she'd called their affair to an end so abruptly.

Jenna moved closer to Cole. Bright green eyes stared at him questioningly.

"Hello, Jenna."

"Hi," she returned shyly, a hesitant smile tugging at the corners of her lips.

"You're almost as tall as your mother."

Jenna cast him a full grin. "Mom always said I had your eyes."

Marni's heart wrenched with pain. She'd always known Jenna resembled Cole, but she'd never realized exactly how much until now. She'd pictured them together in her mind at least a zillion times over the years, but never had she imagined she would feel such a confusing mixture of joy and pain. Jenna deserved to know her father, but that knowledge would change all their lives forever.

Marni needed time to recompose herself. "I'll make some coffee." Neither Cole nor Jenna acknowledged her, and she slipped quietly out of the room.

In the kitchen, she moved around automatically, filling the coffee maker with water, setting mugs on a serving tray. Fragments of conversation from the living room drifted into the kitchen, and she tried to discount the easy relationship developing between father and daughter. What had she hoped for? That Jenna would despise her father? She should be happy they seemed to be getting along so well, but she couldn't bring herself to enjoy what she'd dreamed about for so many years. At least keeping Cole at a distance had been safe.

Marni returned to the living room with tray in hand, coffee for her and Cole and a mug of cocoa for Jenna. Her daughter sat next to Cole on the sofa, telling him about her friend Denise while Cole listened with rapt attention, only casting a cursory glance in Marni's direction when she set the tray on the oval table.

"You need to tell her," Cole said to Jenna.

Jenna turned to face Marni. "Mom, I'm sorry. I gave Dad the address. It's my fault he's here."

Marni's heart twisted, not because Jenna had given him the address but because of her easy reference to Cole as "Dad." Any time they had spoken of Cole, Jenna had always referred to Cole as "him" or "my father."

She cast Cole a scathing glance before answering Jenna. "We can talk about that later. Why don't you go on to bed. Your—Cole and I have a lot to talk about."

Jenna nodded in agreement, a smile on her face. "I am sleepy," she admitted, and smothered a yawn. The girl turned to face her father. "Can I kiss you good-night?" she asked him shyly.

Cole smiled. "I'd like that," he answered softly.

Marni poured coffee from the carafe, wishing she could ignore the exchange of emotion between parent and child. She added cream to the steaming mug of black brew with the concentration of a chemist.

Jenna picked up the mug of cocoa from the tray. "Thanks, Mom."

Marni kissed her daughter good-night. "I'll be in later."

"Mom," Jenna wailed. "I'm too old to be tucked into bed. Geez, I'll be a teenager soon."

Marni lifted a brow at Jenna. "Well, indulge me, anyway."

Jenna left the room and called Arlo, who'd resumed his nap near the tiled entryway. The shepherd trotted off behind Jenna, leaving Cole and Marni alone.

Turning her attention back to Cole, Marni shuddered at the dark expression on his face. "Coffee?" she asked, unsure what to say to break the uncomfortable silence hanging between them.

He sighed heavily. "Don't you have anything stronger?"

"There's an old bottle of Jack Daniel's around here somewhere," she offered, not really wanting to continue their conversation.

"That'll do."

Cole waited while Marni disappeared to get the liquor. She returned from the kitchen with the whiskey and a small glass, setting it on the tray beside the carafe of coffee. He poured himself two fingers of the Daniel's and tossed it back, savoring the heat of the liquid burning its way down his throat.

"She's a great kid, Marni. You've done an excellent job raising her."

The yellow flecks in her eyes seemed to flash at him. "Gee, thanks."

"I mean it," he said, not rising to the bait of her derision.

Marni lowered her eyes. "I'm sorry," she said, the heat gone from her voice. "I'm a little edgy."

"Why didn't you tell me?" He waited, hoping she would finally give him the answers he needed to hear. She had to have a good reason for not telling him he'd fathered a child.

She set her mug down on the table. "I thought I explained. By the time I learned I was pregnant, you were on your honeymoon with Elizabeth."

"No, I mean yesterday. Today."

"I don't know."

She knows, she just won't tell me. He wasn't sure where the thought came from, but he knew as well as he knew his own name she was lying. Something was keeping her from

telling him the truth, and he was determined to find out
what. Perhaps a different approach... "I'm sorry you had
to go through all this alone. If I had known..."

"What, Cole? If you had known, what?" she snapped
at him. "You would have divorced Elizabeth and come
running to me and Jenna? Would you have tossed aside a
woman of your own class to assume your role as father in
Jenna's life?"

Cole remained silent. His marriage to Elizabeth might
have been a sham, but Cole honestly could not imagine
how he would have handled the news Marni was pregnant.

"I didn't think so." Her tone was scathing. "Jenna and
I have done fine by ourselves all these years and we'll
continue to do so. *Without you.*"

"Jenna needs a father."

"Jenna has a mother. She doesn't need anyone else."
The heat returned to Marni's voice, and yellow anger
flashed in her deep brown eyes.

"I beg to differ." He set the empty glass on the table
with more force than he intended.

"Beg all you want, Cole. Jenna is my daughter." Her
voice rose slightly. "Get it straight. She's *my* daughter. I
had her, I raised her."

"And I'm her father," he growled, unable to keep his
temper in check. "Just a little fact you forgot to mention."

Marni glared at him. She had to make him understand
he couldn't be a part of her life again. She'd made a bargain with the devil and now she was paying the consequences for the deal she'd struck. "We don't need you."

"I really don't care what you *think* you need. Jenna is
mine, too, Marni. You've kept her a secret from me far

too long. Did it ever occur to you what *I* might want? Or Jenna, for that matter?''

Guilt reached out with icy fingers to grip Marni's heart. Did Cole really think she was so callous she didn't realize how much her choices had hurt him, and Jenna? "Why can't you just leave us alone?" She hated the pleading note in her voice.

"I don't turn my back on my responsibilities. I never have." His eyes flashed dangerously and he flexed his hands, gripping his knees until his knuckles turned white. Marni knew he had a volatile temper; she'd seen it the day she ended their affair, and the thought of facing his wrath again wasn't a happy one.

"I'm not about to start ignoring my obligations now. I have twelve years to make up to my kid and I plan to start immediately. Like I said, you've done a great job with her, but she needs a father as well as a mother."

"We don't want you in our lives," she whispered.

"That may be *your* opinion but it certainly isn't Jenna's." Cole's voice was deceptively calm, belying the green fire burning in his gaze.

Fear and irrational jealousy settled in the pit of Marni's belly. "How do you know what Jenna wants?" Could she lose Jenna to Cole emotionally as well as physically? Suddenly the threat seemed very real indeed. And, of course, there was Carson. The wild card.

Cole stood abruptly and ran a hand through his hair. "Look, I'm tired of this. I'm going to be a part of my daughter's life, Marni. *An active part.* And nothing you can say will stop me." With long strides he reached the entryway. "I'll see you tomorrow."

Before Marni could object, she heard the front door close more forcefully than necessary. A deafening silence cloaked the spacious living room, settling over her like a black fog. Cole's car roared to life and then the sound was gone, leaving only the soft tick-tick-tick of the anniversary clock on the end table.

For the second time that day, the faint sound implied a ticking bomb waiting to explode in her face.

CHAPTER FIVE

Marni wanted to know who the idiot was who had said "Things look better in the morning." Her black mood was in sync with the gathering storm clouds rolling in off the ocean. Nothing looked any brighter today than it had last night when Cole had stormed out of the beach house.

She poured herself a mug of strong black coffee, forgoing her usual cream. Taking a sip, she waited for the caffeine to revive her. Nothing happened.

Leaving the kitchen, she crossed the den toward the sliding glass door leading onto the deck. Arlo nearly knocked her over in his haste to get outside and complete his morning routine. Stepping onto the deck, Marni inhaled deeply. The scent of sea and sand wafted over her but didn't have its usual calming effect. This morning the fierce pounding of waves upon the shore matched her mood. Dangerous and reckless.

Striving for a semblance of calm, she curled onto the deck chair and snuggled into her red hooded sweatshirt. The January morning air held a bite to it, and Marni welcomed the slight sting against her cheeks. She wanted nothing more than to curl up into a ball and sleep for a few days. To regroup and restore her sanity so she would be emotionally prepared to deal with Cole and his rapidly developing relationship with Jenna.

Unfortunately, life didn't work that way. And not today. There was work to be done, and even Cole Ballinger had to take second place to a serial killer who might soon find himself free to kill again. Well, not if she could help it.

Arlo trotted up the steps of the deck and laid his large head on her lap. The dog looked at her expectantly and waited for his morning scratch behind the ears. A few sea gulls engaged in battle over scraps of food while Arlo groaned his pleasure at Marni's ministrations.

"Good morning."

Marni jumped at the sound of Cole's deep voice. She'd been so lost in thought, she hadn't even heard the rusty hinges on the back gate.

"You're here early," she said, careful to keep her tone even and controlled. "It's not even eight o'clock yet. I have work to do."

Cole stood on the steps leading to the deck, his hair ruffled by the wind. "Sorry. I couldn't sleep." He stepped onto the deck and sat in the chair opposite her. Leaning forward, he clasped his hands together, his elbows resting on denim-covered knees. Even the heavy ski sweater covering his thick muscled arms and broad chest emphasized his rugged good looks.

"Coffee?" she offered, conscious of her own appearance. She hadn't bothered to apply an ounce of makeup and her hair was pulled away from her face in a ponytail.

Cole nodded.

"Black?" she asked, wondering if he indulged in cream now like she did. Running her gaze over his body convinced her otherwise.

"That's fine."

He looked a little ragged around the edges, as if he'd been up half the night. A spattering of crow's feet fanned outward from his eyes, and he hadn't shaved. She couldn't deny his distress made her feel just a tiny bit better. Misery loves company, she mused.

She gently urged Arlo out of her way. "I'm gonna trade you in for a Doberman," she told the dog, and went into the house.

She returned a few minutes later with Cole's coffee. "Jenna's already gone," she said.

He took a sip of coffee, then wrapped his long, brown fingers around the mug. "I know. I came to see you. We need to talk, Marni."

She sat back in the deck chair and curled her feet beneath her. "I thought we did that last night." She wasn't emotionally equipped to endure his demands right now. There had been no time to lick her wounds or come to terms with her new circumstances.

Cole leveled his gaze at her. The look he gave her told her he was not in the mood for a debate. "We need to resolve this."

She sighed. How could she argue with him? He was right. They did need a resolution to their problem, but for the life of her, Marni didn't know where to begin. "What do you want from me?" she asked, gazing at the ocean.

When he didn't answer her question, she looked at him. He was staring at the deck between his feet, lost in his own thoughts. He appeared as defeated and dejected as she felt. Finally, he lifted his head. The pain in his eyes reached into her soul and squeezed a part of her that had lain dormant for twelve years.

"I told you last night. I want to be part of Jenna's life."

She opened her mouth to protest and he raised a hand to stop her. "Let me finish. I've missed twelve years of her life and I want to start making it up to her."

"How do you plan to do that?" she asked cautiously. Was this it? Was this where he told her he planned to sue for custody? *Please, God, no.*

"By being there for her when she needs me, for one."

"That's very noble." The sarcasm in her voice veiled her fear. Where was her cool courtroom demeanor now, when she most needed it? "But I've got a question for you. For how long? Until your dad decides it's time for you to move on to another division of Ballinger Electronics? What happens after you've saved the software division from bankruptcy? Do you go to Boston or Texas or God knows where? What happens to Jenna when that happens, Cole?"

Cole's eyes glittered dangerously. "It won't."

No matter how much conviction she detected in his voice, she found it difficult to believe him. "Really? How do you know that? Please, leave us alone before Jenna really does get hurt."

Cole tamped down his anger and frustration. "You're just going to have to trust me."

She laughed harshly, the sound grating on his already-taut nerves.

He took a deep breath in an effort to calm his rising anger. "Look, why don't we just take this one step at a time. Don't look too far into the future."

"I have to, Cole. We're talking about Jenna's future, and if you're just going to waltz into her life and then dance out again, it's going to break her heart." She paused and took a sip of coffee. "I won't allow you to do that to her."

The frustration hit him full force. Why couldn't he make her understand he'd never hurt his daughter? "How can I convince you?"

She looked at him as if he wasn't there. "I don't know that you can."

"Let's just take today and get through it, all right? I'm tired of arguing about this. Jenna's my daughter, Marni. You can't deny that. Don't make this difficult, for any of us." He didn't mean the words to sound so harsh, but he was quickly losing his patience. Damn, but the woman was stubborn. "I promise I'll never do anything to harm Jenna."

A wry grin canted her mouth, and her expression softened. "You made me another promise once, too. Remember?"

He remembered, and he wanted to cringe at her softly spoken words. If she'd spat them at him, they couldn't have been a more hurtful reminder of another time, another place.

The simple words of love they'd exchanged thirteen years before rang with clarity through his mind. He could still see Marni on his father's small sailboat on the lake, her wild blond curls pulled back into a tight ponytail, her eyes shining with adoration.

I love you, Marni.

Oh, Cole, promise me we'll always be together.

I promise.

He tried to shake the memory from his consciousness. "You broke a few promises yourself. *You* were the one who called it off, then left town without a trace. What was I supposed to do, wait forever for you to come back to me?"

She looked away from him, her gaze slipping to something beyond his shoulder. When she finally spoke, her words were soft. "We can have this conversation over and over, Cole, and we'll never settle it. Leave it alone."

"You brought it up, lady," he shot back, finding refuge in his anger. Anything to keep from feeling the other emotions trying to surface.

Marni stared at the mug in her hand, silently cursing herself for initiating this discussion. What possible good could it do? And angering Cole was far from the best strategy. Rebecca had warned her to tell Cole about Jenna before he found out on his own. Thus far, he'd never once mentioned custody. Now, she had to wonder how long it would take if she continued to provoke him.

This was Cole, not Carson—but how long would it be before Cole told his father about Jenna?

One step at a time, one day at a time. They could go on arguing and fighting each other until Jenna turned eighteen and probably never resolve their own personal issues. "I'm sorry, Cole. I wish things could have been different." Marni swallowed convulsively. "But what happened between us has nothing to with Jenna."

"It has everything to do with Jenna. I've missed so much of her life."

She glimpsed a flash of torment in his eyes, and his words almost pierced her resolve not to let him into their lives. He had indeed been cheated of precious time with his daughter. A fresh wave of guilt assaulted her conscience.

The dark clouds overhead threatened to burst. "Come on," she said, pushing herself up from the deck chair. Several droplets of water descended from the heavens. In another minute they'd be soaked if they stayed outside. "I've got photo albums for you to look through. It won't replace what you've lost, but at least it'll bring you up to date."

COLE SAT ON THE SOFA in Marni's den and picked up the first volume, the year printed with a bold black marker on the binding.

Marni had retreated to her study to prepare a brief on the Kendell case. Though thankful for the private time with Jenna's early childhood, he couldn't forget that the mother of his daughter was nearby. A part of him wanted her with him now, as he caught a glimpse of his daughter's life within the pages waiting to be explored. He shook the sensation off. Better to go it alone.

Taking a deep, steadying breath, he opened the first album. Behind the velum covering, the opening page held a birth certificate, and the phrase ''suitable for framing'' trotted through his mind. The certificate proudly displayed prints of the tiniest feet and hands Cole had ever seen. He laid his own hand next to Jenna's little handprint. Hers was smaller than his own pinkie finger.

He read the certificate. *Jenna Coleen Ballinger!* Marni had never said a word to him about Jenna's last name. Of course, he really hadn't given her a chance, he supposed. He'd been too busy berating her for not telling him about Jenna in the first place.

Turning the page, he found a copy of Jenna's baptismal certificate. He smiled, remembering a discussion he and Marni had had years ago. Marni's Catholic convictions ran deep, while Cole's family were occasional Baptists who'd only attended church services when it suited Carson Ballinger's needs. ''Looks like you won that round, sweetheart,'' he chuckled.

Continuing through the first volume, he stared at a photo of Marni in late pregnancy. Her small frame ballooned from the baby she carried. *His* baby. A surge of tenderness and longing swept over him. God, he wished he could have been with her. He'd heard about the hor-

rors women went through in childbirth, and a sixth sense
told him Marni must have had a really tough time. She
was simply too big. There was no sign in the picture of the
slim girl he'd memorized with his hands in the moonlight.

With a sigh, he turned the page. An assortment of
photos of Jenna were organized beneath the velum, the
date and age printed neatly below each snapshot. Jenna's
hospital photo, Jenna when she came home from the
hospital, Jenna, with her grandmother beneath a huge
shade tree. Jenna at three months, wearing a pink sun-
suit and a polka-dot bonnet to protect her head from the
August sunlight. Marni holding Jenna in her arms in the
middle of a swimming pool, an expression of pure delight
on Marni's strikingly beautiful face.

He continued to flip through the pages that recorded
the life of his daughter. Marni had even managed to capture one of Jenna's first steps. By the time he reached the
third volume, he felt as if he'd never missed a second of
his daughter's early years. Now, included with the various photos and mementos, were report cards and awards,
her first school photo, revealing missing teeth, and pictures of Jenna's first communion. She looked like a pre-
mature bride, dressed in white with a small veil covering
her sable hair. Her green eyes twinkled mischievously as
the priest offered her the sacrament.

Marni had seized every important moment of Jenna's
life and kept it safe, almost as if she had known he would
one day look through these volumes in an attempt to regain a fragment of what he'd lost.

MARNI REREAD THE SAME paragraph for the fourth time.
She tossed the transcript aside in disgust and listened to
the heavy rain pelting the roof. Usually the steady rhythm
and distant thunder relaxed her, but today she only found

the sounds irritating and she couldn't concentrate. A quick glance at her watch told her Cole had been poring over Jenna's past for nearly three hours.

When she'd started the albums, she'd told herself they were for Jenna. Now she wasn't so sure. Had she really done it for Cole? Had she known, deep down, one day he would learn of his daughter's existence?

Picking up the transcript again, she tried to concentrate on the testimony of the witness in the Kendell case. She'd been over it twice and knew she was missing something. Where, she had no idea.

The hairs on the back of her neck tingled, and she looked up from the transcript to find Cole standing in the doorway, pain etched on his perfectly chiseled features. "Cole?" she asked, concerned at the unusual brightness of his eyes.

He held the scrapbook in his hands and stared at the cover for a long time. "I should have been there for her." His words were whisper-soft but no less painful.

"Cole..."

"No, Marni," he said forcefully. "I should have been there for her. When she cut her first tooth, I should have eased her pain. I should have helped her take her first steps, played Santa Claus for her at Christmas." He ran a hand roughly through his already-tousled hair. "God, did she even learn to say 'da-da'?"

Marni tried to blink back the tears burning her eyes.

Cole took a deep breath. "When she went from kindergarten to the first grade, I should have been there to see it. I should have been the one to sneak into her room and replace the tooth she hid under her pillow with a quarter. Who taught her how to ride a bike, to roller-skate? I wasn't even around to walk her through the neighborhood on Halloween. She's nearly ready to start dating and I've missed so damn much of her life."

God, how Marni understood Cole's anguish. How many times had she wished for the same thing? Too many, she thought. "Jenna won't be dating for a while," she said, trying to lighten the atmosphere.

"You know what I mean," he said.

Marni sighed. "Yes, I know." She stared at him, unsure what to say to ease the ache in his heart. An ache she understood all too well. "Cole, if it makes you feel any better, there must have been a million times when I—"

The phone rang and Marni reached for it. "Hello?" She gazed at Cole, unable to believe what she'd almost revealed to him. The pain on his face was too much for her to bear, and she looked away, concentrating on the desk blotter. "This is Marni. Yes, I've been waiting for your call. Can you hang on a minute?" She pushed the red button on the phone and placed the caller on hold.

Cole stood abruptly. "I need to get out of here for a while."

"This won't take long."

He shook his head. "No. You have work to do. What time will Jenna be home?"

"Late afternoon or early evening."

Cole sighed and shoved his hands into the pockets of his jeans. "I'd like to take Jenna to dinner if that's okay. Both of you," he added almost as an afterthought. "Nothing fancy, just a burger."

"Cole, I..." Marni closed her eyes. Then she opened them and gave him a slight smile. "Sure. Seven okay?"

Cole nodded. "I'll see you then." He laid the photo album on the corner of her desk and headed for the doorway. He stopped and turned to face her. "Marni? Thank you," he said. He turned and was gone.

Tears stung the back of Marni's eyes. Those two simple words had finally destroyed her resolution to keep Jenna from Cole.

Pulling herself together, she choked back a sob and punched the blinking light on the phone. "Thanks for waiting. I have one question, Sergeant Rodriguez. Just what exactly did you promise Monvale for his testimony? Thanks to you and Officer Harding, I've got a serial killer headed for freedom instead of death row."

CHAPTER SIX

MARNI WALKED INTO THE DEN to find Jenna restlessly pacing the spacious room. Arlo lay near the sliding glass door, his furry head moving back and forth, following each step Jenna took.

"He's late," Jenna announced.

Marni glanced at her watch. "Jenna, it's only five after seven." Although she'd never admit it, she, too, was nervous. She'd taken nearly an hour and a half to get ready, discarding one outfit after another. Either she was too dressed up or too casual. No happy medium. Finally, deciding on a pair of black jeans, a thick white sweater and a pair of low-heeled suede boots, she was ready.

"He said seven, Mom. He's late. Do you think he changed his mind?"

The despair in her daughter's voice struck a protective chord in Marni. She had to trust her instincts or she'd drive herself insane with worry. Cole would never intentionally hurt his daughter. Especially after his behavior this afternoon.

The doorbell rang and Jenna darted from the room, clearing the two steps leading into the den from the kitchen in one quick jump. Arlo groaned, laid his head down, and closed his eyes. His services were not required.

Marni followed at a more reasonable pace. By the time she reached the living room, Jenna had already commandeered Cole and was guiding him toward the sofa.

"How was the skiing?" he asked Jenna.

The man who'd been in her home earlier today had been replaced by the Cole she remembered. An air of confidence surrounded him. Marni wasn't sure if he was putting on an act for Jenna's benefit or if he'd come to terms with the circumstances. Nevertheless, she was pleased to see some of the old Cole again.

"Great." Jenna grinned broadly, a definite sparkle in her eyes. "I graduated to one of the bigger hills today."

"Jenna, I thought we discussed that." Marni frowned. Her daughter had no sense of danger. "You were supposed to wait until I could go with you before you moved on to the larger hills."

Jenna sighed impatiently and snuggled closer to Cole, looping her arm though his as if she'd been doing it for years. "Oh, Mom. You worry too much. I know what I'm doing."

Marni glanced at Cole, wondering if he was going to offer an opinion on the matter. He remained uncharacteristically silent.

Their eyes locked and something flickered deep in his gaze. A distinct tingle shot through her, and she struggled to ignore the way her insides skittered.

"Did you get your brief finished?" The question may have been innocent, but the soft, velvety tone he used was more seductive than champagne and candlelight.

"Uh, no," she stammered, unable to tear her eyes from him. "I still have some research to do, and I need to discuss a few things with Dorlan."

Jenna tugged on the sleeve of Cole's well-worn leather jacket, breaking the spell. "Dad, I'm starved."

"Ready?" he asked Marni, pulling his keys from the pocket of his jeans.

Twenty minutes later they entered a fifties-style burger house on the pier. Rock music from another era played in the background, just loud enough to be heard over the din of voices and clatter of dishes. The waitresses were dressed in old-fashioned cheerleading uniforms from a multitude of universities across the country. A hostess dressed in an old UCLA uniform greeted them with a smile and led them to a banquette near the window overlooking the ocean.

Marni slid into the booth, expecting Jenna to sit next to her. Instead, the girl scooted into the bench seat opposite Marni, sitting in the center. Certainly Jenna didn't expect Marni to sit beside Cole, did she?

Cole attempted to sit next to Jenna, but the girl wouldn't budge. "Scoot over, kidlet," he told her.

"Um, I'm left-handed, Dad. We'll be bumping elbows all over the place."

Marni looked from Cole to Jenna and back again. She frowned, a feeling of dread passing over her. There was no way she could sit so close to Cole for the next thirty minutes. Nope. Out of the question....

"Why don't you sit next to Mom? That way I can talk to both of you," Jenna suggested.

Marni took a deep breath. *I'm an adult. I can handle this.* She slid further into the booth and glanced at Jenna, expecting to find a triumphant expression on her daughter's face. Instead, Jenna innocently examined the menu, seemingly oblivious to her mother's discomfort.

The hostess left and Cole sat next to Marni. The aroma of his after-shave tickled her memory, evoking images of a moonlit night and water lapping lazily against the shore, converging with whispered promises and hot, erotic kisses that took her breath away. *Stop it!* she reprimanded herself.

Marni picked up the menu and quickly scanned the fare. Burgers, with or without cheese, onion rings, fries and every variety of fountain drink contrived to tempt even the most conscientious dieter. Everything sounded good, and fattening, and she finally settled on a chocolate malted surprise. Maybe if she concentrated on rich chocolate destined to add an inch to her hips she could get through the night.

"What's good?" Cole asked Jenna.

Jenna laughed and smiled at her father. "Burgers," she said, her voice alight with amusement as a young waitress outfitted in Stanford red and white arrived to take their order.

Jenna rattled on to Cole about her ski trip, Arlo, school and any other subject that came to her mind. He listened patiently to her exuberant explanation of her first year at junior high, glancing at Marni occasionally. The look in his eyes spoke of love. Love for his daughter.

The waitress delivered their drinks while Jenna flipped through the metal pages of the miniature jukebox set on the rear of the table. "I don't know any of these," she said, her brow wrinkling. "They must be really old."

Cole reached into his pocket and pulled out some change. "I bet your mom and I know a few of them." He moved closer to Marni, slipping his arm behind her. Leaning over her toward the jukebox, he pinned her to the back of the booth. Her stomach somersaulted when his knee accidently brushed hers.

"Here's one I know she'll remember." While he spoke the words to Jenna, he looked directly at Marni, his warm gaze full of expectation.

"What is it?" she asked, unable to help herself.

"Tonight's the Night." His voice dropped to a husky purr, as warm and intimate as a lover's caress.

The Rod Stewart song brought to mind images that caused an instant surge of heat to speed through her veins. One corner of Cole's mouth tipped upward in a beguiling, rakish grin, and Marni knew he, too, remembered the passionate lovemaking they'd shared while the song played softly in the background. Marni swallowed convulsively, unable to escape Cole or the recollection of their lovemaking. "I remember." The whispered admission flew from her lips before she could prevent it.

Jenna giggled. "Was this *your* song?"

"No," Marni said.

"You could say that," Cole answered easily.

Much to Marni's relief, Cole leaned back into the seat. Her comfort, however, was short-lived. He kept his arm on the edge of the booth behind her. If she leaned back, only an inch or two, his fingers would no doubt brush against her neck. She was grateful when, a few minutes later, the waitress delivered their meal.

An elderly couple strolled past their table and smiled. Marni supposed from the outside looking in, they appeared to be the ideal family. How easy that would be to believe, she thought. How many times had she dreamed the same thing?

She'd done more than her share of *that*. When she was younger, a student in college with a baby and an ill mother to take care of, she'd spent many a night fantasizing she and Cole were happily married.

Delusions.

She'd been foolish to believe she even had a right to harbor such silly dreams. She'd given up that privilege when she'd left Cole and Elk Falls. Each and every month she'd been reminded of her decision when the hefty check from Carson Ballinger was deposited into her bank account.

Carson!

She'd been so caught up in her own emotional turmoil and the disasters the defense in the Kendell matter was causing her, she hadn't given Carson Ballinger a conscious thought all evening. What would he do when he learned Cole had a daughter, and that he, Carson, was a grandfather? No doubt he'd tell Cole about the money and how he'd paid her off to get out of his son's life. She could easily imagine the picture Carson would paint.

No, Marni resolved firmly. She had to tell Cole, and quickly, before Carson beat her to it.

"Could we, Mom?" Jenna asked, dabbing the last of her french fries in the glob of ketchup on her plate.

Marni pulled herself back to the present. "Could we what?"

Jenna sighed impatiently. "Dad said we could go to the arcades if it's okay with you."

Marni looked at Cole. "Are you sure?" she asked him. Jenna could be fairly persistent when she set her mind to something.

He turned to face her and his knee brushed hers again. Marni flinched at the light touch. She wondered if he did it deliberately, especially since he didn't bother to move. Other than his breathtaking smile, he seemed oblivious to the contact.

Cole nodded, a look of indulgence in his eyes. "It's been a long time since I've played a game of Space Invaders."

Her insides fluttered again at the intensity of his gaze. She reached for her chocolate soda, hoping to quell the tingling sensations.

Marni remembered the hours they had spent in the arcades at the Farmer's Faire in Elk Falls. Cole had won a ridiculous amount of stuffed animals and other carnival favors, which she'd had to leave behind when she moved to California because there hadn't been room in the small rented trailer for such frivolities.

"Okay, but only for a while." Sooner or later she'd have to have a talk with him about spoiling Jenna. They needed to discuss boundaries or Jenna would run roughshod over him.

"Great. Can we go now?" Jenna said, reaching for her jacket.

"Why don't you let your mom finish her dinner first," Cole said gently.

"It's okay. I'm done."

While Cole paid the bill, Jenna and Marni waited outside on the pier. The earlier storm had passed, leaving behind clean, fresh air. The evening was chilly, but that didn't stop the public from patronizing the local pier on a Saturday night.

Cole exited the restaurant. "Where to?"

"This way, Dad." Jenna grabbed Cole's hand and pulled him toward the arcade games.

Marni followed behind at a slower pace. She'd been here hundreds of times with Jenna and knew exactly where she could find her daughter—at the end of the pier in the video game room.

"Coming?" Cole called over his shoulder as Jenna tugged on his arm.

"I'll catch up."

"Sure?"

Marni nodded. "Go. Have fun."

They disappeared in the crowd, leaving Marni alone with her thoughts.

She tried to shake off her melancholy by concentrating on the various tourist traps along the pier. Wandering through the shops did little to keep her mind off the thing that bothered her most. Cole.

She was slowly coming to terms with his intrusion into her life. He was the father of her daughter, and as such, he deserved to be part of Jenna's life. There was no denying he had parental rights, but that wasn't really the problem, no matter how much she had protested. The crux of the matter was his father—and the possibility that Cole could come to mean far too much to her again.

There wasn't a thing about Cole she didn't notice. She didn't need to close her eyes to envision the way his jeans clung to his firm thighs, the way the wind tousled his hair or the way his eyes sparkled when he looked at her. Those images were firmly implanted in her consciousness. Her woman's senses were definitely under attack, whether or not he was near. How could that be? she wondered. Thirteen years had come and gone.

Yeah, and changed your life forever, Rodgers.

When she finally reached the arcade, bright, flashing colored lights and the pings and bleeps of the games washed over her. She stepped through the door and spotted Cole right away. Funny how some things never seem to change.

Marni approached, unseen by either Cole or Jenna. Cole's attention was on a video screen as he saved a make-believe planet from total destruction by a giant spider. Jenna shouted encouragement to her father.

Standing off to the side, still unnoticed, Marni waited while Cole fired missiles at the alien force threatening the planet Zagon.

"Look out, Dad," Jenna yelled when the spider released a large egglike bomb.

"I see it," he said, moving his ship to the left and firing at the same time. He wasn't fast enough. The giant egg shifted at the last minute and landed on Cole's ship, sending tiny sparks of red and yellow across the video screen.

"Aw, Dad, you died."

Cole turned and smiled at Marni. "I got distracted."

There was something very direct and very male in his gaze. Her heart hammered in her chest. She looked at her watch, uncomfortable under his intense scrutiny. "It's getting late."

"Mom, it's early," Jenna whined.

Cole put his arm around Jenna. "She's right, Jen. It's nearly nine and you were up early this morning."

Jenna's shoulders sagged. "All right. But will you come over tomorrow?"

Cole and Jenna both looked at Marni, waiting for her approval. How could she deny either of them? "Jenna would like that."

"And you?"

Marni looked away, unable to answer his question.

Jenna yawned loudly, glancing from Cole to Marni. She covered her mouth with her hand, but not before Marni caught a glimpse of the smile curving her daughter's lips. "I think I'd like to go home now, Dad."

Cole drove the short distance to Marni's beach house. He glanced in the rearview mirror. Jenna had fallen asleep in the back seat, and there was a comfortable silence inside the Jag. An unfamiliar sense of contentment filled him.

Having a family of his own was something he'd always wanted. While he might have missed Jenna's early years, at least he had her now. Marni was slowly coming around, and she seemed to have stopped fighting him. How long that would last, he didn't know, but he was definitely going to take advantage of the situation.

He foresaw a period of adjustment for the three of them, but he was confident everything would work out eventually. He didn't relish the idea of being a weekend father. The thought of picking Jenna up at six on Friday and bringing her back to Marni on Sunday evening held no appeal. Being a part of his daughter's life meant being there for her every day. Only he wasn't sure how to accomplish his goal.

Marni sighed, and he glanced at her. He had no idea what she was thinking or feeling, but her open response at the drive-in restaurant two days ago told him she was still attracted to him physically, at least.

They'd reached an impasse about their past, though. Marni still refused to tell him why she'd left. But that was their past. What about their future? Would they even *have* a future, or was Jenna the only link between them?

He pulled the car into the driveway and killed the engine. "I'll get her," he told Marni, glancing back at Jenna.

Marni reached for her bag and pulled out her keys while Cole carried the sleeping Jenna.

"You could have woken her up," Marni said, unlocking the door.

"Let her sleep. She's had a long day."

Cole followed Marni through the living room and down a corridor to the first door on the right. Marni flipped on the light and Cole approached the pink-canopied bed, where he gently laid Jenna on the spread.

After untying her tennis shoes and slipping them off her feet, he gently took off her jacket. He unfolded an old patchwork quilt lying on a small, scarred cedar chest at the foot of the bed and laid it over her. Staring at his daughter, he was filled with a warmth so great he thought his heart would burst. "She really is a beautiful girl, Marni," he whispered.

"I know."

Tearing his gaze away from Jenna, he said, "I should be going. Walk me to my car?"

Silence stretched between them. A sense of nervousness plagued him, like a schoolboy on his first date. "I had a nice time tonight," he said when they stepped onto the porch. "I'd like to spend the day with Jenna tomorrow. Is that okay with you?"

She sighed, and Cole thought for a moment she was going to argue with him again. "That's fine. I appreciate your asking, Cole."

Did she think he would come and go as he pleased? As much as he would like to, their situation prevented any such liberties. "Care to come with us?"

Marni reached for the gate and followed him through. "I can't. I have work to do." She wanted nothing more than to go wherever Cole planned to take Jenna, a feeling that had nothing whatsoever to do with her overprotective maternal instincts. *Fool,* she thought, knowing she wanted to spend as much time as possible with Cole before reality intruded.

Pulling his keys from his jacket pocket, he shook his head. "All work and no play, Marni." His voice was light, but even in the moonlight Marni could see the intensity in his eyes.

She struggled for something to say. "Jenna had a wonderful time. She really cares about you." *So do you, Rodgers.*

Cole reached forward and gently pushed a wayward curl off her face. "Me, too."

He brushed his knuckles along her jawline, sending little shivers of awareness coursing through her, then he cupped her cheek in his warm palm. "What about her mother?"

Marni turned toward the warmth he generated as if it were the most natural thing in the world. "We were a long time ago."

Using his thumb, he pushed her chin up so she had no choice but to look into his eyes. "Not that long."

One simple touch and he had her wanting him. This was ridiculous. "Cole, we have a twelve-year-old daughter!"

Cole stepped closer, his gaze traveling from her eyes to her mouth while his hand massaged the muscles tensing in her neck. "Hmm, we do, don't we."

Marni stepped backward until she came into contact with the fence surrounding the beach house. "Cole—"

"I always thought you looked beautiful in moonlight."

He cupped her neck and pulled her close. When he lowered his head and sought her lips, her eyelids fluttered closed. The moment his lips touched hers, all thoughts of refusing him disappeared and she opened her mouth for his gentle intrusion. Tiny shivers of delight thrummed through her and settled in the pit of her stomach. His slow, sexy kiss said, I want to make love to you.

He was hard and hot and all man. He was no fantasy, no long-treasured memory. This was Cole, passionate and real. Marni slipped her arms around his neck and sank against him, giving in to the flash fires of sensation.

His hand slid from her jaw, over her shoulder, and down to her breast. She cursed the thick cotton sweater, wanting to feel his hands on her breasts, to feel him run his palms over her pebble-hard nipples. She arched against him.

Dear God. What am I doing?

She pulled away. The clouds of passion slowly parted and Marni attempted to regain her equilibrium. "We can't." Her voice sounded strained even to her own ears.

Cole rested his forehead against hers, trying to get his breathing under control. In a way, he was glad she'd ended the kiss. Otherwise who knew what might have happened? God, he wanted her!

Marni flicked open the latch on the gate and stepped through decisively, closing it behind her. "Good night, Cole."

He chuckled. "It could have been." He reached forward and pushed that wayward curl off her face again, tucking it behind her ear. She sucked in a breath at his light touch, but didn't move away. "Sweet dreams, sweetheart."

BRIGHT AND EARLY Monday morning, Cole sauntered into the outer office to his executive suite. Balancing his briefcase and a box containing a cheese Danish in one hand and a professionally gift-wrapped package in the other, he greeted his secretary. "Good morning, Liz." He smiled and deposited the box on her cluttered desk.

Liz looked up from the computer screen, a puzzled expression on her face. "Good morning. You're in a good mood."

Cole chuckled. He *was* in a good mood today. Even his father's impending visit couldn't dampen his spirits. He crossed the plush, dark blue carpeting toward his private office and issued a list of instructions. "I need a florist who specializes in rare flowers, the Cenpaxx contracts and the report on that new game we're considering."

Liz peeked into the pink baker's box. "Destruction Force?" she asked, eyeing the sweet with enthusiasm.

"That's the one."

With a melodramatic sigh, Liz set the Danish aside and picked up her steno pad. "Uh, Cole?"

Cole stopped at the door leading into his private sanctuary. He knew what she was going to ask him. After nine years together, from Kansas to Seattle and now Los Angeles, they knew each other well. Liz had originally transferred with him to Seattle to escape an abusive husband. When Carson had requested Cole take over the software end of the business and transfer to Los Angeles, she hadn't hesitated to relocate.

"A florist?" Liz asked hesitantly.

Cole smiled. "A florist," he reiterated.

Setting his briefcase and the package on his desk, he slipped out of his overcoat and tossed it over the arm of one of the white leather chairs opposite his desk.

Liz knocked once and opened the door without waiting for a reply. File folders tucked under her arm, a coffee mug in one hand, and her steno pad in the other, she approached the desk. "Cenpaxx, Destruction Force and a florist in Beverly Hills that handles rare flowers." She set the coffee in front of him and laid the files beside the mug. "Oh, and your father's secretary called. Carson won't be arriving until next Monday around ten."

"I thought he was coming in on Wednesday." Cole snapped open his briefcase.

Liz settled into the empty chair opposite the desk. "His secretary said some minor disaster occurred in Orlando. He had to take care of it first. Shall I arrange for a limo or will you be picking him up?"

"Send a car for him." He retrieved the files from the attaché. Examining the labels, he pulled two from the pile and handed them to Liz. "These have been approved and need to go down to Legal. Set up meetings for me later this week with the production and advertising heads. I want Kanga released by late summer."

Liz held up the file labeled Astrological Processing. "You're not serious about this one, are you?"

Cole reached for the mug of coffee. "I take it from that sour expression you don't approve."

"Why would people waste their money on this junk?"

"It's entertainment, Liz, and it's selling." He sipped the strong black coffee, then set the mug aside. "Don't you want to know what the future holds for you?"

"I know what the future holds for me. Twenty more years of putting up with you before I can retire. And if I'm *real* lucky, you'll give me a gold watch so I can see the remaining hours of my life tick slowly away."

Cole didn't take offense. He enjoyed her quick and often sassy wit. "I guess you don't want to hear about the computerized tarot card reader I'm thinking of buying."

Liz rolled her eyes in disgust. "I suppose you're going to tell me forewarned is forearmed."

He pulled a photo of Jenna Marni had given him from the briefcase, then snapped the lid shut. Moving his Out box to the credenza behind him, he angled the photograph of his daughter on the corner. He would have liked one of mother and child together.

"Liz, you have no faith." He glanced at the photo of Jenna and wished *he* had the ability to see into the future, his future with Marni in particular. Damn, he silently cursed. He couldn't stop thinking about the woman.

"Cute kid." Liz glanced at the picture. "Who is she?"

"My daughter." He couldn't help the pride in his voice.

Liz stood and approached the desk. She picked up the frame and stared hard at the photograph of Jenna.

"You're kidding!" Astonishment crossed her lightly tanned face.

"Nope."

She set the frame back on the desk. "Never mind. It's none of my business."

Cole chuckled. "No, it's not, but you're going to ask me, anyway."

Liz laughed, unoffended by his gentle rebuke. "I didn't know you had any kids."

Cole sipped his coffee. He didn't quite know how to explain about Jenna. "Neither did I until this weekend."

"Interesting."

"Complicated."

"An old flame?"

Cole ignored the unasked questions burning in Liz's dark blue eyes. "I guess you could say that."

"And she likes rare flowers."

"Don't you have some menial task to take care of?" he grumbled.

"No," she returned. "But you have a meeting in an hour with the designer of Destruction Force and you still haven't read the reports."

"I need the prospectus from Marketing."

"It's with the report. Is there anything else? I've got a cheese Danish waiting for me."

Cole dismissed Liz and waited until the door closed before picking up the telephone. He dialed the number for the florist and placed the order, requesting the bouquet be delivered to Marni on Friday.

Replacing the receiver, he picked up the prospectus for the new computer game, Destruction Force. Marketing plans for the war game, advertising budget, production costs and packaging expenses held no interest for him to-day. Glancing at the telephone, he thought about calling

Marni but stopped himself. He needed to take things slow. She was so damned skittish when he was around, he worried about frightening her away before he ever had a chance to win her over.

With the same tenacity he used in business, he considered his options. A subtle but overwhelming seduction was in order, and he'd already set his plans in motion. Tossing down the report, he turned his attention to the wrapped package. Soft floral paper and a matching elaborate bow covered the small lingerie box. He'd bought the gift for her on impulse when he'd taken Jenna shopping yesterday, but he hadn't had the courage to give it to her. Too intimate, he'd thought at the time, but when Marni opened the box, she would have to understand the meaning behind the gift. And the flowers.

At least with Carson's visit delayed until next week, Cole would have some time to spend with Marni and Jenna. He wasn't ready to tell Carson about his daughter yet. There had been no love lost between Marni and his father, and Carson had already indicated his displeasure when Cole told him he'd run into her. How would he feel when he learned she'd had Cole's child? His granddaughter.

What happens to Jenna when you have to move on, Cole?

Would he be moving on soon? The software division was growing daily. Sales were high and their stock secure once more. Would Carson transfer him to some other division of Ballinger Electronics? There'd been talk at the last board of directors meeting of branching into radio. Cole had expressed an interest, but now he wasn't so certain. The last thing he wanted to do was leave Los Angeles. There was too much to lose. No, transferring to another division of Ballinger Electronics wasn't the answer, but moving out on his own *was*. After all, he'd been thinking about it for quite a while.

The buzz of the intercom interrupted his thoughts. He pushed the button on the phone. "Yes."

"Glasser is here for your meeting. Hanna Masters and Ross Stevens are already waiting in the conference room."

"Tell them to get started. I'll be there in a minute."

"You got it, boss."

He released the intercom button and leaned back in the soft leather chair. His planned seduction took shape. He'd ply Marni with gifts, one item after another. Little tokens of their time together to evoke memories of their past, and their passion. Cole grinned and reached across the desk for a notepad. He jotted down a few items then sprang from the chair, picking up the wrapped package on the way out.

He stepped into the outer office just as Liz returned to her desk. "Would you find these and have them delivered to Marni Rodgers?" He dropped the box on the desk. "Have this one delivered on Thursday."

Liz examined the note. "To the D.A.?"

Yup," he answered, unable to keep the smile out of his voice.

"Where am I supposed to find a green dragon? Purple dinosaurs are hot right now, but a stuffed green dragon?"

"Just find me one, Liz."

"How about something nice, instead? A crystal vase to go with the exotic flowers. I'm sure she'd appreciate the thought."

He frowned at his secretary. "Can you do it or not?"

Liz tossed the list on her desk and sat down. "I knew that course I took in scavenger hunting would come in handy one day," she answered with a disgruntled glare.

Cole rested his palms on the edge of her desk and leaned forward, trying to look threatening. "One of these days I'm going to get tired of your smart mouth."

A warm smile lit her attractive face. "No one else would put up with you, Cole, and you know it."

He pushed away from her desk. "Just have that dragon delivered to Marni Rodgers before five today."

She flipped through the Rolodex, ignoring him. "God, I hate it when he's in a good mood," she grumbled.

"I'VE READ THE DEFENDANT'S appellate brief, Marni." Walter Dorlan poked his head inside Marni's open door. "We could be in trouble."

Marni motioned her boss into her office, clicking off her dictation machine. She set the microphone on the desk. "That's not the worst of it," she said as Walter seated himself across from her desk. "The press has gotten wind of the situation, and they're sniffing around like a bunch of hounds. They're digging up everything they can about the witness, and April Burnell is making this her own personal mission. She's actually trying to garner sympathy for Kendell. Surely she must realize what a monster this guy is."

Walter's brows creased and he leaned forward, resting his elbows on his knees. "You've handled Burnell before. What's the problem?"

"Monvale lied on the stand during his trial. What's to say he didn't lie during Kendell's trial?"

"Especially if Rodriguez and Harding offered him something worth lying for," Walter finished for her.

"Exactly." No one liked to fight an uphill battle, but they needed to start working on damage control in case the appellate court ruled in favor of the defense. The thought of retrying Kendell wasn't something she was looking forward to. She hated the thought of putting the families of the victims through another trial.

"What's your strategy at this point?" Walter asked, lacing his fingers together.

"During the trial when Monvale was brought in as a witness, the defense didn't object to his testimony, except when I asked how Kendell looked when relating the details of the murders. I'm using that as my argument in the reply brief. Peg should have it finished before she goes home today, and we're going to file it tomorrow."

"Have you requested preference? There's a jury on call, you know."

Peg knocked on the doorjamb, then stepped into the office, a stack of papers in one hand and a brightly colored gift bag in the other.

Marni eyed the colored bag curiously.

"Here's the Kendell reply," Peg said, setting the brief in front of Marni. "And this just arrived for you. I don't see a card."

"A secret admirer," Walter teased, leaning back into the chair.

Marni gave him a weak smile and took the bag from her secretary. Peg stood to the side of Marni's desk. Obviously neither her boss nor her secretary planned on leaving until they had viewed the contents of the bag.

Peg had been right, there was no card. Curious, Marni moved the tissue paper aside and lifted an adorable stuffed green dragon from the bag. She didn't need a card to tell her the toy was from Cole. He'd won a similar stuffed animal for her at the summer carnival in Elk Falls. That night, he'd kissed her for the first time.

Walter laughed and stood. "It must be from April Burnell."

"Why would Ms. Burnell send a dragon to Marni?" Peg asked Dorlan.

"She's probably using it as her calling card. From the dragon lady."

Peg laughed and Marni winced. What was Cole up to?

By Friday evening, Marni was as confused as ever. She pulled her Prelude into her driveway beside his Jaguar. Each night when she came home from work, he was there. Telling herself that he'd only come to see Jenna did little to quell the anxious feeling that had plagued her all week, but she had to admit that knowing he'd be there when she arrived gave her a tiny thrill. He'd stay long enough for dinner and then for a couple of hours afterward, either helping Jenna with her homework, watching television or just getting to know his daughter. He always left before Jenna went to bed, promising he'd be back again the following day.

Not once did he mention the barrage of gifts he'd been sending her all week. Each one had some small meaning behind it, a gentle reminder of their brief affair. She always made a point to thank him, but he'd simply smile at her, then turn his attention back to Jenna, as if the subject was of little or no importance.

On Tuesday afternoon, shortly after lunch, another messenger had arrived, this one bearing a cheesecake, her favorite dessert. She'd brought it home and wasn't overly surprised to find that Cole had prepared dinner. The mouthwatering aroma of lasagna had filled the house. Another delicate hint of the past. Cole had taken her to an Italian restaurant in Lawrence, complete with candles, checkered tablecloths and Dean Martin on the jukebox. He'd ordered cheesecake for dessert.

Wednesday morning, an overnight courier delivered the next gift. Cole had really given this one some thought.

She'd opened the box from FAO Schwartz in New York to find a wooden sailboat, again with no note attached. Peg had eyed her curiously, but hadn't asked any questions. The last thing Marni wanted to do was explain the meaning behind *this* one. The first time they'd made love had been on his father's boat. They'd taken it out on the lake, just the two of them, and hadn't returned until after dark. Cole had shown her all the joys of lovemaking that day. Just the memory of that long, hot summer day did funny things to her insides.

When she'd returned to the office after a grueling morning in court on Thursday, she hadn't been surprised when Peg handed her a small, prettily wrapped box with a frilly bow on top. Only apprehensive. After receiving the sailboat the previous day, she was nervous about what Cole would send next. She took the gift into her office and closed the door.

She sat at her desk and stared at the box for a good five minutes before she finally summoned the nerve to open it. Pale pink tissue paper surrounded a beautiful off-white cotton camisole edged in handmade Irish lace and a pair of matching tap pants. This time, a card had accompanied the gift. With shaking hands, she opened it and read Cole's bold scrawl. *I promised you I'd replace it.* As if it had been yesterday, she recalled how Cole had accidentally torn her simple cotton camisole in their haste to make love. That had been the last time she'd made love to Cole. Twenty-four hours later, she'd been on her way to California.

Friday, Marni gathered her briefcase and the most recent arrival—a bouquet of pink dogwoods and foxgloves. While the other gifts evoked memories of their passion, the flowers brought to mind the love they'd once shared. Whatever doubts Marni might have had about

Cole's feelings for her during their short time together were dashed with this one simple gesture. On a lazy Sunday afternoon, Cole had picked the wild dogwoods and presented them to her with a declaration of his love.

She entered the house and Jenna met her at the front door.

"The Lamberts are going to Palm Springs for the weekend and invited me. Can I go, Mom?"

Marni frowned at her daughter. "How was your day, Mom?"

Jenna smiled sheepishly. "I'm sorry." She leaned forward and placed a kiss on Marni's cheek. "Did you have a good day?"

"That's better, and, yes, I did."

"So can I go to Palm Springs? Denise'll be so bored if I don't go. She'll have no one to keep her company. Her mom's going shopping and Dr. Lambert will spend the day playing golf."

Marni deposited her briefcase in the entry hall and moved toward the kitchen. "Let me call Mrs. Lambert, then I'll let you know." She gently laid the bouquet on the counter and opened cupboards in search of a vase. Flowers were something she rarely received and vases were in short supply.

She finally found what she was looking for. A heavy, broad-bottomed brass vase. Standing on tiptoe, she reached for it, but came up short.

"Let me," Cole whispered huskily, coming up behind her.

His large body pressed into her back as he retrieved the container from its perch on the top shelf. His hand rested casually on her hip. Marni clung to the tiled counter for support, straining away from his touch. Then, before she realized it, the intimate contact was broken, and she felt strangely disappointed.

Turning to face him, she saw blatant desire burning in his eyes. Somehow, she managed to find her voice. "Thank you," she said, taking the proffered vase. "For the flowers," she added, then looked away hastily.

He chuckled lightly, as if he enjoyed her discomfort.

"Mom? Can you call Mrs. Lambert now?"

Jenna's voice jarred Marni out of the spell Cole was weaving around her. She turned on the tap to fill the vase with water, willing the trembling in her hands to stop. "Did you ask your dad if he had any plans this weekend?"

Jenna perched on a stool at the tiled serving bar. "He said he didn't care as long as you didn't mind. Gee," Jenna added brightly, "I never thought I'd have to ask both of you. This is kinda neat."

Marni turned off the tap and looked at Cole. He leaned against the counter, his arms folded across his chest, watching her. "This okay with you?" she asked him.

He nodded. "I didn't have any plans for the weekend, if that's what you're asking."

"All right, Jenna. You can go. But I still want to talk to Mrs. Lambert first."

"*Yes!* I'll call Denise and tell her. They'll be picking me up about seven for dinner and then we'll head out to the desert. Dr. Lambert doesn't like to sit in traffic." Jenna disappeared into the den to make her phone call.

With Jenna away, maybe she could finally tell Cole about the money from his father, Marni thought. She hadn't had an opportunity to talk with him alone all week. Now was her chance.

But first, she'd have to ask him to stay.

CHAPTER SEVEN

GATHERING HER COURAGE, Marni turned to face Cole. "I hate to eat alone." She despised the shakiness in her voice and hoped he didn't notice. "Would you like to join me?"

She must have surprised him with the invitation, because the expression on his face could only be described as astonishment.

"Yeah, that'd be great. I have some contracts I need to read over," he told her. "I could do that while you fix dinner."

She let out the breath she'd been holding. "Yes, sure, I mean no problem," she stammered. *You idiot!* she chastised herself. *It's not as if he's a total stranger, for crying out loud.*

Cole sauntered into the den as Jenna bounded into the kitchen with the cordless phone attached to her ear. Marni pulled a couple of steaks from the freezer, popped them into the microwave to defrost, then retrieved the makings of a salad from the fridge.

"It's Mrs. Lambert, Mom." Jenna handed Marni the phone.

The confirmation took only a few minutes, Jeanine Lambert assuring Marni the girls would be supervised the entire weekend. After a nod of approval from Marni, Jenna disappeared into her room to pack.

Marni busied herself washing the lettuce, tomatoes and mushrooms for the salad. In her mind, she went over and over the best approach for telling Cole about her deal with Carson. Much like preparing for a closing argument, she mentally rehearsed her speech, only this time, *her* future hung in the balance.

She cast a surreptitious glance into the den toward the object of her thoughts. Cole was leaning over the hearth, placing logs into the fireplace. With each movement, the muscles of his back bunched and rippled beneath his crisp white dress shirt. He'd rolled the sleeves back, exposing his strong forearms. She bit back the overwhelming urge to trace the corded flesh with her fingertips.

He glanced over his shoulder and grinned. "It's getting chilly."

Chilly? Hardly. Her temperature was definitely rising! She turned away, embarrassed that he'd caught her admiring him.

The vegetables for the salad needed chopping. She kept her eyes locked on her task, slicing mushrooms with the concentration of a neurosurgeon.

The fine hairs on the back of her neck tingled, and she didn't need to look up to know Cole had entered the kitchen. The man had an uncanny effect on her senses.

"Sweetheart, I need your legal opinion on something."

Marni's heart swelled at the casual endearment. He wasn't making things easy for her, no matter what his intentions. Her life was becoming more complicated by the minute.

"Mom," Jenna wailed from her bedroom. "I can't find my bathing suit."

"Bathing suit?" Cole exclaimed, tossing the sheaf of papers he held on the bar. "It's the middle of January!"

"She's going to *Palm Springs*," Marni reminded him, a little surprised by his attitude. She wasn't accustomed to having to explain Jenna's whereabouts or actions. She supposed Jenna wasn't the only one who had a few adjustments to make now that Cole was a part of their lives.

A wry grin canted his mouth. "Sorry."

"Mom!" Jenna wailed again.

Marni looked from Cole to the doorway leading to the opposite end of the house. "Sit down." She gestured toward the bar stools. "I'll be right back."

Fifteen minutes later, Marni returned with Jenna. No sooner had she tossed the last of the salad makings into a glass serving bowl than the doorbell rang, signaling the arrival of the Lamberts. Jenna darted out of the kitchen to answer the door.

Denise, with her mother in tow, entered the kitchen. Jenna excitedly made the introductions. Marni couldn't blame her. Having a father was still a novelty, and she could see Jenna was enjoying every moment of it.

"We'll have her home around six or seven on Sunday," Jeanine informed them, herding the girls out the door and into the minivan.

After their departure, Cole seemed as uncomfortable with the silence as Marni, and he flipped on the stereo. Soft country music drifted into the kitchen.

Marni pulled the steaks from the microwave and added a few seasonings as Cole rejoined her there.

"Okay, what was your question?" she asked over her shoulder. She mentally kicked herself for not taking the opportunity to tell him about her deal with Carson. *I'll tell him after we eat,* she promised herself. Why spoil their dinner?

Marni scrubbed a large potato and Cole sat at the bar, scanning the contracts. "There's a clause in here I'm not too sure about."

"Why not tell me what the contract is for first," she suggested.

"A new computer chain wants to sell our games. Everything is pretty standard, except I don't quite understand this line about 'sole and exclusive remedy pursuant to Uniform Commercial Code, Section 2719.'"

"What are the terms for damaged goods?" Marni glanced his way. With his attention on the paperwork in front of him, she had ample opportunity to appreciate the lean strength of his body. All week she'd seen him dressed casually, wearing jeans and cotton shirts or sweat suits. Tonight, he hadn't changed before coming over. He was still dressed in a suit, although his tie was loosened and his shirtsleeves were rolled back. He still appeared every inch the high-powered executive.

His brows drew together in concentration. "Uh, says something about replacement only, no refunds."

"That seems pretty straightforward." She scoured the potatoes, then moved to the microwave. After setting the controls, she turned to face Cole, only to find him watching her intently. Her heart pounded. "Why would you *not* offer them a refund if the goods are damaged?" she asked, trying to regain her equilibrium. "Seems like bad PR to me."

"They're buying last year's product at a substantial discount," he explained.

"Why would anyone want last year's video games?" she asked, setting the temperature gauge on the oven, then slipping in a loaf of French bread.

"It's one of those membership warehouses," he said. "They buy up last year's products at huge savings and sell them at reduced prices."

After turning the steaks she'd placed in the broiler, she faced him, hands on hips, and pinned him with a suspicious glare. "Cole, you don't need my legal advice. Is this your way of making conversation?"

He tossed the contract on the bar. "That transparent, huh?"

She straightened at the laughter in his voice. His eyes sparkled, reminding her of happier times. "Uh-huh. We don't have to talk legalese to have a conversation."

He laughed then, a low, throaty sound that poured over her like warm honey.

"Need a hand?" he asked, gathering up his papers and setting them aside.

"Sure. You can set the bar."

Cole enjoyed the companionable atmosphere, thankful the old animosities were, for once, dispelled. They worked together, chatting easily about a variety of topics.

Every time she came near him, reaching for some utensil or spice, his pulse beat just a little faster. She moved around the kitchen in her stockings, pink toenails peeking through her stockings. He'd always liked her feet, especially when she curled her toes. No, he amended. He liked *making* her toes curl, a sexy little habit she had when he kissed her.

"Any word on that Kendell case you've been working on?" he asked, trying to change the unsettling direction of his thoughts.

"Not yet," she said. "It shouldn't take too long for the appellate court to make a decision, though."

"Civil rights and all that?"

"Sort of. Until the higher court makes their ruling, the jury is on call. That means twelve citizens have to put their lives on hold until they're needed for the penalty phase. Can you hand me the pepper?"

He retrieved the pepper from the stove and brought it to her. He hitched his hip against the counter next to her. The sight of her breasts gently swaying as she stirred salad dressing in a mixing bowl made his mouth go dry.

Damn, it was getting warm. He tugged on his already loosened tie, then reached into the cabinet for two dinner plates. After setting the bar, he found a bottle of wine. Marni tested the steaks one last time, finally proclaiming them ready, sliced a loaf of crusty French bread, and he opened the wine. The simple domesticity of the scene stirred him deeply. A wave of loneliness washed over him. He'd had too many dinners alone in cold, impersonal apartments over the years.

Settled across from Marni at the tiled bar, Cole cut into the thick steak. "I've got an appointment with a real estate agent tomorrow," he said offhandedly, pretending interest in the food. He'd thought a great deal about the future this week and had made a few decisions. The first was to find a house, a place of permanence. A home for his daughter.

"A real estate agent?" she asked, taking a deep drink from her wineglass.

The caution in her voice alarmed him. He wanted her to be happy about his decision. "I think it's time I looked for something more permanent. I hate that condo."

"You're staying in L.A.?" She eyed him warily, her fork poised in midair.

"I was hoping to find something close. To you."

Cole winced when she forcefully stabbed a tomato. "Does that bother you?" he asked, disappointed in her reaction.

"Jenna will be happy."

He reached across the bar and laid his hand over hers. When she looked at him, confusion burned in her eyes. "Marni? What about you? What'll make you happy?"

You! Marni wanted to shout. *You can make me happy!*

She'd never stopped loving him. She'd always known he was more than a fond memory of her first romance and the father of her child. She'd always loved him, no matter how much pain she'd felt when he married Elizabeth. The past no longer mattered. What was important now was whether they had a chance at a future together. For the first time, she dared to hope.

How could this be happening to her? One week in his company and she'd completely lost her mind—and her traitorous heart. The gentle look in his eyes while they'd cooked dinner together, the easy banter between them, as if they'd never been apart, as if they'd never hurt each other, had annihilated her resistance. Was she crazy?

So what if I am? she argued with herself. Didn't they deserve this chance? Didn't Jenna? But what if he broke her heart again? What about Carson?

She pulled her hand from his grasp and moved to the sink. Before whatever was happening between them went any further, she had to tell him about his father. Maybe, if she was damned lucky, Cole would understand.

Marni closed her eyes and shored up her courage. Finally, she turned to face him. "Cole, I need to tell you something."

He pushed his plate away and approached her, his steps slow and deliberate. "You're right. You still haven't thanked me for the dragon."

The sultry, husky note of his voice sent a shiver racing down her spine. She sidestepped, but he altered his course.

He stood in front of her, only a breath away. He braced both hands on the counter behind her, pinning her against the tiles. Trapped within the confines of his thick, muscled arms, she had no hope of escaping.

"Cole, I'm serious."

His deep chuckle sounded more like a muted roar. "So am I." He placed light, teasing kisses on her neck.

She turned her head. "Cole, I can't think when you do that."

He nuzzled her ear. "That's the whole point," he growled, his breath hot against her neck.

"Cole, please," she begged in a breathy whisper.

"Oh, I plan to, sweetheart."

Her breath caught at his erotic promise. Before she could utter a response, his mouth covered hers. She opened to him, any thoughts of denying him, no matter how fleeting, banished. Wrapping her arms around his neck, she clung to him, wanting him with a need so intense and urgent it took her breath away.

He deepened the kiss, probing, tasting. Marni's head spun as her body responded to the searing heat traveling at the speed of light through her veins. The teasing dance of their tongues, his hands moving seductively down the length of her back, imprisoned her in a web of growing arousal.

He unbuttoned her blouse and slipped his hand inside the mauve silk, running his fingers over her slim waist before lifting her onto the counter. Her gray skirt crept up her thighs, and she hooked her legs around his hips, pulling him close. With a dexterity that didn't surprise her, he unclasped the front hook of her lacy bra and pushed it aside.

She moaned when he gently outlined her breasts with his hands, lifting and kneading. The gentle massage conflicted with the hard, hot demand of his kiss. The pleasure was pure and explosive, and not nearly enough.

As if he sensed her need, he trailed hot kisses down the column of her throat, tickling her too-sensitive flesh, until his tongue caressed her swollen nipple. Marni arched toward the delicious sensations. Her breath came in shallow gasps as he flicked his tongue expertly over her pebble hardness. A heaviness settled between her thighs. She wanted more.

Her hands gripped his broad shoulders and she dug her fingers into the hard muscle, cursing the shirt he wore. She wanted to feel his skin against her hands, wanted to feel his chest pressed against her.

His hands and mouth left her breasts, and she groaned in frustration until he captured her lips again in a fierce, drugging kiss, his hands resting teasingly on her thighs. With frantic fingers, she tugged at his shirt, popping a few of the buttons in her haste. She ran her fingers over the firm wall of his chest. Pulling him close, she pressed her exposed and tender breasts against him. Heat cascaded within her, and the aching emptiness of the past began to ebb.

He shuddered as she arched against his torso. Finely honed muscle twitched and jumped everywhere she touched. He tore his mouth from hers, and her heart beat in triple time when she saw the carnal desire blazing in his eyes. It had been thirteen long years since he'd looked at her that way.

"I want you, Marni." Cole's voice was harsh, emphasizing his need.

Her hands stilled. She should end this. Right now, right this second. Tell him the truth about the deal she'd made with his father before they went any further. Before either of them got hurt.

She couldn't do it. Once, she told herself, just this once. Then she'd tell him the truth. No more secrets between them. But not now. Tonight nothing mattered but Cole and this exquisite moment of pleasure.

"I've wanted you for so long," she finally whispered, ignoring the exasperated sigh of her conscience.

Cole groaned his pleasure and pulled her into a fierce embrace, crushing her against him. His hands found her hair and he gently tugged on her French braid to expose her slim neck. He kissed the pulse at her throat, darting his tongue over the gentle vibration. A low moan of pleasure escaped her, and a surge of powerful need crackled inside him like wildfire. A throbbing, pulsing heat settled low and deep inside him, hardening him beyond endurance.

His hands explored the lines of her back, her waist, her hips. Reaching beneath the hem of her skirt, he pushed the barrier higher until he found the lacy edging of her stockings. Slowly, he rolled first one, then the other, down her thigh and over her calf before tossing the silken garments carelessly on the floor.

His gaze captured hers, and her breath audibly caught in her throat. Her soft brown eyes were filled with passion. Never taking his gaze from hers, he slowly moved his hand up her leg, gently kneading the silken flesh, lightly brushing his fingers against her white lace panties, moistened by her own need.

Marni sucked in a breath at the feather-light touch. Heat rippled under her skin at the flush of sexual desire Cole had awakened in her. He stood between her parted thighs, his sinewy hand gently massaging the sensitive flesh. Arrogantly he held her gaze while his long fingers occasionally brushed against her most intimate place. Each agonizing touch added to the smoldering heat inside her, sending electric shock waves to her already scorched nerve endings.

"Tell me what you want, sweetheart."

His softly spoken words made her grip the counter with such force she feared she might break the tiles. "You."

He chuckled and moved his hand further up her thigh, his finger lifting the elastic band of her panties. "You always were impatient."

Anticipation made her squirm. "I wasn't the only one," she said huskily.

"I could tease you all night," he said, his head moving closer, as if he planned to capture her swollen lips once again.

"I was hoping you would."

His eyes darkened, turning a deep forest green at her sensual challenge.

"Make love to me, Cole," she demanded before she lost her nerve.

He pulled her into his arms and slid her off the countertop. His lips locked hard on hers, his tongue demanding entrance. The kiss was wet, hot and filled with sensual promise—and more.

Cole growled in frustration when she stepped away from him. Before he could protest, she grabbed his tie, flicked off the overhead light and led him into the den. She stopped in front of the fire, then turned to face him.

The confusion he'd seen earlier had disappeared. Only passion, earthy and hot, burned in her eyes. With deliberate slowness, she unfastened her skirt and let it fall to her feet, exposing her shapely legs.

Not taking his eyes from her, he held his breath as she slipped out of the silk blouse and discarded the matching lacy bra on the floor with her skirt. She stood before him, unashamed, the firelight casting a golden hue over her gentle curves.

He was afraid to move. Afraid that if he did, she would disappear like a phantom. But this was real, and the aching hardness straining against the zipper of his trousers served as a wonderfully painful reminder.

She reached up behind her head, her full breasts swaying with the gentle movement. Seconds ticked by as she shook her hair loose, the long blond curls cascading over her shoulders. She reminded him of a white tigress, poised and confident and just a little dangerous. His body strained with need, and he ached to touch her, to lose himself inside her. She reached forward and grasped his tie again, pulling him slowly toward her. Cole needed no further encouragement.

"Marni," he whispered. His lips found hers, and then he slowly eased her down to the carpet.

Marni clung to him, impelled by the passionate embrace. His clothes scratched her sensitized skin, and she quickly helped him remove them. Her eyes drank in the sight of his magnificent body outlined by the firelight. He reminded her of a dark and powerful knight.

He came back to her slowly, covering her with his large body. She sighed, running her hands over his bare back, a beautifully sculpted landscape of solid muscle. Sliding her hands into his hair, she guided his mouth back to her lips.

This time, she kissed him, with all the passion and love she'd kept bottled inside her for years. This was Cole, at last, in her arms again.

His hands moved over her body, his movements as frantic as her own. Together they touched, explored and rediscovered each other's bodies. He slid one hand down her stomach to the swell of her hips, grasping the top of her lacy panties and disposing of the last barrier between them. He gently stroked her moist curls, sending jolts of pleasurable anticipation through her as his hand moved closer to the place she wanted him to fill. Her body ached for his touch, craving the release she knew only Cole could grant her.

Too soon, his gentle stroking wasn't enough. He'd awakened her long-repressed sensuality, and her body screamed for fulfillment. He teased her open, then, before she could find what she so desperately craved, he retreated. Unable to bear the aching emptiness any longer, she pleaded in a voice she hardly recognized as her own.

"Not yet, sweetheart." Cole said huskily. "We have all night."

His lips traced a path over her stomach to her hip, then kissed and teased her inner thigh. She cried out when his tongue lightly grazed the place his hand explored. He tortured her with quick, darting kisses until involuntary tremors of ecstasy gripped her, pulling her into a cyclone spiraling out of control. Her unexpected release was hard, fast, and left her panting for more. Cole continued the intimate torture until she cried out again, her entire body shaking with the force of her orgasm. Unable to hold back any longer, he positioned himself above her.

Her eyes opened suddenly, a frisson of alarm in her gaze. "Cole? I'm not using birth control."

He couldn't help but smile. "I've already taken care of that." With a quick kiss he left her, sheathed himself and returned before her passion cooled.

He kissed her again, gathering her into his arms, enjoying the feel of her body close to his. Rolling her beneath him, he nudged her knees apart, sliding between her thighs. Without restraint she offered herself to him. Cole greedily accepted her silent proposition, lifting her hips slightly and burying himself in her soft, warm flesh.

Her quiet moans of pleasure urged him onward. He made love to her slowly, wanting to prolong the pleasure. His lips captured hers, delving deep inside, drinking in the sweet, honeyed warmth as he thrust his body into hers. Finally they found the tempo that bound them together in exquisite harmony.

Cole buried his head against her shoulder. "You're so hot...sweet...I..." The words died on his lips as she shuddered and arched wildly beneath him. He understood completely, and moments later, he drove into her one last time before finding his own shattering release.

Marni held him close, his heart beating in rapid cadence with her own. Muscle and bone ceased to exist, and hot, golden liquid flowed swiftly through her veins. She wondered if she'd ever recover, if she ever *wanted* to recover.

He rolled off her but kept her wrapped in his arms. She laid her head against his chest and snuggled into him, entwining her legs with his. Her nerve endings still tingled from their reckless lovemaking. Well, not so reckless, she thought, smiling, reminded of Cole's prudence.

"You're smiling," he softly accused, kissing the top of her head.

"I was just wondering if your Scout leader would be proud of you."

With a gentle hand, he tilted her chin so he could look into her eyes. "My Scout leader?" His brows drew together.

Marni nodded. "Isn't the Boy Scout motto Be Prepared?"

He chuckled, the sound deep and rumbling inside his chest. "Not enough, sweetheart. If I had known we'd end up like this, I'd have bought out the damned drugstore."

Rising up, she eyed him suspiciously. "Do you mean to tell me you only have..." Too embarrassed to continue, she changed tactics. "Cole Ballinger, you've been planning this all week. The dragon, the cheesecake, the *sailboat*."

His hands cupped her face, guiding her lips down to his, his lips slanted in a cocky grin.

"This was premeditated seduction and you know it."

"I confess, counselor. Guilty as charged."

An hour later Cole added wood to the dying fire while Marni retrieved their still-full wineglasses from the kitchen. She padded into the den and stared at the breathtaking sight of Cole. He wore only his trousers, as she had confiscated his shirt. The man had a body she could stare at all night and never get tired of. How long had it been since she'd felt so wonderful, so content?

Handing him the glass, she curled up on the floor in front of the fire, watching the flames jump and lick over the logs. Cole came to sit behind her, cradling her between his thighs. She leaned against him, reveling in his musky scent as he draped an arm around her, pulling her close.

They stayed that way for a long time, neither speaking, lost in their own thoughts. Marni knew she was letting a golden opportunity pass her by, but she didn't want the aftermath of their lovemaking tarnished by the past.

"What did you want to tell me earlier?" he queried, as if reading her mind.

Marni's heart stopped. It resumed with a thump so loud she was certain he could hear it. "Uh, when?" she hedged.

"During dinner, before I distracted you. You said you had something to tell me."

"I... it must not have been important. I can't remember." Marni drained her glass of wine. She reached for the bottle. "More?" she asked, hoping to distract him.

"No, I'm fine." He eyed her curiously.

She poured more wine for herself and set the bottle aside. The look in his eyes told her he was not convinced. Nervously, she lifted the glass to her lips and swallowed, returning her attention to the flames.

"I'm supposed to get you drunk first, *then* have my way with you." He took the glass away from her, setting it on the carpet. "What's wrong, sweetheart?"

The concern in his voice chilled her, despite the warmth of his body pressed against her back. "I'm just a little nervous," she answered honestly.

He brushed her hair aside and nuzzled the nape of her neck. "A little late for that, don't you think?"

"Mmm," she muttered, laying her head against his chest so he could place tender kisses on her throat. The arm surrounding her waist moved, and he cupped her breast in his large hand.

"What's got you so nervous?"

She scooted closer, her bottom rubbing against his arousal. The man was amazing. "Jenna's not coming home tonight."

Chicken, her conscience taunted.

"I know." His tongue traced the outline of her ear, causing Marni to squirm against him. He nipped her lobe, sending tiny shivers of delight cascading over her.

Tell him! that voice nagged her again.

"What were you going to tell me?" His hand slid from her breast to caress her inner thigh, inching higher and higher until it settled between her legs.

She said the only thing she could think of when he touched her so provocatively.

"Make love to me, Cole."

CHAPTER EIGHT

MARNI OPENED HER EYES and stretched, then snuggled deeper beneath the covers. Despite the long hours spent loving Cole, she felt surprisingly rested, but too lazy to get out of bed at such an early hour on a Saturday. She reached across the bed and wasn't surprised to find him gone. From the warmth of the sheets, she suspected he'd left recently. She vaguely recalled something about him having an appointment today.

Just as well, she thought, reaching for his pillow and pulling it close. At least with him gone she'd have an opportunity to rehearse her speech. Today she'd tell him about her deal with his father. No more stalling.

She shivered suddenly, and hugging the pillow tight, she absorbed the scent of Cole, replaying in her mind the passionate memories of the night they had shared. Soon, she promised herself. She'd tell him soon. And she drifted off to sleep again.

"SWEETHEART, it's after ten."

Marni opened her eyes and found Cole casually sitting on the edge of her bed. "I thought you'd left," she said, releasing her death grip on his crumpled pillow.

He shook his head and grinned tenderly at her, running his index finger down the slope of her nose. "Nope. Can't get rid of me that easy. Cream, right?" he asked, looking entirely too handsome in faded, body-hugging Levi's and a beige chambray shirt.

She smiled up at him, and her hand snaked out from under the covers, lightly tracing the tendons of his muscular forearm.

Blatant desire smoldered in his eyes. "You take cream, right?" he asked again, his voice huskier.

"Excuse me?"

"In your coffee." He nodded toward the night table.

Marni turned her attention to the mug of steaming brew waiting for her. "Thank you," she answered cautiously, starting to wake up. Something wasn't quite right. His hair was damp, as if he'd just showered.

Cole handed her the mug. "We're meeting with the real estate agent in an hour and a half. Drink this and get moving. We'll be late."

"We will?" She took the coffee and sipped it, waiting for the caffeine to take effect. "It's only ten."

"I remember how much you hated mornings." He leaned forward and brushed a light kiss over her lips. "Time to get up. You want breakfast?"

"Hmm." Marni sighed. She could get used to this. "Breakfast in bed?" she asked hopefully.

Cole braced his arms on either side of her and leaned forward. His gaze darkened with wicked promise. "Is that an invitation?"

His sexy grin rendered her momentarily breathless. She set the mug on the table, then slowly wove her fingers through his hair, pulling him closer. "Do you need an invitation?" she whispered, pressing her lips to his.

Cole kissed her, deep and long and hard. A warm cascade of sensual heat slipped over her the instant his tongue touched hers. Oh, yes, she could definitely get used to waking up to Cole.

All too soon, he ended the kiss. Marni groaned in protest.

Playfully, he squeezed her thigh, then reached for the emerald silk robe crumpled on the floor and tossed it to her. "Come on. Up."

"I really don't see the hurry," she grumbled, slipping her arms through the sleeves. She pulled the garment around her before tossing the covers aside. "Why do you need me to meet with the real estate agent?"

"Women know more about kitchens and closet space."

"Oh, now that's..." The intended upbraid at his chauvinistic reply trailed off as she looked at the overstuffed chair in the corner. A black gym bag rested on the mauve chintz. She tied the sash of her robe and frowned at Cole, realization dawning on her. "You really earned your merit badge last night," she said, stepping toward him.

Cole backed toward the door, his hands raised as if she held a gun. "Now, sweetheart..."

"Don't 'sweetheart' me, Cole Ballinger," she said, poking his chest. "I was suspicious when I saw the condom, but this is..." The words died in her throat at his lazy grin.

"Premeditated seduction?" he suggested.

Marni reached behind her and tossed a pillow at him. He caught it easily. "I just want to know how you got the Lamberts to take Jenna to Palm Springs," she said, unable to prevent the laughter from creeping into her voice.

He threw the pillow back on the bed and stepped in front of her. His hands resting gently on her shoulders, he pulled her toward him and placed a light kiss on her lips. "Fate, my love. Get dressed or you'll miss the game. Kansas City held the lead with a field goal at the end of the first quarter."

Twenty minutes later Marni joined Cole in the den. He sat on the sofa, his attention divided between the football game and the financial page. The remainder of the newspaper lay scattered around his feet.

"I thought you were cooking breakfast," she said, pulling the newspaper from his hands and tossing it on the floor. She climbed onto his lap, surprised by how comfortable she felt with him. There was none of the usual "morning-after" shyness between them. It was almost as if they'd been married for years.

"First down," he updated her, giving her a quick kiss. "The Chiefs just rushed forty-three yards."

"Did they score?" Marni snuggled beside him on the sofa. On the screen, the Chiefs inched closer into field goal range.

If the Chiefs score a touchdown I'll tell him.

The quarterback handed off to the running back, who charged up the middle of the Raider defense for an eight-yard gain. Marni had never realized the seduction of procrastination until now.

Hold 'em, defense!

Another ten-yard rush by the tailback put the Chiefs in position for a field goal.

"Damn," Cole complained, pulling Marni closer to his side. "They should have gone for the touchdown."

Marni expelled a long breath. Okay, so she didn't want to tell him about the deal she'd made with Carson. What was wrong with that? Why ruin a good thing?

Because, her conscience reminded her, *you already made love to the guy with that lie between you, and an omission of facts is still a lie.* Cole would not take it well.

She remembered the one time she'd seen him lose control. After he'd ranted and raved, a deadly calm had taken over, frightening her more than his outburst had. A shiver stole down her spine at the memory. Cole had been furious with her. His hands had clenched and unclenched at his sides until he'd finally turned and walked away from her. She'd never seen him again.

Okay, she promised herself, shaking off the dark recollection. *I'll confess to him before the weekend is over. I just want one day of loving him before he walks away again.*

"Let's go to breakfast," he said, pulling her off the sofa and into his arms.

"And here I thought you were going to cook for me." Marni feigned a pout.

He kissed the tip of her nose. "Sorry, love. Unless you like charred bacon and rubber eggs."

Marni wrinkled her nose. "I'll get my coat. There's a great little coffee shop a few blocks from here. We can walk."

Fifteen minutes later, hand in hand like a couple of teenagers, they walked into the cozy seaside diner. The hostess seated them at a table with a view of the ocean, brought coffee and left them with menus.

"Mornin', folks. What'll ya have?" a young waitress asked a few minutes later, her pen poised over her pad.

After they placed their order, Marni returned her attention to Cole, who regarded her with fierce intensity.

"What are you staring at, Ballinger?" she blurted out. She resisted the impulse to straighten her hair.

"You."

"And do you like what you see?" she asked flirtatiously.

Cole raked his gaze over her delicate features, the gentle swell of her breasts beneath the soft flannel of the pink-and-white plaid shirt. She'd left the top two buttons undone, exposing her slim neck. "Very much," he said, bringing his gaze back to hers. "Which makes me wonder why you never married."

Not that her past relationships were any of his business, he thought, but curiosity was eating him alive. After the night they'd spent together, and the nights he planned to spend with her, he didn't want anything between them. Especially a man from her past.

Her huge brown eyes widened a fraction. "Just waiting for the right guy to come along, I suppose."

He drew his brows together. "I'm serious." And he was. Not to mention jealous of any other man who'd shared Marni's passion.

"So am I." She laughed, the sound too brittle and her smile a tad too bright.

The waitress approached and refilled their cups before disappearing again. Marni busied herself by adding cream and sugar. Cole knew she was avoiding his gaze.

"You mean you've gone to school, raised Jenna and worked. That's it? No social life?" he persisted.

Marni shook her head and took a sip of her coffee.

He wanted to know if lack of time or lack of interest was the reason. His ego hoped for the latter. "No relationships at all?" he pressed. "I find that hard to believe."

"No one worth writing home about," she answered, avoiding his eyes. "I dated occasionally."

So what did you think, Ballinger? She'd spent the last thirteen years waiting for you? "What happened?"

"Didn't work out," she answered offhandedly.

A wave of profound relief surged through him. "Did you see anyone for very long?"

"I dated one man for a couple of years." She toyed with her napkin, making neat accordion folds in the paper.

"And?"

She returned her attention to the folded napkin, completing her sharp folds before turning the napkin over. Holding the center, she pulled it apart, layer by layer, until a paper rose lay in her hand. "He wasn't ready to take on the responsibilities of having a ready-made family," she finally answered, not bothering with the details. A quick snap of her wrist, and the paper rose disappeared. A serviceable, if slightly wrinkled, napkin took its place.

Cole bristled. Jenna was a great kid and he couldn't imagine anyone not finding her adorable. He wondered what his father would say when he told him about her. Somehow, he doubted Carson would be overly jubilant at the thought of his son and Marni having a child together, let alone a future. He wasn't looking forward to breaking the news that Marni was back in his life. To stay.

"What about you?" she asked as the waitress delivered their breakfast.

"After Elizabeth, nothing too serious," he said, adding a healthy dose of Tabasco sauce to his scrambled eggs. "But I dated, too. Was there anyone else in your life besides the guy who didn't like kids? I can't believe you only had one relationship in thirteen years."

"Really?" she shot back, becoming irritated. "And why is that?"

He set aside his fork. A smile tugged at the corners of his mouth until he finally gave in and flashed her a full grin. "Because, you're a very passionate woman."

Marni coughed and reached for her water. "I dated an accountant for about six months," she replied haughtily, hoping the heat in her face wasn't a glowing blush.

He chuckled, a smug expression on his face. "Oooh, I bet that was exciting."

"He was a nice guy, Cole."

"What happened?" he asked between bites of rye toast.

Marni toyed with the sausage on her plate. Finally she lifted her gaze to his. She couldn't keep the laughter out of her voice. "He was boring."

His laughter was a full-hearted sound that warmed her from head to toe.

She thought for a moment about her relationships and how they compared to her affair with Cole. Being completely honest with herself, she admitted there simply *was* no comparison. She'd never have been happy with either Kyle or the accountant. Could any man besides Cole make her truly happy? Sadly, she didn't think so.

Cole's deep voice interrupted her thoughts. "What do you want, Marni?"

"Excuse me?"

"What do you want out of life?"

Try as she might, she couldn't define the expression in his eyes. They burned her with hot fire and chilled her with green ice.

She turned her attention to the landscape. What *did* she want? She wanted a family, a real family. Another baby would be nice, and a husband. As much as she loved Jenna, there were times when she wished she had someone to come home to, someone to share her day with, to curl up on the sofa with, to snuggle next to each night. Someone to hold her and tell her everything would be okay when times were tough. And she wanted that someone to be Cole. Same old song and dance, she thought irritably.

"Just like everyone else, I want to be happy," she finally answered with more sarcasm than she'd intended.

His hand slipped over hers. She turned to face him, and the gentle look he gave her was nearly her undoing. "What would make you happy, sweetheart?"

Marni's breath caught, stopped by a lump in her throat. *You!* her heart cried. *You could make me happy.* She braved a smile. "Spending the next twenty-four hours in your company would help." For now, that was all she would allow herself to think about.

He pulled his hand away from hers and contemplated her across the table. She saw a man who was intelligent, caring, loving and passionate. A man who knew and understood his purpose. A man who never thought twice about the decisions he made about his life or his business. A man who would never find himself in her position.

"Is that all?" His voice broke through her reverie.

"That's all I'm willing to risk for the moment," she answered honestly.

A sensuous light shone in his deep green eyes. "Then that's what you shall have, my love. For the next twenty-four hours, I'm yours."

Marni grinned. In the space of a second she imagined all sorts of deliciously wicked ways she planned to enjoy Cole.

By MONDAY MORNING, Marni still hadn't told Cole about the deal she'd made with the devil. She'd planned to tell him Sunday night, but after Jenna had gone to bed, Cole had done his best to distract her. Again. And now it was work as usual.

"You're late," Peg barked from behind her computer monitor, the telephone receiver sandwiched between her shoulder and cheek.

Marni looked pointedly at her watch. "So I am," she said, not the least bit concerned.

Peg held out a stack of messages. "Dorlan's been asking for you, Judge Gladstone's clerk has called three times already, defense counsel on the Whitford case wants a meeting this morning at eleven and Mr. Ballinger is on line two.''

Marni froze. *Mr.* Ballinger? Carson? ''Mr. Ballinger?'' she squeaked.

''Yeah, the sexy voice.''

''Cole?''

Peg nodded, clearly exasperated. ''And it's only nine.''

Marni took a deep breath and ordered her racing heart to slow down. ''I'll take line two and deal with everything else in a minute.'' She ignored Peg's scowl, made more ferocious by the awkward slant of her glasses.

Marni picked up the contents of her In box and headed straight for the privacy of her office, and Cole. She closed the door and rushed to the phone, punching the blinking light with her index finger. ''Good morning.''

He chuckled, the deep, rough sound doing strange things to her insides. ''You sound chipper for a Monday.''

''Better enjoy my mood while it lasts,'' she warned him good-naturedly. ''From the stack of messages Peg had waiting for me, it's bound to be a bitch of a week.'' She set her briefcase on the floor, dropped the contents from her In box on the desk and shrugged out of her coat.

Cole sighed. ''I know the feeling. I'll call Jenna later, but I wanted to let you know I won't be coming over tonight.''

Damn, she thought. She had to tell him. The tension was killing her. ''Jenna's going to be disappointed.''

''What about you?'' His voice was a throaty growl, filled with innuendo.

Marni laughed. ''I'll be *very* disappointed.''

''I promise, I'll make it up to you.''

Images ran though her mind of just how he would make it up to her. A pool of heat settled in her stomach at her erotic fantasies.

Once again, she prayed he would understand when she told him. But what if he didn't? "Cole, there's something we need to talk about."

"I'm listening."

"No. Not on the phone. When can I see you?"

"Sounds important."

"It is."

Silence. Finally he spoke. "Today is shot. How's lunch tomorrow?"

Marni flipped through her calendar. "Can't make it. We could talk after Jenna goes to bed tomorrow night."

"I can't promise anything right now. I'll have to see how... my meetings go today."

She detected a note of apprehension in his voice and could only wonder at the cause. "Problems?" she asked, concerned.

"I don't anticipate any." He sounded as if he refused to *allow* any.

What else could she do, short of blurting out the awful story over the telephone? It just wasn't the sort of thing one conveyed via Ma Bell. "Well, call me, then. Jenna's going to want to know when you're coming over, anyway."

"All right. I've gotta run. I have to get to the office. Busy day ahead."

"I know. I've got alligators nipping at my heels, too." She sighed, not wanting to let him go just yet.

"Marni?"

"Yes."

"I... I'll miss you."

The hesitation in his voice startled her. Almost as if he were about to tell her he...loved her? One weekend of great sex, and her fantasies were getting out of control. "Me, too," she told him.

Cole hesitated a moment longer. "I'll call you tonight," he finally said, and then the line went dead.

Marni replaced the receiver and forced her wayward thoughts aside. The alligators needed her attention.

COLE ENTERED THE OUTER office of his executive suite and deposited another pink baker's box on Liz's desk.

"Oooh, twice in the same year. You're not really Cole Ballinger. You're an alien who's taken over his body." Liz dropped a stack of contracts on her desk and peeked into the box. "Yum. Blueberry muffins."

"Can't I show my secretary how much I appreciate her?"

Liz laughed, a light tinkling sound. "You want something. Last week you sent me on a scavenger hunt. What is it now? Your father's already here, so I know you don't want me to pick him up at the airport."

Cole's body tensed. "What?"

"You couldn't tell? He's been in your office all morning. The staff's been walking on eggshells ever since."

Cole let out a string of curses that would have made a sailor blush. *Damn him!* Jenna's photograph!

Liz lifted a perfectly arched brow. "Cole?"

"Just hold my calls," he said, then strode purposefully into his office.

Carson sat behind Cole's desk, his hands folded in front of him, resting on top of a thick file folder. Staring at the wall, he didn't even acknowledge his son's presence.

In the six months since Cole had last seen his father, the man had aged visibly. His thick hair was more gray than brown, and there were deep lines etched in his face, especially around his trademark green Ballinger eyes. Carson looked every bit his sixty-two years.

Cole stepped deeper into the office and set his briefcase on one of the white leather chairs facing the chrome-and-glass desk. "You're early."

Carson didn't answer, and Cole wondered if the older man had even heard him. He appeared distracted, a look of...regret?...etched on his strong features. At this moment, Carson Ballinger seemed almost—defeated. Cole mentally shook himself. Defeated was not a word used to describe the powerful head of Ballinger Electronics.

"I took an earlier flight," he finally said, his commanding voice uncharacteristically soft. He unfolded his hands and reached for the photograph of Jenna. An eternity later, he lifted his gaze to Cole. "Who is she?" he asked.

Resentment coiled deep inside Cole at his father's intrusion. He hadn't planned on telling Carson about Jenna until his role in his daughter's life was secure, but he couldn't refute the truth. Aside from the fact that they looked too much alike, he had no intention of denying the existence of the child he'd come to love so much.

"My daughter." Pride filled Cole's voice.

Carson didn't so much as flinch. "Does she have a name?"

"Jenna."

Carson returned his attention to the photograph. A wry smile curved the older man's lips, and an emotion Cole couldn't define flashed briefly in his eyes. Slowly Carson shook his head as if he'd half expected to discover he had another grandchild today.

"Who's her mother?" he asked dispassionately.

"Marni Rodgers."

Carson sighed and set the photo of Jenna back on the desk. When he turned to face Cole, his eyes looked hard, but he schooled his expression so quickly, Cole wondered if he'd imagined it.

"So," Carson began, resting his hands on the arms of the executive chair. "I see Marni didn't get the abortion after all."

Cole stared at his father in shock. Abortion? Marni? "What abortion?"

"You'd better sit down, son."

Cole ignored him. Instead, he loomed over the desk and braced both hands on the edge. "What the hell are you trying to say?" *Not Marni!* his heart cried out. She wouldn't. *She didn't.*

Carson looked down at the file in front of him. "I'm sorry, son. This isn't easy for me."

Cole didn't move. He didn't think he could if his life depended on it. "Get to the point, Dad," he ordered harshly.

"Marni came to me when she found out she was pregnant. She said it was yours and she asked me for the money for an abortion."

Cole pushed away from the desk. Fury demanded he do something, *anything,* or he would explode. He strode to the window, then turned. "Marni would never do that."

"It's the truth, son."

Running a hand roughly through his hair, Cole paced the office. His hands flexed, balled into fists, then flexed again. Straining for control, he finally shoved them into the pockets of his trousers. *No!* he wanted to shout. Marni was not the kind of woman who would do what his father was suggesting. "I'm not buying it, Dad. Marni isn't the type to sweep her problems under the rug."

"Cole, I know how painful this must be for you."

Painful? Pain didn't begin to describe the agony Cole was feeling right now. More like someone had ripped his heart out and run over it with a truck. *Could* it be true?

"Cole?"

Cole composed himself and turned to face his father.

"I have proof." Carson picked up the folder in front of him.

"What proof?" Cole asked.

"Take a look at this," Carson said, holding the file out to him.

Cole hesitated. Those papers could destroy him.

"You need to know the truth, son," Carson said gently, waiting for Cole to retrieve the file. "You need to know the kind of woman Marni truly is. When you told me you'd run into her again, I had a feeling she might try to use you again. I'm sorry, son, but you deserve to know *everything* about Marni Rodgers."

Reluctantly Cole stepped forward and took the file. Rounding the desk, he sat in the chair across from Carson and opened the manila folder. Inside were copies of canceled checks. The first one had been issued the day before Marni ended their relationship.

Anger surged through Cole. The force of the fury built with each copy he reviewed. "What the . . ." he muttered. The amounts were staggering, and all payable to Marni Rodgers over a period of five years. "An abortion would have cost a few hundred bucks."

Carson sighed heavily. "Cole, there's more. My part in it . . ." He shook his head regretfully. "I'm ashamed."

Cole tossed the file on the desk. He'd seen enough. "What the hell is going on?"

"When Marni came to me after she learned of her pregnancy I asked her why she didn't tell you. She explained that if she did, you would insist on doing the right thing."

"Damned right." He would have married Marni in a second.

His heart contracted when he thought of Marni and Jenna, how it might have been. He could have, *should* have, been with them all along. He'd been cheated, and the thought burned his gut.

"The last thing she wanted was to be saddled with a husband she didn't love and a baby she didn't want," Carson said bluntly.

Cole bounded out of the chair. "I don't believe this."

He didn't *want* to believe that Marni could make love to him so passionately with this lie between them. But doubt had been planted, and each revelation was turning it into a noxious weed. Maybe he'd never truly known Marni at all.

Cole moved restlessly through the office, pacing like a trapped animal. He didn't want to hear any more.

"Cole, sit down."

Cole shook his head, not trusting his voice at the moment. The anger coursing through him prevented rational thought. Strangling Marni was definitely not a good idea, but it held appeal.

"I asked her what she wanted to do," Carson persisted.

A weight the size of a two-ton brick settled in Cole's stomach. He didn't want to know. He really didn't, but he couldn't let it go. "And?"

"She wanted a career. She'd always dreamed of being an attorney. You know that. It's all she ever talked about."

Icy fingers gripped what was left of his heart. There were simply too many truths to Carson's story to deny it.

Being a lawyer *had* been Marni's dream, a dream she'd accomplished. He'd wondered how she'd done it—college, law school, taking care of an ill parent *and* raising a child. God, he'd even felt guilty because he hadn't been there to help her carry the burden.

"If she'd asked for an abortion, why the hell did you give her so goddamn much money?"

"She told me that if I paid her way out of town, and provided for her education, she'd get an abortion and never see you again."

"And you did it?" Cole said incredulously.

Carson nodded. "Cole, she wasn't right for you. If you'd married her you'd have been miserable. She didn't love you—you were merely a bank balance to her." Pointing to the folder, he asked, "Doesn't this prove it?"

"Then why did she keep Jenna?" Cole asked, hoping to find a flaw in Carson's story. "Why didn't she get the abortion?"

Carson shrugged his wide shoulders. "Who knows what goes through a woman's mind? She could have had a twinge of conscience at the last minute. Maybe she never planned on the abortion at all. Maybe she just used the child to gain what she wanted most—her career."

"Marni loves Jenna," Cole argued. Of that, at least, he was certain. He recalled with clarity each gesture of affection and respect. This was not a woman who could have planned to destroy her unborn child.

"I'm sure she does, in her own way. But remember, that child, *your daughter*, was a pawn, Cole." Impatience filled Carson's voice. "Marni used an innocent life, her own flesh and blood, to extort money from us."

Cole strode to the desk and picked up the damning folder again. The things his father told him made sense. And as many times as he'd asked her, Marni had never answered his questions about why she'd left Elk Falls without any explanation. Looking at the astronomical figure in front of him, he finally understood. Bitterness filled his heart, slowly pushing away any tenderness he held for her.

Carson stood and rounded the desk, then placed a comforting hand on Cole's shoulder. "I never meant for you to find out, especially like this. I'm not proud of what I did, but I thought it was for the best."

Turning to face his father, Cole asked, "When did she tell you?"

"It's not important."

"It's damned important," Cole snapped.

"The Fourth of July party. You'd gone upstairs to change and Marni asked to speak with me."

"Did you agree to her terms right away?" he asked, needing to know every last detail.

Carson closed his eyes briefly, as if the answer pained him. "Yes."

Cole shook his head, confused. "Fourth of July?"

"That's right."

"But Marni didn't leave town until the middle of August."

Carson spoke so softly Cole had to strain to hear him. "She was waiting to see if she was accepted at USC."

Carson removed his hand, then turned his attention to the photo of Jenna. Cole's gaze followed his father's. Jenna. She was the innocent party in all this. Had Marni truly used their daughter as a pawn for her own gains? The thought sickened him.

He set the file aside and dropped into the soft leather chair, feeling like the biggest fool ever to walk the face of the earth. He thought pain was supposed to be numbing. He wished to hell it was.

He massaged the back of his neck, trying to ease the tension, while memories of another time, another place, played through his mind. A dejected Marni, crying softly in his arms because her application for a full scholarship had been denied. God, he'd comforted her, told her that if she really wanted to go to college, she'd find a way. Apparently she had. His heart turned to stone.

"Cole?"

Carson's voice reached him, but he chose to ignore it, wondering what else Marni hadn't told him. What else had she lied about?

"Cole, what are you going to do now?"

"What am I supposed to do? That—" he angrily pointed to the photograph of Jenna "—is my daughter."

"Yes, but her mother..."

"Will be hearing from my lawyer. Today."

CHAPTER NINE

PEG ENTERED MARNI'S office late Monday afternoon. "Dorlan wants to see you."

"Can't," Marni returned, shoving her arms into her cream-colored jacket. "I've got to get to the courthouse right away. The judge on Kendell wants to see counsel in chambers in ten minutes."

"Uh-oh." Peg placed a file in Marni's briefcase. "That doesn't sound good."

No, it didn't, Marni thought, adjusting the high collar of her turquoise silk blouse. Judge Gladstone's highly unusual request worried her. As far as she knew, the appellate court hadn't handed down its decision, but there was a possibility the judge had received word. Especially if the decision was that the witness had been coerced.

Peg pushed her glasses back up the bridge of her nose. "I've got motions for you to review for tomorrow and attorneys calling me for answers on plea bargains you offered. What'll I tell them?"

Blowing out a frustrated breath, Marni left her office. "I'll handle them when I get back." She didn't think the day could get any more hectic. She stopped short to avoid bumping into a blond young man standing near Peg's desk.

His hesitant gaze met hers. "Ms. Rodgers?"

"I'm Marni Rodgers," she said briskly. Judging from the blue uniform he wore, she realized he must be a courier of some sort.

"This is for you, ma'am," he said, a brown envelope extended in his hand.

"My secretary can sign for it." Marni stepped around him, anxious to be on her way.

"I'm sorry, ma'am." The courier hurried after her. "I'm to give this directly to you."

"Fine." Exasperated at his insistence, Marni took the envelope from him. "Where do I sign?"

"No signature required, ma'am. You've just been served." The young man turned and hurried toward the exit.

Marni ripped open the envelope in irritation, certain this was just another attempt at grandstanding from some rookie defense attorney. The word *summons* appeared at the top of the form. She flipped the page, and the floor tipped. She reached for Peg's desk for support. The words she'd dreaded since Cole's return swam before her eyes.

Cole was suing her for joint custody of Jenna.

Trying to hold back the panic threatening to overwhelm her, she scanned the document a second time. She'd been ordered to appear in court in five days for a custody hearing.

"Oh God," she moaned. Loud humming reverberated through her head, growing louder by the second.

"Marni? Are you all right?"

Peg's voice filtered through the thick fog enveloping Marni's mind, but she couldn't speak. This had to be a joke. A sick joke. Hadn't Cole sworn he'd never hurt Jenna? Did he think this wouldn't affect their daughter?

Someone guided her to a chair and pushed her into it. She didn't protest. The papers were snatched out of her hand, replaced by a paper cup.

"Drink." The order came from Peg.

Somewhere in the back of her mind, she heard Peg arrange to have someone cover her immediate appearance in judge's chambers. Marni didn't care. Nothing mattered now except Jenna. Her worst nightmare had become reality.

A deep chill settled inside her. She lifted the cup to her lips and sipped the water Peg had forced into her hand. She tasted nothing. A stiff belt of whiskey would do the trick, she thought. Something to burn away the numbness so she could at least feel something. Briefly she wondered if she was going into shock.

Peg returned and took the cup from her hands. "Come on, Marni. I'm taking you home."

"I have to get to court," Marni mumbled, but couldn't remember why.

"Dorlan's covering it for you. He said he'd call you tonight."

"You told him?" Marni asked. She didn't want her boss to know her world was caving in around her. She didn't want him to think she couldn't handle her job!

Peg gave Marni a sympathetic squeeze. "It's okay, Marni. He understands and said for you not to worry."

She wasn't worried. She was terrified. What would she do if the judge granted Cole's petition? *Die,* she thought. *I'll just crawl away somewhere and die.*

"Jenna," Marni whispered. "I have to get to Jenna."

"I know you do," Peg agreed. "I've called Ms. Parks. She's going to meet us at your place."

No one could help her now, not even Rebecca Parks. Her world was coming apart at the seams.

"Come on," Peg ordered, Marni's purse and briefcase in her hands. "Let's get you out of here."

MARNI PACED THE CARPETING in front of the fireplace in the den. The same den where she and Cole had made love only three days before. "I should kill him," Marni announced for lack of a better plan. Her earlier numbness had faded, replaced by a burning anger at Cole's betrayal. He'd made love to her the entire weekend, knowing full well he intended to break her heart on Monday.

Rebecca chuckled. "Attorney-client privilege should hold up if you're actually considering that as an option."

Marni glared at her friend. "I'm serious," she said, thankful Peg had taken Jenna home with her. No matter how angry she was with Cole right now, she didn't want to become one of those parents who ran the other into the ground in front of the children. Kids were the real victims in situations like this.

The laughter left Rebecca's eyes. "So am I."

Marni sighed and continued her pacing. Murder, no matter how gratifying, was out of the question, but the thought of putting Cole through the same hell she was experiencing gave her pleasure, no matter how illogical or immature. An eye for an eye.

"Can't you do something, Bec? Isn't there a way to stall him?" But Marni knew the answer before she even asked. They'd been over her options, and until she appeared before a judge, there wasn't a damn thing Marni could do. She only prayed that Carson wasn't involved somehow, but with the way her life was going lately, she seriously doubted she'd be spared.

She couldn't take Jenna away. Cole had seen to that. An order preventing Marni from taking her daughter out of the country, or out of the state, for that matter, had been included with the summons and notice to appear.

"Are you sure you don't have any idea where this is coming from?" Rebecca asked her for the third time.

"Dammit, Rebecca, I've already told you everything. We spent the weekend together, the *entire* weekend. I had no idea Cole was planning anything like this." Marni walked to the sofa and plopped down next to her friend. She rested her elbows on her knees, cradling her head in her hands. The tears she'd been fighting all evening finally won the battle and flowed down her cheeks. "We even looked at houses together," she said through her tears. Marni raised her head and looked at Rebecca. "He almost told me he loved me this morning. Why, Bec?" A note of hopeless despair filled her voice. "Why is he doing this?"

Rebecca scooted closer and wrapped her arms around Marni's shoulders. "Go ahead and cry, kiddo. It won't change a thing, but you'll feel a helluva lot better."

And she did. Marni allowed the tears to flow unchecked. Great wrenching sobs tore from her body until she ached. When she finally exhausted herself, Rebecca handed her a snifter of brandy and urged her to drink.

"There are a couple of possibilities. On an up side," Rebecca drawled as Marnie sipped, "there's a chance that this could all be a mistake."

Marni gave a choked, desperate laugh. "Oh, yeah. And I made it when I trusted Cole."

"Listen a minute before you start cursing again," Rebecca continued, taking the snifter from Marni's tight grasp. "What if Cole originally planned to sue for joint custody of Jenna only to establish his parental rights but changed his mind, and the papers couldn't be stopped before they reached you? It happens all the time. Things get lost in the legal system and sometimes it can't be helped. You haven't even talked to him yet."

Marni flopped back in defeat against the cushions, her legs stretched out in front of her. "You tried to phone him and he wouldn't take your call, remember? Besides," she argued, "don't you think he would have warned me?"

Now it was Rebecca's turn to sigh. "His secretary said he was in a meeting. That's not necessarily refusing to take my call. He could have thought everything was taken care of."

"You believe that?"

"What I believe doesn't matter."

"You're supposed to be my attorney."

"I am. But right now I'm your friend. You need to talk to Cole. Make sure this isn't all a big mistake before you do anything stupid."

Marni digested Rebecca's suggestion. Maybe her friend had a point. There was a chance, no matter how slim, that Cole had filed a week ago when he'd first found out about Jenna and forgotten to dismiss the action before she'd been served. But there was a greater chance for a Los Angeles snowstorm in the middle of August.

Turning to look at Rebecca, she said, "There were two things. What's the other?"

"He's only suing for *joint* custody, not full."

The thought of losing Jenna even for half the year gnawed at her insides. "And that's a plus? Six months with me and six months with Cole?"

Getting off the sofa, she walked to the slider and stared out at the evening dusk. There was a churning in the pit of her stomach that went hand in hand with the heaviness settling in her chest. She hadn't even told Cole about his father's money yet. What would he do when he found out about *that* little secret? Amend the petition from shared custody to full? Her stomach lurched at the prospect.

Rebecca's voice broke into her thoughts. "In a joint custody matter, the judge often allows the child to reside permanently with one parent while the other has the right to come and go at mutually agreed times. Seeing Jenna on a daily basis could be all Cole wants. An open invitation for visitation."

Marni strode across the room, heading toward her bedroom.

"What're you doing?" Rebecca called after her.

"The only thing I can do. I'm going to see Cole," she said, stopping on the steps leading to the kitchen. She turned around and faced her friend. "If I'd listened to your advice a week ago, I might not be in this mess right now. Maybe I can reason with him."

"And if that doesn't work?"

She gave her friend a rueful grin. "Then I just might end up killing him after all."

COLE LET HIMSELF into the apartment after dropping his father off at his hotel. He'd offered his spare bedroom to Carson, but the elder Ballinger had declined. Now Cole was thankful, glad to be alone.

He flipped on a lamp. Incandescent light spilled over the room. He stood for a moment and surveyed his surroundings. He found them cold and stark, and for the first time, it bothered him. He was glad he'd decided to purchase a house. This definitely wasn't the kind of home he wanted for his daughter.

After leaving his attorney's office, assured Marni would be served with the papers today, he'd made an offer on one of the places in the hills overlooking Malibu. His agent had been confident the owners would accept his offer. By the end of the day, Cole had purchased the property. A home where his daughter could possibly live for six months of the year.

Loosening his tie, he set his briefcase on the sofa, then slipped out of his blazer, carelessly tossing it on top of the attaché. After turning on the television for background noise, he wandered into the kitchen and opened the fridge. He reached past the chef salad his housekeeper had left for him and grabbed a beer. He took a long pull, trying to wash the bad taste of the day's revelations out of his mouth. After the conversation with his father, Cole had operated on autopilot for the remainder of the day, completing each task with cold precision, determined not to allow his emotions to get in the way. If he could control his feelings, he wouldn't suffer the pain of Marni's betrayal. Again.

The doorbell sounded, and Cole sighed. Only one person he could think of would be coming to his apartment, and it wasn't his father. He took another swig of beer and the bell sounded again. Marni was a fool to want to face him now. She must realize he was itching for a fight. Setting the bottle on the countertop, he stalked through the living room to the front door.

He swung open the door and Marni stepped through the portal without waiting for an invitation. Before he could stop her, she drew her hand back and slapped him hard across the face.

"You son of a bitch," she whispered hoarsely, her voice thick with unshed tears.

Fury, dark and dangerous, gripped his insides. Grabbing hold of her upper arm, he slammed the door before jerking her roughly around to face him. Her eyes rounded in surprise, then she pulled away, taking a few steps back.

He gingerly touched his stinging jaw. Bitter satisfaction flowed through him, mingling with the anger he'd kept at bay for so long. He hoped she was feeling the same sense of betrayal that had gnawed at him since the enlightening conversation with his father. "I take it from your greeting, you've been served."

Marni's fingers flexed, and Cole wondered if she was going to slap him again. He wasn't about to give her a second chance.

"You knew," she stated, a hint of resignation in her voice. "It wasn't a mistake."

He laughed, a cruel, harsh sound even to his own ears. "The only mistake I made was believing your lies."

Marni flinched, then shoved her hands into the pockets of the leather bomber jacket she wore. "Cole, I didn't tell you about Jenna because I was afraid."

"Afraid I'd find out you never wanted her to begin with?" he returned contemptuously.

A flash of confusion crossed her face. "I've always wanted Jenna," she stated emphatically, each word spoken succinctly.

Cole stepped more fully into the living room and snapped off the television. "Save it. I know better."

She pulled her hand out of her pocket and ran it shakily through her hair, pushing the curls away from her face. The light-blond tresses hung loose, bouncing around her shoulders in wild disarray. She was dressed in a pair of stonewashed jeans that hugged her slightly rounded hips, and he responded to her even through his anger. He swore softly.

She spun away from him. Standing before a wildlife print of Arctic foxes, she wrapped her arms around her middle, hugging herself. When she finally spoke again, her voice was feather soft. "I'll admit when I first found out I was pregnant I was worried, but I've always wanted my daughter. She's everything to me and you have no right to do this."

"I'm her father. I have every right, dammit."

She whirled to face him, her deep brown eyes glistening with moisture. "You can't mean to do this."

He didn't want to see her tears or hear any more of her lies. "Get off it, Marni." His voice rose, but he was powerless to stop the surge of anger. "I know the truth. Jenna was a means to an end."

Her delicate brow creased in puzzlement. "What are you talking about?"

Bracing his hands on his hips, he glared at her. "I know. I've seen the evidence, counselor. You used Jenna to get what you wanted."

"Why won't you listen to me?" Her voice shook and panic filled her eyes.

"I've listened to enough of your lies to last me a lifetime, lady." Cole spun away, not wanting to look at her. "For years I've wondered why you really left me. Now I know. I've seen the canceled checks."

All remaining color drained from her face. "Carson," she choked out.

"Yeah, Carson," he drawled. "Did you think I wouldn't find out? Did you plan to extort more money from my father?"

She closed her eyes, as if in intense pain. "Cole, it wasn't like that."

"Then how the hell was it, Marni?" he growled.

She skirted the room to one of the leather chairs and sat down. Resting her elbows on the arm, she clasped her hands together and brought them to her lips, then closed her eyes. Cole wondered if she was praying.

Minutes passed but Marni didn't say a word. The silence drove him crazy. With each second her guilt grew in his mind. "Did my father pay you off or not?" he finally asked, unable to bear the quiet any longer.

After what seemed like an eternity, she raised her gaze to his. Despair clouded her eyes. "Yes, but—"

Cole swore viciously, cutting her off. "I didn't want to believe it. I really didn't."

"I can explain." Desperation laced her tone.

"Can you? How? With more lies?" He ran a hand roughly through his hair. "Damn you, Marni!" He didn't care if he was shouting. He didn't care if the entire city heard him.

She got out of the chair and approached him slowly. "Don't do this, Cole. Don't hurt us. Don't hurt Jenna."

Cole stiffened. The pain in her eyes mirrored his own. His heart momentarily twisted in anguish. He hated the part of him that still wanted to hold her, to chase away her doubts and fears. Instead, he struck out verbally. "There is no us," he said, his voice deadly quiet.

"What about—"

"The weekend?" he finished for her. "Great sex, Marni." He purposely raked her with his gaze, aiming for insolence. "You're a great—"

Cole stopped his tirade at her shocked gasp. She spun away as if he'd struck her. He wanted to recall the cruel words but couldn't. "Doesn't spell happily ever after, does it," he said, his tone returning to normal.

Marni stood silent for a long time, staring at the entrance to the bedroom, where they'd made love late into Saturday night after their house-hunting excursion.

An unexpected wave of longing swept over him. Telling himself it was only physical, he said the one thing he knew would hurt her. "I want my daughter."

She raised her eyes to his, and the anger he saw there seared his soul. "Why are you doing this to Jenna? Don't you realize how much this is going to hurt her?"

"And you haven't?" he shot back. "What about keeping her a secret from me for all these years? Hasn't growing up without knowing her father hurt her?"

"We've been over this before," she reminded him tersely.

"I think you'd better leave," he said, and strode past her into the bedroom, closing the door with more force than necessary.

Marni fought back tears, surprised she had any left. She could no longer tell whether the ache in her chest stemmed from Cole's demand for custody or her shame that he'd learned about the money from Carson. Despite his anger, she'd seen pain in his eyes. Pain at her betrayal. As long as he cared, she still had hope.

She couldn't leave like this. A driving need to come to some sort of understanding steered her toward the closed bedroom door.

She took a deep breath and slowly turned the knob, unsure what she would find. Cole stood facing the window, his hands thrust deep into his pockets, his broad shoulders hunched forward. Her stomach clenched in fear but she forced herself to enter the room.

"Cole?" she whispered.

The visible tensing of his body was the only indication he'd even heard her.

"Please, Cole," she ventured. "You can see Jenna any time you want, just don't take her away from me. She's all I've got."

She resisted the urge to turn and run when he finally faced her. His eyes glittered dangerously in a face that could have been made of stone. Not an ounce of compassion softened him. Her steps faltered for a second, then she continued until she stood before him.

"What are you willing to sell this time?" he demanded savagely.

Marni swallowed convulsively, his question stabbing what was left of her heart. Compelled to reason with him, she asked, "What do you want, Cole?"

With deliberate slowness, he raked his gaze up and down her body, giving Marni the distinct impression he was taking inventory of her imperfections. If she'd been stripped naked and placed on the auction block, she couldn't have felt more humiliated.

He took a threatening step toward her, but she held her ground, unwilling to back down until she convinced him what a mistake he was making.

He reached for her, his hand cupping her chin. A wave of fear passed over her, but she willed herself not to move. With as much courage as she could muster, she said, "Cole, I need—"

"I know you have needs, lady. Very *powerful* needs." There was nothing seductive about his tone, only cold contempt.

Without warning, he gripped her upper arms and pulled her against him, crushing her breasts against the firm wall of his chest. Momentary panic filled her when his lips descended on hers. There was nothing soft or coaxing in his insistence that she open to him. Despite her fear, an unwanted thrill of anticipation thrummed through her veins.

He ran his hands up her shoulders and cupped her face, deepening the unyielding kiss. Hot electric waves sparked inside her at the uncompromising thrust of his tongue, and despite herself she slid her arms around his waist. God help her, she wanted him. Despite all the pain, she wanted Cole with a fierceness that scared the hell out of her.

With jerky movements, he tugged her T-shirt out of her jeans, then slipped his hand beneath the fabric. His fingers skittered across her skin, reaching upward to cup her breast. His thumb rubbed against the lace of her bra, teasing her nipple into a hard peak. She groaned and pressed her hips against his thigh. Desire wrapped around her in a blinding, intense light.

He tore his mouth from her and she whimpered in protest. Opening her eyes, she gasped at the feral gleam in his gaze that had nothing to do with passion.

"Sorry, sweetheart," he said, pushing her away. "I don't want what you're selling."

Ashamed, she shook at just how far she might have gone. Her desperation frightened her almost as much as her physical reaction to Cole.

Running a shaky hand through her hair, she said, "I'm sorry." Spinning away from him, she crossed the room. She reached for the door, but his cold voice stopped her.

"I'm sorry, too. But you can't change the past."

Marni's temper snapped. She might deserve his anger for taking money from his father. She'd expected him to be furious when he'd learned about Jenna, but she'd never once regretted her affair with Cole. "I loved you, Cole, and no matter what you think of me now, don't you realize that if I hadn't we'd never have Jenna at all?"

Cole swore viciously. "You're damn lucky I don't sue you for full custody. You don't *deserve* Jenna."

"And you do?" she returned sharply, reacting to the loathing in his voice. "I'm a good mother and you know it."

Cole advanced, and Marni backed away. She'd pushed him too far this time. Her anger quickly evaporated, leaving cold, stark fear in the face of his fury.

"A good mother wouldn't have used her own daughter as a bargaining chip."

"Bargaining chip?" What the hell was he talking about?

"I'll tell you something right now, *counselor*. If you so much as attempt to use Jenna again, I won't hesitate to take her away from you. And I'll make damn sure you won't have so much as supervised visitation."

She swallowed hard, trying not to reveal her fear at his threat. "You can't do that!" she cried in a choked whisper. "No judge in the land would give you that right!"

"Just try me, lady." The coldness in his eyes matched the chill of his threat.

The words echoed into silence with the finality of a twenty-one-gun salute. She turned away from him and walked out of the apartment. Carson had to be behind this, but how much could his money buy? A deep, familiar pain gripped her heart, and her throat ached with the tears she held back.

She raced down the two flights of stairs and ran through the lobby to the front door of the building. Slipping inside her car, parked alongside the curb, she rested her head against the steering wheel and gave vent to her agony.

She cried with gut-wrenching sobs that made her stomach ache and her throat raw. If she'd had any hope of trying to reason with Cole, she'd blown it. The moment she walked in and slapped him across the face, she'd sealed her fate.

IF MARNI HAD LEARNED anything in the past couple of weeks, it was the terrible results of procrastination. She'd brazenly tempted fate, and her hesitation had brought forth disaster. And now she had to try to explain everything to Jenna.

Marni rapped softly on the door and pushed it open. Jenna sat on top of the frilly pink bedspread, surrounded by stuffed animals. Posters of the latest teen idols adorned the walls between the shelves of books and an antique doll collection. A set of red-and-gold pom-poms vied for position with a battered teddy bear in a white wicker rocking chair. The room clearly stated the current stage of Jenna's life. She was a little girl standing on the threshold of young womanhood.

Jenna cast her gaze in Marni's direction. Tears brimmed in her eyes. "What's going on, Mom? Why did I have to go to Peg's while you and Rebecca talked?" The catch in Jenna's voice ripped Marni apart. "It has something to do with Dad, doesn't it?"

Sighing deeply, Marni sat on the bed beside her daughter. "Yes, sweetie, it does." Marni silently cursed Cole. She wished he were here now so he could see what his damned petition was doing. "Jenna, when two people are married, sometimes they get divorced."

Jenna's brows drew together in confusion. "But you and Dad aren't married," she responded logically.

"I know," Marni answered, taking Jenna's hands in her own. She thought she finally understood the pain of divorce even though she'd never experienced the sense of loss herself until now. "But when two people divorce and they have children, sometimes the parents argue over who the children will live with."

"But you guys aren't married," Jenna repeated.

Marni gave her hand a reassuring squeeze. "That's true, but when both parents want their children to live with them and they can't reach a decision together, they have to go to court and ask a judge to decide for them."

Jenna snatched her hand away and hugged a stuffed orange cat to her breast. Her eyes widened and filled with tears. "Is that what you and Rebecca talked about? Do we have to have a judge?"

"Yes." The harsh reality of the one, simple word tore at Marni's insides.

"But why?" Jenna cried. A single tear fell from her lashes onto her freshly scrubbed cheek. Her lips quivered as she bravely attempted to hold her emotions in check.

"Because your dad wants you to live with him part of the time, too."

"But I want to live here. With you." Jenna tossed the stuffed animal aside and flung herself into Marni's arms. "This is my home," she wailed, the words muffled against Marni's T-shirt.

Marni swallowed hard and held Jenna tight. Hot tears slipped down Marni's cheeks. She was completely destroyed by the deep, racking sobs of the child she cradled in her arms. *Damn you, Cole Ballinger.*

Marni soothed her daughter as best she could, whispering words she hoped would ease Jenna's fear. But trite phrases had little meaning when their lives were on the verge of disaster.

Jenna took a shuddering breath and pushed away from Marni. Wiping her eyes with the back of her hand, she asked, "Why is he trying to take me away from you, Mom?"

"He's not trying to take you away from me, sweetie."

"Rachel Harper has a fifty-fifty split. It's a mess, Mom. She's always moving. Other kids live with their mom and then visit their dad on the weekend. Why can't we do that?"

"Maybe we can, Jen," she answered. "Rebecca thinks your father is doing this so he can see you whenever he wants without my permission."

"But he already does," Jenna argued. "Dad comes over all the time. I don't understand." She looked at Marni hesitantly. "Did you... make him mad?"

Marni rubbed the throbbing in her temples in an attempt to relieve her headache. Not wanting to lie to her daughter, or malign Cole, put Marni in a precarious position. The tightrope she was walking had just gotten thinner, and someone had yanked away her safety net. "Your dad and I have some things we need to work out," she answered cautiously, not willing to go into detail.

"What'd you do to make him mad?" Jenna demanded, her Ballinger eyes hardening.

"Oh Jenna, it's so complicated." Hopelessness settled over her.

"You made him mad and now he's going to take me away," Jenna accused, shooting off the bed. She paced the room in agitation. "I'll probably have to move to that little town you and Nana ran away from and go to school with a bunch of stupid hicks. They probably don't like dogs, either, and I'll have to get rid of Arlo."

"I did not run away," Marni said. "And you won't have to get rid of Arlo," she added, hoping to lighten the atmosphere a fraction.

Jenna spun around to face Marni. "Nana said you ran away because my grandfather was a mean old bastard."

Marni's brows rose a fraction. "Jenna!"

"It's true, isn't it?"

Marni might have sworn not to malign Cole's character, but she had no such qualms about Carson Ballinger. "Yes. I left because of Carson, but that was a long time ago."

"Nana said he *made* you leave town."

Marni froze. She knew her mother and Jenna had shared a close bond, but the intimacy of their conversations stunned her. The fact that Jenna and her Nana had been close had always pleased Marni. But she couldn't help wondering what other enlightenments Sally Rodgers had shared with Jenna.

"It's true," she finally answered. "He promised me he'd help Nana if I left Elk Falls." Marni hated being so evasive, but how exactly did one explain such a complicated situation to a child?

Jenna began her agitated pacing again. Marni could almost see wheels and gears churning inside Jenna's head as she thought about the latest development. "You mean you left Kansas to help Nana? Because she was sick?"

"That's only part of it, punkin. Nana was right. Carson was a mean old bastard and I believed his lies. I was young and foolish and I made a mistake." She hoped her daughter could understand, but Marni wasn't even sure *she* understood the reasons any longer.

Jenna stopped her pacing and faced Marni. A mixture of emotions crossed her young features. Anger, indecision, and then fear. "I don't want to see him."

"Sweetie, he's your father. You might not have a choice."

"No. My grandfather. I don't want to see him, Mom. Ever." The determination flashing in her eyes reminded Marni of Cole.

Carson Ballinger was the last person Marni ever wanted to see again, either, but he was a part of Jenna's life, and all too soon, the choice might no longer be hers to make. "Jenna, he *is* your grandfather," she said hesitantly, knowing Cole would want Jenna to meet his family.

Jenna crossed her arms over her chest, her chin set mutinously. "I don't care. He's mean."

"He's determined to have the best for his family." And she hadn't been the best for Cole, she thought with a stab of old insecurities. "Besides," she said, forcing a brightness she didn't quite feel, "I remember your grandmother. Miss Shaylene was a very special lady."

Jenna giggled. *"Miss Shaylene,"* she exclaimed. "She sounds like one of those funny old ladies from Georgia."

Marni smiled. "She's from South Carolina, and I'm sure when you meet her she'll tell you all about the Carolina Davises and their kinship to Jefferson Davis."

Jenna's stance relaxed. "You mean the Civil War Jefferson Davis? The phony president?" Her voice filled with awe at the prospect of lineage dating as far back as the Civil War.

Marni stood and crossed the room. She rested her hands on Jenna's shoulders. "Sweetheart, I know this is a lot for you to try to understand, but we all have things in our past that we're not happy with. I made a mistake a long time ago, and I'm so sorry that you're caught in the middle."

Jenna looked up at Marni, indecision and fear battling within her gaze. "Mom?" Her young voice was whisper-soft and filled with trepidation. "I'm scared."

Marni pulled her daughter into her arms. A suffocating sensation tightened her throat at the fear in Jenna's voice. Facing the harsh realities of her own deception was one thing, but for Cole to put their daughter through this frightening anguish was beyond anything she'd ever imagined.

There was no doubt in Marni's mind about Cole's feelings for Jenna. While he might despise *her,* she knew he loved his daughter. She *had* to find a way to make him understand the torment he was putting Jenna through and convince him to drop the custody suit.

She tightened her hold on her precious daughter. "We'll be okay, baby," she whispered. "I promise. Somehow, we'll be okay."

CHAPTER TEN

FOR THE SECOND TIME that day, Marni was in court. But this time she sat at the defense table. No, she amended, the respondent's table. She traced the outline of the arm on the smooth wooden chair with her index finger, keeping her eyes straight ahead, reading and rereading the judge's nameplate situated atop the bench. Judge Kenneth Russo had the power to change her life, and Jenna's, forever.

She thought the entire situation ironic. Every day of her career she bargained with defense attorneys regarding the lives of the people she prosecuted. She convinced judges or juries that those people were responsible for misdemeanors and great atrocities. It was her job.

Today the lives of three people were about to be decided by one man. She prayed he saw that she, Jenna and Cole were living, breathing human beings, and not just one more case on his busy agenda.

Marni took a deep, steadying breath and folded her hands on the table to keep them from shaking. She resisted the urge to look over her shoulder, afraid she'd see Carson Ballinger standing in the rear of the courtroom. There was no statute of limitations on promises or deals with the devil, she thought defeatedly. Carson had paid her to stay out of his son's life and she'd reneged. Somehow he'd found out, and now she was being forced to pay the price for seventy-two exhilarating hours with Cole.

Fortunately, the court had recessed until the following week on the penalty phase of the Kendell trial. Monvale's testimony had been found legitimate, and the appeal filed by the defense had been denied. Walter had been concerned about her covering the penalty phase of the trial, but she'd promised to let him know if she had any problems. The fact that her boss was worried about her abilities didn't sit too well, but as long as she managed to convince the jury to issue the death penalty to James Kendell, she'd have done her job—despite the flack from the press and the custody hearing hanging over her head.

The bailiff's baritone suddenly reverberated throughout the courtroom as he swore in the parties before announcing the arrival of Judge Russo. After instructing everyone to remain seated, he sauntered across the carpeted forum to his perch beside the court clerk.

Marni glanced across the courtroom at Cole. He was staring straight ahead, his expression unreadable.

"Are you ready?" Rebecca whispered.

Marni nodded, not trusting her voice, and lifted trembling fingers to her lips. An attempt to summon all her courage to face the moments ahead took her mind off the churning in her stomach.

Judge Russo entered the courtroom and lowered his thin, wiry body into the large executive chair behind the bench.

"I have read the petitioner's request for joint custody of the minor child, Jenna Coleen Ballinger, and the opposing papers filed by respondent." Judge Russo's surprisingly strong voice commanded attention. He glanced at Cole and Marni as if to reassure himself of the identity of the players before continuing. "Ms. Rodgers. Is there any question as to the child's paternity?"

Marni had dreaded this question and knew from the hours she and Rebecca had spent going over the proceedings the matter had to be resolved before they could commence with the custody issues. Even though Rebecca had strenuously advised against it, for a wild, crazy moment, Marni considered lying. The truth would eventually come out, of course, probably in six weeks or so after the judge ordered blood tests, so all she would accomplish would be a delay in the hearing... and more stress to her and Jenna's lives. Still...

"Ms. Rodgers?" Judge Russo asked again impatiently.

"No, Your Honor." She spoke so quietly she feared the court reporter hadn't heard her and she'd be asked to repeat her answer. She didn't think she'd be able to. But a quick glance at the stenographer's fingers flying over the keys of the transcribing machine reassured her.

Russo addressed his next question to Cole. "Mr. Ballinger, am I correct in my assumption that until three weeks ago you had no knowledge of the minor child's existence?"

No one understood legalese better than Marni, but she hated Jenna being referred to as a minor child. This was *her* child. A loving and bright twelve-year-old girl. The child she'd been in labor with for seventeen hours. The infant she had cared for in the middle of the night during her final exams. The toddler she'd walked the floor with when four teeth had broken through her gums at one time. The little girl she soothed after bad dreams. This was her daughter, dammit!

Peeking around Rebecca, she stole another glance at Cole. Nothing.

Look at me, dammit, she ordered silently. *Show me a glimpse of the man I fell in love with all over again. Wake me with a kiss and tell me I'm just having a horrible nightmare.*

As if he heard her thoughts, Cole turned and faced her. She gasped, and Rebecca automatically reached over and clasped her hands.

He was regarding her with utter contempt. A combination of fear and anger knotted inside her, warring for control of her shattered emotions. She tried to tell herself the hardness in his eyes was a facade; he had to possess some feelings for her. This man staring at her with such disdain was not the same who'd nearly told her he loved her a few days ago. This man looked as if he wished she were dead.

Cole sensed Marni's torment but hardened himself against her. The flash of fear in her eyes gratified the part of him that wanted to hurt her. Hurt her as she'd hurt him, not once, but twice.

Samuel Wetzel, his $200-an-hour attorney, stood and faced the judge. "That is correct, Your Honor. Ms. Rodgers kept the subject minor's existence from Mr. Ballinger."

"Objection." Marni's attorney stood abruptly. "Counsel is implying my client intentionally kept the child a secret from the petitioner."

"What would you call it, Ms. Parks?" Wetzel asked sarcastically. As if anything Ms. Parks had to offer in opposition lacked importance, Wetzel returned his full attention to Judge Russo. "Your Honor, the minor is approaching her thirteenth birthday. My client only learned of her existence less than twenty days ago. In fact, the respondent did *not* inform my client. Mr. Ballinger discovered his daughter's existence by accident. Ms. Rodgers never had any intention of advising my client that he was a father."

Cole despised the impersonal formalities of the courtroom. He understood the proceedings, but the constant reference to petitioner, respondent and minor child irritated him. *Marni* had kept his *daughter* a secret from *him*. It was that simple.

"My objection stands, Your Honor," Ms. Parks argued. "Mr. Wetzel is assuming facts not yet in evidence."

The facts were that Marni didn't tell him he had a child because she'd taken a ridiculous amount of money from his father. She'd held out her hand and left town in search of her career with a fistful of Ballinger money. And that was only the beginning of her deceit.

Judge Russo raised his hand for silence but kept his eyes riveted on the open file. His stern features set and his mouth in a grim line, he examined the documents in front of him. "Sustained."

Looking at Marni, the judge asked, "Ms. Rodgers, may I ask why the petitioner was not informed of the child's existence?"

Now there was an answer Cole had wanted weeks ago. Maybe the judge could succeed where he had failed. Somehow he knew there was more to the issue than he'd already learned. Not that he cared, he reminded himself.

Her attorney stood again, and Cole knew the question wouldn't be answered. "Your Honor, Ms. Rodgers did attempt to inform the petitioner of the child's existence on two separate occasions. The first occurred when my client discovered her pregnancy, the second, shortly after the birth of the minor."

Cole glanced at Marni. She'd never attempted to let him know about Jenna. She claimed to have called when she learned she was pregnant, but he already knew that was a lie. How could he believe her, since he'd discovered Marni already knew she was pregnant when she'd left Elk Falls?

"I object," Wetzel announced. "There is no evidence to support the respondent's claim."

"On the contrary, counselor," Rebecca replied smoothly, flipping open a file and producing an envelope, which she held out to the bailiff.

Cole's brows drew together, his gaze resting on Marni. She fiddled with some papers in front of her, and Cole could swear she looked paler than she had a few moments ago.

The bailiff retrieved the envelope from Rebecca Parks and handed it to the judge. "This is a sealed envelope, Ms. Parks. I'm not a clairvoyant."

Rebecca handed a piece of paper to Cole's attorney, who examined it and finally passed it to Cole. He stared in disbelief at the photocopy of an envelope addressed to himself.

"If you will notice the postmark, you will see that it is dated more than twelve years ago and addressed to the petitioner." Rebecca cast her cool blue gaze in his direction. "Of importance, Your Honor, are the words Refused—Return to Sender handwritten on the face of the envelope."

Leaning close to Wetzel, Cole whispered harshly. "Get me that envelope."

Wetzel nodded his agreement.

"Are you entering this into evidence, counselor?" Judge Russo asked, his brows drawn in consternation.

Rebecca nodded. "Yes, sir. Respondent's exhibit one."

Sam Wetzel jumped to his feet. "The petitioner objects, Your Honor."

You're damned right I do, Cole thought angrily. He'd never seen this before. If he had, he certainly wouldn't have returned the damned thing. He needed to get his hands on the contents of that envelope.

"My client has not had an opportunity to review the respondent's exhibit," Wetzel argued.

"The contents of the envelope are not being offered, Mr. Wetzel, only the envelope itself. The respondent has provided a copy to counsel," Rebecca replied.

"I have your copy, Ms. Parks. It is the contents of the envelope we're objecting to. Your Honor?"

Judge Russo glared at Wetzel. "Overruled," he barked.

Marni released the breath she'd been holding. The last thing she'd wanted was for the court to allow the letter she'd written to Cole years ago to become public record. She'd die of humiliation.

"The contents are relevant to this action," Mr. Wetzel argued.

"Ms. Parks, have you seen the contents of this envelope?" the judge asked, pointedly ignoring Wetzel's protest.

An uneasiness settled in the pit of Marni's stomach. *Please, no,* she prayed.

"No, sir."

"Do you have knowledge of the contents?" Judge Russo pressed.

"Yes, I do."

"Would you mind sharing your knowledge with the court?"

Marni winced at the judge's heavy sarcasm.

"A hospital photograph taken the day after the minor child's birth and a personal letter written by the respondent, to the petitioner, two weeks later."

Marni resisted a strong temptation to look at Cole. She couldn't bear to see the distrust and scorn in his eyes.

The judge leaned back in his large swivel chair and laced his fingers together. "So I'm to understand you haven't seen these documents for yourself."

"No, sir, I haven't," Rebecca answered.

Judge Russo sighed irritably. "Ms. Parks, the court cannot admit the evidence on your client's behalf without seeing the contents."

Rebecca tapped her pencil on the table. "Your Honor, my client doesn't—"

"I need to see the letter, counselor."

"But, your Honor—"

Judge Russo raised his hand, stopping Rebecca's argument. "I understand the respondent's reluctance. However, I propose to review the contents, not to make them a part of the record." The judge leaned his arms against the bench and looked at Marni. "Ms. Rodgers, is that acceptable to you?"

Marni bit her lower lip until it nearly bled. He wanted to open the letter, to read the words she wrote to Cole, telling him he was a father, telling him that she still... Oh, God, why was this happening to her?

"Marni?" Rebecca whispered.

Marni nodded.

Rebecca rested her hand on Marni's shoulder. "Are you sure?"

"He won't read it into the record. Do it."

Rebecca turned her attention back to the judge. "My client agrees with your proposal, Your Honor."

Marni shifted uncomfortably in the hard chair and looked around the courtroom while Judge Russo read the letter. The court reporter's hands stilled over the keys of the transcribing machine, waiting for someone to speak. The bailiff stood near the clerk, an expression of boredom on his face while the clerk whispered something into the telephone.

"Very well," Russo's voice boomed over the sound system. "I will accept the exhibit as it stands."

Marni closed her eyes briefly, thanking whatever guardian angel was looking over her for that one small victory. She'd known the move had been risky when Rebecca first mentioned it when they'd planned their strategy, but she'd reluctantly agreed. There'd been no doubt in Rebecca's mind that Cole's attorney would bring up the fact that Jenna's existence had been kept a secret. This was the one way to *prove* that Marni had at least attempted to inform him. At least now the judge knew the truth.

"Your Honor, I object," Wetzel argued. "The contents of that envelope are addressed to my client, and as such, he has a right to review them."

Judge Russo leaned forward again and glared at Cole's attorney. "Your objection is duly noted, counselor, but my ruling stands. The respondent is not offering the contents as evidence, only the envelope itself. Ms. Rodgers obviously does not wish to have the contents entered into evidence, and until such time as she does, the letter shall remain inadmissible. I assure you, Mr. Wetzel, the letter to your client does address his paternity and is in fact dated ten days following the birth of the minor child. I'm sure I do not need to remind you of the appropriate Evidence Codes, now, do I?"

Cole stole another look in Marni's direction. The relief on her face was so blatant, his curiosity tripled. What could possibly be in that letter she didn't want him to see? Probably more lies, he told himself angrily.

Judge Russo cleared his throat. "Since there is no question as to the child's paternity, a ruling would generally be in order."

Cole turned his attention back to the judge. The time had come for his decision, and Cole suddenly had very mixed feelings about what he was doing in the courtroom. If victory was his, would he lose as well? He'd already sensed a distance in his daughter when he'd come by the beach house to see her. Her usual exuberance had faded, and it tore at Cole's heart knowing he was the cause. No matter how he tried to rationalize that Marni's betrayal was the real cause, he couldn't shake the guilt that plagued him. He decided to wait until Jenna brought up the subject, but he knew that after today he would have to make her understand his reasons for fighting for shared custody. But how did he make a twelve-year-old understand her parents had no future together and legal intervention was a necessity to guarantee him his rights?

The judge's voice called Cole out of his musings. "However, since the child has been in the constant care of the respondent, forcing her to live with a parent whom she hardly knows may prove detrimental to her welfare. It is with the child's best interests in mind that I will forgo a ruling in this matter for ninety days. During this time, the parties are required to meet with the court liaison. I will also order a psychological evaluation of the minor child."

Sam Wetzel leaned back in the hard wooden chair. "My client has a right to his child, Your Honor."

"Mr. Wetzel, I'm not denying your client his parental rights, but I'm sure he doesn't wish to cause the child irreparable harm."

"No, Your Honor," Wetzel conceded.

"Sir, the respondent wishes to note," Rebecca said, her eyes taking on a hard gleam, "that the petitioner may be *forced* to relocate again. As such, I feel this is grounds for denial of his suit for joint custody, and we request only visitation for the petitioner."

Wetzel shot out of his chair. "Mr. Ballinger has purchased a home, Your Honor, near the minor child's current residence. I believe this refutes the respondent's claim."

"Very well, Mr. Wetzel. The court recognizes the petitioner's claim. Therefore, it is hereby ordered that the petitioner shall be deemed unsupervised visitation daily from 3:00 to 6:00 p.m., and alternating weekends from 6:00 p.m Friday to 6:00 p.m. Sunday. Visitation will commence immediately."

Ninety days! Marni couldn't believe the court could be so cruel. For the next three months, her life would hang in the balance. Every single day she would have to live with the knowledge that soon Jenna could be ordered to move in with Cole for six months of the year. How could he do this?

Rebecca leaned toward Marni. "I'm sorry, kiddo."

Marni couldn't speak. An unexpected numbness gripped her insides. A decision had been handed down and there wasn't anything she could do about it. Within a matter of seconds, Cole's legal rights to his daughter had been established. While Jenna still primarily resided with her, twice a month, for an entire weekend, Jenna would be with her father. She leaned into the hard wooden slats of the chair, a sense of deep loss slowly shattering her anesthetized state. With feeling, came pain. An emotion she knew only too well.

She'd always feared that Cole would someday learn about Jenna. But no matter how much she'd dreaded the moment, she'd never actually believed they would be sitting in a courtroom while a judge decided their fate. Fears that sneak up on a person in the middle of the night weren't supposed to be real. Night terrors, nothing more, gone with the light of day.

She turned to look at Cole. His gaze caught hers, but she could read no emotions in the deep jade eyes she'd always loved. They were cold. Empty.

She'd lost two things today and knew she'd never have them again.

Her daughter. And Cole.

COLE LET HIMSELF INTO his apartment. He needed to be alone and couldn't face returning to the office. He'd call his secretary to let her know where he could be reached.

He slipped out of his jacket and loosened his tie. The blue digital lights on the VCR indicated eleven o'clock. He couldn't see Jenna for another four hours, he thought, plopping down onto the couch. The court dictated the rules and he had to follow them or chance losing what liberties he'd been granted.

But then what? What if the court denied his petition after three months? Would he be relegated to occasional fatherhood until Jenna turned eighteen? Or would his daughter live with him for six months at a time? Would he have visitation when it was Marni's turn to be the parent? How would Jenna feel about all this damn volleying back and forth? That was one question he hadn't pondered until now.

Disgusted with the turn of his thoughts, he kicked off his shoes and propped his feet on the low glass cocktail table. Carson was expecting his call. He'd spoken to his father briefly this morning before he left for the courthouse. The old man would be waiting in Denver to hear from him. For reasons Cole didn't want to examine, his father was the last person he wanted to speak to at the moment.

With a heavy sigh, he reached for the cordless phone on the glass end table and punched in a familiar set of numbers.

"Ballinger residence."

The housekeeper's Southern drawl drifted over the phone lines, and he smiled for the first time that day. "Gertie, this is Cole."

"Cole?" she squealed excitedly. "How y'all doin'? How's California treatin' ya?"

He chuckled. An unexpected pang of homesickness assailed him. He suddenly missed the quiet of the small town he still called home. "I'm fine. Is Miss Shaylene home?" he asked. Even his father called her Miss Shaylene.

"Your mama's gonna be so pleased ya called. Hold on a minute, darlin', and I'll track her down for ya." The line clicked as Gertie placed him on hold.

Moments later his mother's soft voice came on the line. "Cole? Is everything all right, dear?"

"Hello, Mother." He didn't know why he'd called, only that he wanted to hear her voice. Leave it to Miss Shaylene Davis Ballinger to know there was a reason for his call home. "How have you been, Mother?"

"I'm fine, dear."

"How's Janelle?"

His mother was quiet for a moment before answering. "Janelle is doing well. So are the girls and Don. Gertie is healthy as a horse and I've never felt better. It's not my birthday, Mother's Day is three months away, and Christmas was over two months ago. Now, tell me what's the matter, Cole."

Although she kept her voice carefully modulated, Cole sensed her worry. Miss Shaylene *never* raised her voice, nor did she react emotionally to any situation, especially in public. Southern gentility had been imbedded into her soul.

He closed his eyes. He could almost see her delicate brows raised in concern, her hazel eyes watchful. Her artfully arranged blond hair would be swept into an elegant knot at her nape with delicate pearl earrings hugging her lobes.

"Have you spoken to Dad recently?" he asked carefully.

"I speak to your father every night when he's away on business. You know that."

True, he did. Ever since Cole could remember, whenever his father was away from home—which was often—he'd call each and every night. He never asked to speak with either of his children, but his mother always conveyed his affection. Cole had often wondered if his mother had embellished the loving image of his father, and now he realized he'd been right. Where that revelation came from, he didn't know, but he filed it away for later. "Did he mention Marni Rodgers?"

"He did mention that you'd seen her again," she answered.

Cole detected a hint of apprehension in his mother's voice. Exactly what *had* his father said about Marni?

"I suppose he also told you about Jenna?"

"Jenna?" She sounded surprised.

"Yeah, Mom." He hesitated. "Jenna is my daughter."

A distant hum was the only sound coming through the receiver. No gasp of surprise, no tears. Although, he'd known, of course, that wouldn't be the case. When Miss Shaylene finally spoke, her voice was in a whisper. "You have a daughter," she said.

Cole despised the pain he knew he must be causing her. A Ballinger born out of wedlock would be hard to accept for a woman of her breeding and values. "I just wanted to let you know you have a granddaughter."

The seconds ticked by like hours as Cole waited for his mother's response. He wanted her acceptance of Jenna more than he'd realized.

"Tell me about her," Miss Shaylene said quietly, her voice filled with wonder, and a little apprehension.

Relief surged through Cole. A smile touched his lips as he told her about the girl he'd known for only a few weeks. "She's smart. Sassy. Stubborn."

"She sounds a lot like Marni," his mother said with a soft chuckle.

Cole's body tensed. "She looks like the Ballingers," he said, not wanting to discuss the mother of his child. "She'll be a teenager come May."

"How is Marni? I've always wondered how she was doing. She was such a sweet girl."

Cole emitted a short bark of laughter. "Marni's fine," he answered curtly.

"When did you find out about Jenna?"

Cole briefly explained how he'd run into Marni and discovered Jenna's existence, leaving out the more painful details of Marni's duplicity.

"What are your plans now?"

Cole hesitated. He ran his free hand through his hair and massaged the tight knot at the back of his neck. "I've filed for joint custody," he told her.

"I see."

No, he didn't think she did see, but he wasn't about to tell her so. "I'd like to bring Jenna for a visit this summer."

"I think you should. We are her family, after all. Janelle will be so surprised. Karen and Sandy will be thrilled to learn they have an older cousin."

Cole wondered what Jenna would think of his family. He wished, for a minute, she could meet them under happier circumstances.

"I've kept you long enough, dear. Give Marni my best."

"Yeah. I'll do that, too," he responded gruffly.

"And, Cole?"

"Yes?" he said slowly.

"Kiss Jenna for me?"

He smiled. "I'll do that, too, Mom."

AT THE TIME MANDATED by the court, Cole picked up his daughter from the beach house. They drove in silence along the coast highway for a few miles with Arlo stretched out on the back seat of the Jaguar. Cole didn't want to think about the damage Arlo's toenails would do to the imported leather. Jenna had asked if the dog could go with them and he'd been reluctant to deny the simple request.

He guided the sleek sports car onto a secondary road that brought them closer to the ocean. Finding a place to park was easy on the chilly February afternoon.

"Why are we here?" Jenna asked, a tightness in her voice Cole couldn't remember hearing before.

"I thought we'd take a walk."

Jenna shrugged and zipped up her jacket before reaching for the door handle. She slipped out of the car and opened the back door for Arlo, who groaned considerably before lumbering from the automobile.

Cole stepped around the vehicle and approached Jenna. She spun on her heel and headed toward the beach, Arlo trotting after her.

Jenna moved at brisk pace, as if she didn't want to remain in the same vicinity as Cole. The thought irritated the hell out of him, but he knew he was at a distinct disadvantage. He'd never been a parent before, not in the real sense of the word, and he didn't know how best to approach what was troubling his daughter.

He lengthened his stride and easily caught up with her. She kept her eyes straight ahead, not bothering to acknowledge his presence. When he lifted his hand to rest it on her shoulder, she sidestepped to avoid his touch.

He remained silent and matched her stride. The only sounds were the distant hum of automobiles on the coast highway and the waves lapping against the shore. Arlo bounded ahead in an atypical burst of energy, chasing a small flock of sea gulls. The birds squawked and took flight, circling over the huge German shepherd as if planning a strategy for counterattack.

Jenna kept her head down, her hands shoved into the pockets of her jacket. Her hair was unbound, the cool sea breeze whipping the long silky strands behind her. Cole reached out again and rested his hand on Jenna's slim shoulder. She stopped, but didn't look up. Gently he tilted her chin until he could see her eyes. Tearstains marred her pretty face. Fear and anguish brightened her eyes. Lord, what had he done?

Jenna stepped away and hastily brushed the tears from her face before shoving her hand back into her pocket.

"Wanna tell me about it?" he asked gently.

Jenna shrugged, gazing into the distance.

"Is this about your mom and I going to court today?"

Hesitantly, she turned to face him.

"Jenna, I can't help you if you don't tell me what's wrong."

Tears brimmed in her eyes, and a heavy weight on his chest made breathing difficult.

"Why do you want to take me away from my mom? We never did anything to you."

The accusation in Jenna's voice ripped his heart in two. He didn't think he had a heart left after what he'd learned about Marni, but this slip of a child had proven him wrong.

"I don't want to live with you," she announced in a low, tormented voice.

Guilt washed over him for the pain and confusion his daughter was suffering. He had to find a way to make her understand he'd never meant to hurt her. "Jenna, I never dreamed that I'd ever have a daughter. I've always wanted a family, and now that I've found you, I don't want to lose you again."

A light breeze blew along the shore, ruffling Jenna's hair. She pushed it out of her eyes and held the thick length of it in her trembling fingers. "Why can't you be a family with us? Don't you love Mom?"

"It's complicated," he answered evasively.

"That's what Mom says. You're hurting her. She cries all the time. She tries to pretend everything is okay, but I know it's not. She hardly ever cried until you came back."

The allegation made Cole wince. "I'm not trying hurt your mother," he said, and found to his surprise that he meant it. Sure, he admitted, he was angry, and he didn't think he'd ever trust her again, but there was no satisfaction in causing her pain. "It's just that I want you to be a part of *my* life, too. Your mom's had you all these years, and I'm just getting to know you."

Jenna traced the outline of a shell with the toe of her sneaker, her gaze intent on the ground.

Cole wanted to see the girl he'd known for the past few weeks. The bright, happy preteen who was on the verge of discovering boys. The girl who wrestled with an over-large German shepherd, then complained when he'd gotten her jeans dirty. He wanted to see her laugh and look at him as if he were capable of moving mountains just for her pleasure.

"How about if we try to be friends?" he asked. "Spend time together. Let me get to know who you are, and you get to know who I am. If you still decide you don't want to live with me, then we'll cross that bridge when we come to it."

Jenna brought her gaze to his. Tears still brimmed in her eyes. With a quick jerk of her head, she nodded her assent.

A few of the weights on his chest disappeared. He took a chance and stepped toward her. When she didn't bolt, he enfolded her in a loving embrace. He wanted to tell her everything would work out for the best, but he couldn't quite form the words.

The last thing he wanted to do was lie to his daughter.

AFTER THE CUSTODY HEARING, Marni had returned to the office. She'd missed too much work the past few days, only making an appearance when absolutely necessary, choosing to work at home instead. Today she needed the hectic atmosphere of her workplace to take her mind off her problems.

When she returned to the beach house, her briefcase packed full of court transcripts and new cases, she found it dark and empty. Even Arlo was missing. She left her things in the living room and entered the kitchen in search of a note from Jenna. She found one, stuck to the fridge by a souvenir magnet from their summer vacation in San Francisco. Out with Dad. Love, J.

Resentment welled inside her. Coming home to an empty house could very well become a new way of life for her. She despised the silence, and Cole for doing this to them. She filled the teakettle and set it on the stove, adjusting the burner so she'd have enough time to change before it boiled. The house was quiet, too quiet, and Marni felt very much alone.

After flipping on the stereo, she quickly changed into a pair of jeans and an old red flannel shirt. The teakettle whistled loudly, but she ignored it long enough to take the pins out of her hair. Shaking out the curly strands, she scrubbed her fingers over her scalp and padded barefoot back into the kitchen. The sound of the front door opening caused a surge of relief to course through her. Jenna was home.

She turned off the kettle and hurried into the living room, stopping short at the sight of Cole slipping out of his jacket. He couldn't be planning to stay, could he?

Jenna rushed forward and threw her arms around Marni's middle, holding on tightly.

"You okay, punkin?"

Jenna nodded, her head against Marni's shoulder. "I love you, Mom," she whispered.

Marni placed her hands on Jenna's shoulders, setting the girl slightly away until Marni could see her eyes. Streaks stained her cheeks as if she'd been crying. A wave of anger gripped her. Cole had done this. He'd made her daughter cry. She quickly cast him a baleful glare before returning her attention to Jenna. "I love you, too, sweetie."

"I have homework. I'm going to my room."

"Go ahead," Marni said, sensing her daughter's need for solitude. "I'll be here if you need me."

"Do you need any help?" Cole asked.

Jenna stopped, turning to face him. "No, thanks," she said, then disappeared through the doorway.

Cole sighed and tossed his keys and jacket on a chair.

"There's no reason for you to stay. Unless you're here to gloat," she told him, unable to keep the bitterness out of her voice.

Cole leaned his hip against the chair, suddenly tired. Was this the way things had to be from now on? "Why the hell would I want to gloat? Do you think I'm happy about all this?"

"Just leave, Cole. I don't have anything to say to you." Marni spun on her heel and marched into the kitchen.

Cole swore under his breath. Jenna would end up resenting them both if they didn't reach some sort of understanding. Against his better judgment, he followed Marni into the kitchen.

The minute he stepped through the doorway, she rounded on him. "What are you still doing here? You got what you wanted. You won, but your time is up."

"I didn't *win* anything," he told her angrily. "I haven't even been granted what is rightfully mine."

She glared at him, the yellow flecks in her eyes bright with her anger. "Isn't visitation enough for you?"

He braced his hands on his hips. "I don't want to be a weekend father."

"You self-serving, arrogant fool," she said, pulling a mug from the open cabinet. "Can't you see that what you want is hurting people?" She slammed the cabinet door closed.

"Oh, you're a fine one to talk. What about what you wanted? Being a damned lawyer was so important to you, you..." He turned his back on her, unable to finish. What the hell were they doing to each other?

Reason told Marni to leave the subject alone, but she couldn't. "What, Cole? What did I do?" she demanded, setting the mug on the counter with enough force to crack the ceramic tiles.

He pushed away from the countertop and turned to face her. A series of conflicting emotions crossed his features. In the space of a second, she saw anger, pain and even regret. "Why? Why did you do it?"

She knew what he was asking. Not "Why did you keep Jenna a secret?" or even "Why did you leave without telling me?" He was asking about the money she took from Carson. As much as she wanted to, she couldn't hide from the truth any longer. She was no longer an insecure girl of eighteen, and she was tired of running away.

"Because of who I was, I couldn't be the woman you needed. Because if I'd stayed in Elk Falls I never would have amounted to anything. And because my mother couldn't have waited tables in the truck stop forever." Lowering her voice, she aimed for a semblance of calm. "She was a diabetic, Cole. She was already taking two insulin injections a day. After we moved, she didn't have to work and her health improved. She lived nearly ten years relatively pain-free. I thank God every day that Jenna had those years with her. If we'd stayed in Kansas, I honestly don't believe she would have lasted another six months."

Cole stared in disbelief at the woman standing before him. He crossed his arms over his chest and asked, "Are you trying to tell me you took my father's money for your mother? I'm not buying it, Marni."

Her eyes flashed. "I'm not asking you to, dammit."

"Then why the hell did you do it?" he thundered.

"I didn't belong in your world. You want the truth? I did it for you, too," she answered heatedly.

Try as he might, he couldn't quite grasp her logic. How could she think she wasn't good enough for him? "I didn't care where you were from," he told her. Social connections, family wealth, hadn't been important to him and still weren't. "I loved you for who I thought you were." A loving, warm and caring woman. A woman who gave herself to him completely, holding nothing back.

She ran a hand through her hair, her fingernails tangling in the curls. "How long do you think that would have lasted? Another two months, two years? I heard the whispers, Cole. Your so-called friends didn't approve of me. I was never good enough to be one of them. Don't you understand? I didn't fit in. I came from the wrong side of the tracks, and no one minded that I'd crossed them just as long as I remembered to go back at the end of the night."

Marni couldn't stop the words from finally spilling out. "I'll admit, I was wrong to take your father's money, but I cannot regret my reasons for doing it. I bought my mother a few extra years of life and I saved you from making a drastic mistake."

"I never thought we were a mistake, Marni," he said in a low voice.

"Maybe we were, maybe we weren't, but I did what I had to do. And I'm paying for it now. With interest."

His mouth quirked in a half smile filled with bitterness. "I'll be taking Jenna for the weekend," he announced, signaling the conclusion of the bumpy ride down memory lane.

"I know."

They stood staring at each other for a long moment, neither speaking, both lost in their own private thoughts. Finally Cole spoke. "I'll see you tomorrow," he said, and walked out of the kitchen.

He reached for the door, his lightweight jacket slung over his shoulder and his keys dangling from his hand. He hesitated an instant. "Just tell me one thing."

Marni shoved her hands in the back pockets of her jeans and curled her toes into the thick carpeting. "What?"

He raked his gaze over her as if he were imprinting her image on his memory. "You said you loved me. Did you?"

"Yes," she answered in a choked whisper.

He nodded, then opened the door. He turned back one last time before softly closing it behind him.

"And I've never stopped," she whispered to the empty room.

He reached for the door, his hand on it, jacket slung over one shoulder and his eyes deep pools of hurt in a bronzed and finely chiseled face.

Marni slipped her hand into the back pocket of her jeans and curled her fingers . . .

CHAPTER ELEVEN

MARNI LET HERSELF into the beach house late Sunday morning, her overnight bag slung over her shoulder. She couldn't bear the thought of spending the weekend alone, but Rebecca had come to the rescue, offering a weekend of skiing in the local mountains. Marni had quickly agreed. She'd spent plenty of time alone whenever Jenna had been invited by the Lamberts for weekend excursions, but somehow this time had been different. Jenna wasn't off for two days of fun with her best friend. She was away on court-ordered visitation with her father.

The storm that cut short their weekend of skiing had already reached the coast. A light sprinkle of rain streaked the windows. Marni wondered where Cole had taken Jenna. She hoped they'd stayed at his apartment and weren't traveling on the slippery roads.

After unpacking, she ventured into the rain to remove her skis from the rack on top of her car. She issued a string of curses when the latch wouldn't give. A dark cloud overhead opened up, drenching her in a matter of minutes. Angrily pushing her hair out of her face and squinting to avoid the water splashing off the roof into her eyes, she gave the latch a vicious tug. The damn thing wouldn't budge.

The sound of tires on the rain-slick side street caught her attention. She glanced at the late-model Cadillac pulling into her driveway. Probably someone turning around, she thought, giving the catch on the ski rack one last try. Finally the latch popped open.

The Cadillac stopped, the driver turning off the ignition. Seconds later the door opened and Marni stared openmouthed as Cole's mother emerged from the vehicle.

No matter how Marni felt about Carson, she had nothing but respect for Cole's mother. Miss Shaylene had shown her nothing but kindness and Marni was assailed by a fierce stab of guilt. Not only had Cole been denied his daughter, but this woman, whom she'd always admired, had been denied her granddaughter, as well.

A flash of lightning brought Marni back to her senses. "Come in out of the rain," she shouted over the angry roll of thunder, holding open the gate for the older woman.

Miss Shaylene hurried through and waited on the porch while Marni quickly removed the skis from the rack. Setting them aside, she opened the door and followed Miss Shaylene into the house, dreading the recriminations she was bound to hear. Cole's mother could only be in California for one reason—to give Marni a proper set-down.

"You're soaked clear through, dear," Miss Shaylene said with a warm smile, pushing back the hood of her trench coat. "Why don't you take a nice hot shower and then we'll talk."

Marni nodded, a welcoming numbness sweeping over her. "Make yourself at home," she said, disappearing into the bedroom and leaving a trail of water on the floor.

Stripping out of her wet clothes and stepping into the hot spray of the shower, Marni took another dreaded excursion on the emotional roller coaster she'd been riding since Cole had walked back into her life. She thought of his mother's past kindness to her, and suddenly doubted she had the courage to face Miss Shaylene's condemnation.

Her body, at least, warmed from the shower, she dried herself, rubbing the towel roughly over her skin until it turned pink. After a quick makeup job and plaiting her hair, she checked her appearance in the full-length mirror. Satisfied, she left the sanctuary of her bedroom to face another Ballinger. All that was left was a showdown with Carson, and maybe Janelle. By then Marni feared there'd be nothing left of her but an empty shell.

With her courage sufficiently bolstered, she headed toward the family room after a cursory glance told her the living room was empty. She entered the kitchen and found Miss Shaylene near the stove pouring coffee into a carafe. Two mugs, sugar and flavored creamer sat on a teakwood serving tray.

Oh, boy, we're going to have a lecture Southern-style, Marni thought in wild panic. She wondered if she could just ask Miss Shaylene to leave without being rude.

"Shall we take these into the den where we can be more comfortable?" the older woman asked as if she were the hostess.

"Uh...yes. That'd be fine," Marni answered hesitantly, and warily followed Cole's mother into the family room.

Miss Shaylene set the tray on the square coffee table before sitting gracefully on the sofa. She poured coffee into the ceramic mug and smiled at Marni. "I haven't been to California in years," Miss Shaylene said conversationally, handing Marni the mug. "And now that I've managed to escape the harsh winter of Kansas for a few days, I've flown straight into a rainstorm. How have you been, dear?"

Marni detected no animosity in the older woman's soft hazel eyes, only genuine concern. Knowing in a matter of moments the pleasantries would be replaced with hostility only increased Marni's tension. "As well as can be expected under the circumstances, I suppose," she answered truthfully. How much Cole had told his mother she didn't know, but she decided to take matters into her own hands, for once.

"Have you met Jenna?" she asked.

Miss Shaylene sipped her coffee, a warm light passing over her still-beautiful face. "Yes, I have. And I must say, she is a *delightful* child. She was a little shy at first, but by last night, I'd say she'd warmed considerably."

"Last night?" Marni asked, stirring the creamer into her coffee.

"Yes," Shaylene Ballinger answered, setting the mug down on a coaster. She crossed her legs and adjusted the cuff of her silk blouse. "I spoke to Cole a few days ago. He explained the situation to me. I couldn't wait to meet her, so I took a flight out Friday."

"Does Carson know you're here?" she asked, wondering how much Miss Shaylene had been told.

Her gaze held Marni's. "Yes, he knows," she stated quietly.

"But he's not happy about it."

Miss Shaylene reached over and gently laid her hand on Marni's arm. "Let *me* handle Carson, dear."

Too bad she couldn't have handled Carson thirteen years ago. "You said Cole explained everything to you," Marni prompted.

"Yes," Miss Shaylene replied, removing her hand from Marni's arm. "I'm sure there is more to his less-than-glowing version. I'm not certain what happened to the two of you all those years ago, but I do know that my son loved you. He was devastated when you left him.''

Old pain renewed itself within her. ''I didn't have a choice,'' she whispered, her gaze drifting to the sliding glass door. The storm was in full force now, the rain coming down so hard, Marni couldn't see past the deck.

Miss Shaylene's voice drifted over her, her delicate Southern accent somehow soothing. ''We always have choices, dear. Sometimes we choose the wrong option or we take what we assume is the easiest solution. The things Cole told me do not sound like the young girl I knew in Elk Falls. I'd like to hear your side, if you'll let me.''

Why? she wondered dejectedly. What good could possibly come of reliving such painful memories? What was done, was done. ''It won't change anything, Miss Shaylene.''

Cole's mother sighed softly. ''Maybe not, but perhaps you'll feel better getting everything out in the open.''

Marni contemplated Miss Shaylene's offer. She desperately wanted this woman to understand her motives, but she feared the outcome would result in more pain. Did she know the part Carson had played in the past, and possibly the present? Somehow Marni didn't think so, but she knew without a doubt that Carson had been the one to push Cole over the edge.

''I know about my husband's involvement,'' Miss Shaylene announced, as if in answer to Marni's unspoken question. Her voice was carefully controlled. ''Please tell me the truth, Marni. If I can make sense out of this, maybe I can help. What really happened?''

Marni drained the last of her coffee and set her mug on the table. How she wished someone *could* help her. She was so damned tired of the lies and deceit, of the half truths. Without bothering to examine her motives, she told Cole's mother everything. Miss Shaylene sat quietly, only asking questions when a point required clarification. When she'd finished, Marni sighed heavily. "Miss Shaylene, I'm so sorry," she said through the tears burning her eyes. "I never meant to hurt you or Cole."

Cole's mother moved closer and draped an arm around Marni's shoulder, giving her a reassuring squeeze. The simple gesture of kindness was Marni's undoing. Tears fell unchecked and great sobs shook her body. Miss Shaylene pulled her close, her slender arms holding Marni as if she was a small child, murmuring words of comfort.

When her tears were spent, Marni straightened. "I'm sorry."

"Don't apologize, dear," Miss Shaylene said with a smile. "You've been through a lot these past days."

The two women sat in silence, lost in their own thoughts.

"Marni, do you love my son?"

Miss Shaylene's question took her by surprise, but what good would lying do now? She gave a ragged sigh. "I never stopped loving him. I tried, I really did. But there doesn't seem to be a thing I can do about it. It's funny, really. The only man I've ever loved comes back into my life, and for a few days I find myself hoping maybe we can be together again. Now he can barely stand the sight of me. I've been convicted and penalized on circumstantial evidence."

Miss Shaylene reached over and took Marni's hands, clasping them gently. "Then you need to tell him the truth."

Marni shook her head. "I've tried. He won't listen."

"Tenacity, dear. Tenacity. He may not want to hear what you have to say, but he needs to listen. Then it will be up to Cole to make a few decisions."

"I can't force him, Miss Shaylene. He loses his temper and storms away, or he shuts down completely. We can't even have a civil conversation anymore."

Miss Shaylene tugged on Marni's hands to emphasize her point. "My son loves you. He wouldn't be so angry right now if he didn't. You have to find a way to make him understand."

Oh, how Marni wished she *could* make Cole understand, but the odds were against her. A vision of the contempt in his gaze in the courtroom flashed through her mind, and she shivered.

"It seems impossible. And what about Carson? He despises me. Even if Cole forgave me, Carson would always stand between us."

Miss Shaylene raised her delicately arched brows. "Like I said, you leave Carson Ballinger to me. And I want you to stop beating yourself up over this unfortunate business. If you don't, you'll never be able to go forward." The heat in her eyes took Marni aback.

Miss Shaylene looked away, as if embarrassed by the display of emotion. A wry grin tugged at the corners of Marni's lips. Only the Ballinger men could cause such deep passion in the women who loved them.

Cole's mother glanced at her watch and stood. "I have to be going, dear. My flight leaves soon."

Marni rose, reaching for the trench coat Miss Shaylene had carefully folded over the arm of the recliner. Holding the coat open, she helped her into it.

"I'll call you in a few days." Miss Shaylene placed a motherly kiss on Marni's forehead before pulling her into a warm hug.

"Thank you," Marni said.

Miss Shaylene released Marni and stepped back. "For what, dear?" she asked.

Marni attempted a smile. "For believing me."

Miss Shaylene waved her hand, casually dismissing Marni's comment. "Nonsense. *I* should be thanking *you*."

"Thanking me!" Marni said, bewildered.

"For my beautiful granddaughter," Miss Shaylene whispered, her eyes moist.

They said their goodbyes, and Marni waved as the Cadillac headed down the street. Wrapping her arms around her middle, she stood on the porch and listened to the sounds of the storm. She found herself wondering if perhaps there was some truth to Miss Shaylene's claim. Did Cole love her? Could he? Could that explain the reason for his anger?

The thought gave her a faint glimmer of hope. Still, how on earth was she going to get him to listen to her? Short of trussing him up like a rodeo calf, she couldn't make him stay put long enough. She didn't know if she could stand being kicked in the teeth by him one more time, yet if there was a chance, she knew she didn't have a choice. Because one undeniable fact remained. She loved Cole.

And the thought terrified her.

THE PRESS WAS IN FULL FORCE once again as the prosecution and defense gave their closing arguments in the penalty phase of the Kendell trial. Marni tried to ignore them, she tried to ignore the lights and cameras, the microphones and the sounds of pencils scratching down notes as John Middleton, the defense attorney, gave his closing address to the jury. Every sound, every movement, seemed magnified ten times. Her nerves were raw.

"Ms. Rogers?"

"Yes, Your Honor," she said, straightening the papers scattered in front of her as she mentally prepared her closing argument.

She rose and approached the jury box. Resting her hand on the hard wooden partition, she looked at each of the jurors, hoping to gain their confidence.

"Ladies and gentleman, today you are being asked to make what could be one of the most difficult decisions of your life. You are being asked to send a man to his death." With as much poise as she could muster, she crossed the courtroom, her footsteps muffled on the nondescript carpeting until she was standing directly in front of James Kendell.

Marni suppressed a shiver when the defendant looked at her. Forcing herself to return his gaze, she continued, "This...man took the lives of five women. Five young women whose lives had barely begun. The defendant took away their dreams and the dreams of their families. And when he did, he did so without conscience."

Kendell leaned back in the wooden chair as if he was doing nothing more important than relaxing after a hard day's work. His blond hair was slicked back, secured in a ponytail at the base of his neck. No emotion showed in his silver gaze, as if the proceedings held little or no importance to him. From the atrocity of his crimes, he obviously placed little value on human life, and she wondered, briefly, if he attached any more significance to his own.

Marni turned away from Kendell's cold eyes and looked at the jury instead. *This is just another case,* she tried to tell herself, but she couldn't quite believe it. The family of one of the young coeds Kendell had murdered sat in the front row behind the prosecutor's table. The girl's father had broken down during the trial when she'd presented the blown-up police photographs of his daughter's body.

Her heart had gone out to the man, and at that moment, she'd hated her job.

The mother of another victim sat ramrod straight beside one of the reporters from the *Times*. The woman held a crystal rosary, the strands wrapped around her fingers. Marni had the feeling the woman wasn't praying for mercy on Kendell's soul.

A young man of about twenty-five stood in the rear of the courtroom, his arms crossed over his chest. The hatred in his eyes as he glared at the defendant was palpable. He'd been engaged to one of the victims and had learned of his bride-to-be's demise hours before their wedding was to take place. She thought of his pain and knew he'd carry that hurt with him for many years to come. For him, and the others, she had to pull herself together and deliver the most convincing speech of her career.

"The families of these victims have been tragically torn apart," Marni said, stepping in front of the jury box again, determined to win one more time. "The defendant's gruesome acts cruelly ended the lives of five young girls, and it's up to you to now offer some small measure of comfort to those left behind to deal with the pain and loss of their loved ones."

Taking a deep breath, she strolled in front of the jurors, keeping eye contact with each person as she paused in front of them. After summarizing the defendant's crimes, she said, "I don't think I need to remind you of what your verdict must be. After hearing the evidence, you made the only judgment possible. You found the defendant guilty. Now you need to deliver the only conscionable decision available to you. Death by legal injection for James Kendell."

Calmly, she returned to her seat and waited while Judge Gladstone issued instructions to the jury before dismissing them. The jury would go into deliberation again, and once more, Marni would be forced to wait for a decision. Lately, her entire life seemed to be waiting for others to make decisions just as now she was waiting for another judge to decide about the course of her own life.

COLE ANGRILY PUNCHED the intercom button on the phone and buzzed his secretary. "Liz, where the hell are the advertising costs for Dragonmire?" he barked in agitation.

Her sigh was audible. "You gave them back to me twenty minutes ago," she said, impatience lacing her usually soft voice.

"Well, I need them back," he growled before releasing the connection.

Seconds later Liz entered his office, closing the door behind her with a quick push. "Thanks," he grumbled when she laid the file on his desk with a snap.

He glanced up at her, sensing her irritation. Leaning back in the chair, he ran a hand through his hair. "I'm sorry, Liz," he said, figuring she was pretty well fed up with his foul mood lately. He knew he'd been in a hell of a mood since the custody hearing. A seed of doubt had been planted in his mind by Marni's angry confession. Did she really believe she couldn't have made him happy? For what must have been the hundredth time, he pushed the doubts away.

Liz crossed her arms over her chest. "Cole, something's got to give. You've been a pain in the ass for the past two weeks."

"That bad, huh?" he asked.

"The staff would be more comfortable with your father around!"

Cole grimaced and the phone rang, saving him from further apologies. "Take a message," he instructed, not wanting to talk to anyone at the moment. He had too much work to do and he couldn't concentrate as it was. For *that* he blamed Marni, too. As often as he pushed her out of his mind, she just as stubbornly reappeared. And his thoughts weren't about the lies and duplicity, but the passion. The way her eyes sparkled and glowed when she cried out in his arms, the way she clung to him, rubbing her cheek against his chest like a contented kitten.

Liz reached for the phone and nodded. She picked up the receiver, then punched the green flashing light. "Mr. Ballinger's office," she announced. "He's right here. Hold on a minute."

Cole glared at his secretary and punched the Hold button himself. "I just told you to take a message."

Liz returned his glare. "It's your daughter," she said, holding out the receiver.

He snatched the phone from her hand and snapped the blinking button on the console. "Hey there, kidlet. Is everything okay?" His voice softened considerably.

Liz shook her head, mumbling something about Jekyll and Hyde on her way out of the office.

"Yeah. I guess," Jenna said hesitantly.

"I'll pick you up at six. All packed?" he asked. He was taking Jenna to a friend's ranch in Santa Barbara for the holiday weekend. The court order decreed him half of all Jenna's vacation time and President's Day granted him an extra day.

"Dad, I can't go." Jenna spoke the words in a rush, almost as if she feared his reaction.

"Care to tell me why not?" he asked, struggling to keep all signs of irritation from his voice. Half the reason he'd been in such a lousy mood the past two weeks stemmed from his inability to recapture the close bond he'd originally shared with his daughter.

"It's Mom's birthday this weekend, and I don't want to leave her alone. We've always spent birthdays together."

Another harsh reminder, no matter how innocently announced, that Cole was an interloper, that his presence was not as welcome as he'd hoped. Everything had been fine until he'd filed for shared custody. Now he felt as if he were intruding in his own daughter's life. *Damn!* The backlash from his actions had made him wonder if he'd been too rash, after all.

He thought for a moment about canceling the trip, but he'd had such high hopes of reconnecting with Jenna. An irrational part of him wanted to tell her that this was his time with her and she'd just have to get used to the idea that her life was going to change.

"Dad?"

He scrubbed his free hand down his face. He should be institutionalized for what he was about to suggest. "I'll call your mom and see if she'll go with us."

"That'd be great!" Jenna exclaimed. "I bet she'd love to go to Santa Barbara for her birthday. Could we take her to a nice restaurant for dinner? Oh, and maybe buy her flowers?"

The kid was pushing her luck. "Let me ask her first," he hedged, not wanting to commit to anything where Marni was concerned. "She knows you're coming with me for the weekend and she might have made plans."

"Are you going to call her right now?" Jenna asked anxiously.

"Yeah, I'll call her right now." Institutionalized and given electric shock therapy, he amended.

"Thank you, Dad."

Cole shook his head in disbelief. He'd just agreed to invite Marni along for a three-day weekend in Santa Barbara! "You're welcome, kidlet. I'll see you in a few hours."

They said their goodbyes and Cole took a deep breath. *Three days!* Finally he understood what his brother-in-law had meant when he said little girls tended to wrap their daddies around their little fingers. He wondered how in the hell it had happened to him.

MARNI RECHECKED THE LOCK on the sliding glass door for a third time. *I'm not pacing,* she told herself; she was making certain the house was secured.

She'd finished her closing arguments on the penalty phase of the Kendell trial yesterday, and the day had been spent waiting for word from the jury. Usually a few of the jurors had questions on a particular point of law, but thus far, nothing. She adjusted the beeper she was wearing. It was just as well to be prepared. The jury might continue its deliberations through Saturday.

"Mom, he's here!" Jenna yelled from the living room.

"I'm coming," she mumbled, wondering if her spur-of-the-moment decision to accompany Cole and Jenna had been a mistake, and not just because of the Kendell case. But for the past two weeks she'd thought about her conversation with Miss Shaylene. If for no other reason than her daughter's happiness, she had to find a way to make Cole understand her reasons for taking Carson's money.

With wavering determination, Marni entered the living room. Cole stood in the entry hall looking ruggedly handsome in a pair of casual tan slacks and a sweater

Marni would have sworn was the same shade as his eyes when he was deeply aroused.

"I ... I'll just ... uh ... get my suitcase," she stammered, shaken by her thoughts.

"I already got it, Mom," Jenna broadcast happily, nodding toward the two suitcases and overnight bag tucked neatly against the wall.

Cole laid a gentle hand on Jenna's shoulder. "Why don't you get Arlo settled and your mom can help me with the luggage."

"Sure, Dad."

A bright grin split Jenna's face, one of the first genuine smiles Marni had seen since Cole filed for custody. The simple delight on her daughter's face served as a reminder of the need for a resolution of the situation between her and Cole. Maybe they could never recapture the love they once shared, but they had a child. A child they both loved and who deserved to be their first priority.

Jenna called Arlo, and with considerable groaning, the dog followed her out of the house.

Cole chuckled at Arlo's protest. "That dog is a discredit to his breed."

A hesitant grin tugged at the corners of Marni's lips. For reasons Cole didn't bother to analyze, he realized he wanted to see her smile. "We'd better get going," he said brusquely. "Traffic's bound to be heavy until we get out of town."

Gripping the largest of the suitcases in one hand, he bent to retrieve the smaller one just as Marni reached for the same bag. Her audible gasp at the light brushing of their fingers rang in his head. She jumped away from him as if burned.

With a deep sigh, he set both bags down and examined her curiously. Her entire body coiled with tension and something akin to alarm flashed through her eyes, making the tiny gold flecks glow in the dim lamplight. "Marni, we can't keep going on like this."

"I know," she whispered in return.

"We need to come to an understanding."

"I know," she repeated.

He shoved his hands in the pockets of his trousers and regarded her carefully. Her wild curls framed her face, softening her features. A series of emotions flashed in her eyes—fear, apprehension and . . . hope. He'd steeled himself against her, telling himself he'd only asked her along for the weekend to please his daughter. Now, looking at her standing a few feet away from him, he questioned his motives. To cover his confusion, he said, "'Let's be friends' isn't possible for us, and I think you know that as well as I do. There's just too damn much between us for that to ever happen."

She cleared her throat as if prepared to make a speech. "We have to think of Jenna. Her happiness is what's important."

"Exactly," he agreed, a little disappointed that she'd agreed so readily.

"Are you suggesting a truce?" she asked, eyeing him warily.

He gave her one of his best smiles. "A suspension of hostilities."

The anniversary clock chimed the hour. Jenna's instructions to Arlo filtered through the open door. And Cole waited for Marni to agree to a ceasefire.

"I think it'd be a good idea," she said, a hesitant smile turning up the corners of her delectable mouth.

"Good," he said, reaching once again for the bags. "Do you want it in writing, counselor?" he teased. "I know how you lawyers like everything in writing."

"That's not necessary," she said, flashing him a saucy grin. Picking up the overnight bag, she slung it over her shoulder. "The Act of Truth and Fair Business Dealing governs any and all contracts implied or otherwise."

She stepped ahead of him, giving him full view of her jeans-clad bottom. His gut tightened at the sight of her very feminine posterior. Lord help him, he couldn't keep his hormones under control. For the life of him, he couldn't understand why his body craved what his mind told him to stay the hell away from. "I guess all that legal double-talk means you'll sue my pants off for breach of contract if I go back on my word?" he said, trying to sound as natural as possible. He pulled the front door closed, then stepped aside.

"In a manner of speaking," she said, locking the door.

"Wanna shake on it? I heard it's as good as a signature."

She cast him a sideways glance and shook her head. Somehow he had the feeling that touching him was the last thing she wanted to do. He wondered if her reasons were the same as his own. Touching would be like putting a lighted match to dry kindling. The weekend ahead suddenly promised to be very long indeed.

Marni caught her breath at the hunger blazing in his eyes. She quickly stepped around him, needing to distance herself from the spontaneous combustion between them. What was wrong with her? A truce did not mean she had to crawl into bed with the man!

For the next thirty minutes, they drove in relative silence. Even Jenna seemed subdued. Reba McEntire belted out a tune of unrequited love while Arlo snored on the floor behind Marni's seat.

As Cole had predicted, the traffic heading out of Los Angeles was heavy and didn't begin to thin until they reached Agoura Hills. A weather report predicted rain before midnight in the Los Angeles basin.

Marni cast a glance at Cole. He kept his gaze on the red taillights ahead of him, his arm slung casually over the wheel. The man was just too good-looking, she thought. "When did you get the truck?" she asked, suddenly uncomfortable with the silence.

A smile softened his profile, and he looked at Jenna in the rearview mirror before answering. "After Arlo put a hole in the back seat of the Jag I thought it'd be a good idea."

"I like it, Dad," Jenna chimed. "Arlo and I are comfortable back here."

Like she'll have to get used to riding in the back, Marni thought. Family excursions were not something in their collective future.

"The court liaison called today," Cole said. "Liz scheduled her for next week. Have you met with her yet?" It might not be the best topic of conversation right now, but he wanted things to be open between the three of them.

Marni turned in her seat to face him. "Her name's Beth Prentice. She seems friendly enough, but she's a hard sell."

"Oh?"

"She asks very personal questions but doesn't offer any comments. I found her a little disconcerting."

"How so?" he asked.

"What's disconcerting?" Jenna asked, propping her feet on the console between them.

Cole answered her. "Disconcerting means intimidating. Something that throws you off-balance."

Like you do to me, Cole Ballinger, Marni thought a little too desperately.

"Kinda like that weirdo headshrinker I've gotta go see?"

In the dim light from the dashboard, Marni caught Cole's frown. "Weirdo headshrinker?" he asked.

"Yeah. He asks an awful lot of nosy questions. I don't like the way he pokes around."

"How does he poke around, kidlet?" he asked.

"Oh, I don't know." Jenna paused and shifted positions. "He's always asking me questions about you and Mom."

Marni had asked Jenna about the court-appointed psychologist after her first visit, but Jenna hadn't been forthcoming, so Marni had let it drop. She'd figured Jenna would tell her about the visits when she was ready. "I think he's supposed to, sweetie."

"What does he ask you, or aren't you supposed to talk about it?" Cole asked.

"I can talk about it if I want to," Jenna told them, turning her head to stare out into the darkness.

"Did he tell you not to?" Cole looked at Marni, but she simply shrugged.

"No," Jenna said, and looked out the window again.

Marni waited, but Jenna remained silent, obviously not inclined to elaborate on the subject. Music from the radio filled the silence.

"I don't like him," Jenna announced suddenly.

Cole turned to Marni. "Did you know about this?" he asked with a note of accusation in his tone.

She shook her head. "First I've heard about it. She won't talk to me about him."

Jenna gave a loud, frustrated sigh. "Stop talking about me like I'm not here," she grumbled.

Marni smothered a grin at Jenna's impertinence. There were times when she was painfully reminded her daughter was on the threshold of becoming a teenager. Now was one of those times.

Cole looked into the rearview mirror. "What does he ask that you don't like, kidlet?"

"Stupid stuff," Jenna declared, leaning toward the bucket seats. "He asked me if Mom punishes me, and then he wanted to know what I thought about it. The guy's stupid. Like I'm supposed to like being punished."

"What'd you tell him?" Marni asked, curious.

"I told him you just grounded me."

"You grounded her? For what?" Cole's voice took on a steely edge.

Marni ignored his dark look and raised her brows at Jenna, silently prompting her to reveal the indiscretion that had resulted in a week's punishment.

Jenna issued another melodramatic sigh. "Mom told me I couldn't do something and I did it anyway."

Cole hid the smile tugging at the corner of his lips. From the indulgent expression on Marni's face, he quickly assumed the infraction couldn't be too serious. "What did you do, kidlet?"

"I watched a movie I wasn't supposed to," Jenna grumbled.

"What movie?"

Jenna crossed her arms over her chest. "*Basic Instinct.* I didn't think it was so bad, but Mom had a tizzy-fit. I can't watch TV for a week now."

Cole's mouth dropped open. No wonder Marni had grounded her. The highly erotic film was definitely something he didn't want his daughter watching. "I'm about to have a tizzy-fit," he told Marni.

"But *My Fair Lady* is on the Disney Channel this weekend. Can't I appeal for a lesser sentence?"

"No," Marni stated flatly.

"A suspended sentence?" Jenna asked, undaunted.

"No," Cole and Marni chimed in unison.

"Parents can be highly unreasonable," Jenna complained, sinking back into the seat with a distinct thump.

CHAPTER TWELVE

"WILL WE BE THERE SOON, Dad?" Jenna asked from the back seat.

Marni glanced at the dashboard, the digital clock indicating half past nine. They'd stopped for dinner at a family restaurant in Ventura nearly an hour ago. This time, Cole had ordered a table for them rather than a booth, for which Marni had been thankful. Although the tension between them had lessened, she didn't feel quite up to any more of Jenna's matchmaking maneuvers.

"About another twenty minutes, kidlet," he answered, flicking on the turn signal as he neared the off ramp.

Good, Marni thought drowsily. The hum of the engine, combined with a full stomach, had lulled her into a state of relaxation, but when Cole turned the Explorer onto a private road, Marni was confused. "Where are we going?" she asked.

He kept his eyes on the road. "I have a friend who owns a ranch in the valley. He's out of town and loaned me the place for the weekend."

Alarm shot through her. She sat upright in the bucket seat. When he'd invited her along, she'd had no idea she'd be forced to live under the same roof with him for seventy-two hours. "I thought we were staying in a hotel."

He glanced in her direction. "Do you mind?"

Did she mind? What kind of stupid question was that? Of course she minded. She wanted to maintain her sanity, for pity's sake. "No, not at all," she lied. "I just thought..."

"I think you'll like it." He returned his attention to the road to negotiate a turn. "It's an old Spanish-style ranch house. Wide open and plenty of space."

Before she could comment further, Cole slowed the truck. A monstrous wrought-iron gate loomed before them. He put the Explorer in Park and reached across the console to the glove compartment, where he retrieved a card key and a slip of paper bearing a series of numbers. "I'll just be a minute," he said before sliding out of the vehicle.

While Cole proceeded to unlock the gate, Marni devoured the sight of him illuminated in the Ford's headlights. A sense of longing gripped her, so intense she ached in secret places. Dear Lord, how was she going to survive the next three days? She was supposed to find a way to make him understand her past actions, not moon over the man like a lovesick puppy.

"Isn't this exciting, Mom?" Jenna said. "Dad told me we can go horseback riding tomorrow. I can't wait."

"Can't wait for what, kidlet?" Cole asked, easing back into the driver's seat.

"To go horseback riding," Marni answered. "I'll have to keep Arlo with me. Horses are the one thing he does chase."

"Mom, you've gotta come with us," Jenna protested. "It won't be any fun without you."

"We'll see," she answered noncommittally. The thought of getting on a horse for the first time in thirteen years was far less daunting than spending even more time in Cole's company. She took a calming breath as the Explorer started up again.

The drive to the house took another five minutes, and Marni was somewhat relieved to see that Cole hadn't been lying. The house *was* large. She only hoped it was large enough that she wouldn't be running into him any more than necessary.

MARNI STARED AT the contents of her suitcase in disbelief. Where were her comfortable old sweats? And the thick flannel nightgown she'd packed? Even the chenille robe with the ragged collar and torn belt loop was missing.

She picked up a black lace teddy and held it in her hands, eyeing the flimsy garment suspiciously. She definitely had *not* packed this. Nor had she packed the sheer eggshell nightgown.

"Jenna!" she called, realization dawning on her.

Cole rounded the corner leading to the upstairs bedrooms just as Jenna darted across the hall to Marni's room.

"Would you mind telling me how *this* got into my suitcase?"

The sharp edge to Marni's voice surprised Cole. She'd never spoke to Jenna in that tone before. Curious, he stopped outside the open doorway and peered inside. Marni held a black scrap of material in her hands, a look of utter disbelief on her face.

"Gee, Mom. I . . . I'm not . . . sure . . . I mean . . ."

"What *is* this?" Marni asked.

Cole couldn't help but smile. Maybe Marni needed an explanation, but he didn't. He knew right away what his daughter was up to. Hoping for the impossible.

"Aw, come on, Mom. I just thought . . ."

Marni tossed the sexy black teddy on the bed. "Must be the sweats I packed. Oh, and here's my nightgown," she said, picking up the sheerest fabric he'd ever seen in his life and holding it against her. "The thick flannel should really keep me warm tonight," she added with a light touch of sarcasm.

Visions of Marni in the gown, her curves outlined by candlelight, invaded his mind. Cole shifted uncomfortably and pushed the haunting image away.

"Now, I know I put my robe in here somewhere," Marni said, rummaging through the open suitcase. "Ah, here it is," she announced, retrieving an emerald satin robe he recognized. "I really should replace this, shouldn't I, Jenna? Look at how tattered this comfortable old chenille is getting."

Cole stifled a laugh and entered the bedroom. "Problem?" he asked.

Jenna kept her gaze averted, staring at the southwestern bedspread, her hands shoved into the back pockets of her jeans. "I'm sorry, Mom."

Marni tossed the robe onto the bed with the other sexy garments. "As well you should be, young lady," she scolded.

"What's going on?" Cole asked when neither mother nor daughter answered him.

"Nothing," Marni said nervously, her gaze darting to the lingerie on the bed. "Jenna just helped me pack and I couldn't find a few things." She cast the girl a stern look.

Cole stepped up to Jenna and slung a protective arm over her shoulder. "Did you forget something important, Jen?" he asked innocently.

Jenna turned her gaze to his. "I took out some stuff Mom packed," she admitted sheepishly.

He transferred his gaze from Jenna to the tantalizing and filmy nightwear tossed haphazardly over the bed. He gave in to the urge to smile and looked at Marni. A light blush stained her cheeks. "Was it important?" he asked.

Marni sighed. She *would* survive this weekend, she thought. How, she wasn't exactly certain, but she *would* survive. "Jenna didn't approve of my choice of sleepwear and unilaterally decided to make a few substitutions."

"I was only trying to help," the girl cried.

"Help?" Marni said. Help what, or whom?

Cole stepped away from Jenna and reached across the bed. Marni's breath caught in her throat when he picked up the teddy and held it by the thin straps.

"Nice substitution, kidlet." His voice was a low, approving growl.

Jenna giggled, her eyes dancing brightly.

Marni gasped. "Give me that!" She reached for the miniscule teddy, but Cole held it out of her reach.

"What's wrong with this?" he asked, a wicked smile on his face.

Marni wanted to die. When the man called a truce, he really called a truce. No matter how unreasonable, she seriously considered grounding Jenna until she was sixteen. "It's hardly what I would want to lounge around in with a good book," she told him, trying to remain calm. The sight of Cole holding the skimpy lingerie was doing strange things to her insides. She almost preferred the distance between them. At least when he was angry with her, she knew where she stood.

"Hmm. I guess you're right," he said, his grin widening.

"Can I go to bed now?" Jenna asked, inching toward the door.

"Sure, kidlet," Cole answered, tossing the teddy aside. To Marni, he said, "I've got a sweatshirt you can borrow if you need to."

"Thanks," she said, determined *not* to wear the items Jenna had packed.

"I'll see everyone in the morning," Jenna announced, and headed toward the door.

"Jenna?" Marni called.

"Oh! I almost forgot." Jenna spun around and kissed Marni good night, then did the same to Cole. "Good night," she called, then bolted from the room.

Marni returned her attention to unpacking, fearful of what other little delights Jenna had slipped into the suitcase. Cole remained by the bed, making her increasingly uncomfortable with his nearness.

"I made some coffee. Want to join me for a cup?" he finally asked, breaking the silence.

She cast him a nervous glance. With Jenna sleeping soundly, they could talk about all the things she had intended to explain. "Okay, but I want to take a shower first, all right?"

"Sure. Come down when you're ready."

Thirty minutes later, Marni padded down the open staircase feeling refreshed. Dressed in a pair of thick cream leggings and a black sweatshirt that reached mid-thigh, she headed into the kitchen. She found the coffeemaker and the mug Cole had set out for her, along with a bottle of Bailey's Irish Cream. She poured herself a cup, then added a splash of liqueur. As an afterthought, she added a drop more. She needed all the fortitude she could get.

Slipping quietly into the large living room, she found Cole with his feet propped up in a recliner in front of a big-screen television tuned to the evening news. April

Burnell's eyes sparkled as she summarized a train derailment in the Midwest. "She takes too much pleasure reporting disasters," Marni grumbled, curling up on the end of the sofa nearest Cole's chair.

Cole grunted, not looking up from the report in his lap.

A weather update was promised after the commercial break. There was no sign of the storm she'd heard announced on the radio, so at least they wouldn't be cooped up in the sprawling ranch house the entire weekend. Although, she admitted, the house was gorgeous. A mixture of antiques and rustic furniture lent an air of opulence and down-home comfort.

Setting her cup on the rough wood cocktail table, she stood and walked to the full-length glass window. There were no stars in the sky; not even the moon could be seen.

"Have you seen Arlo?" Marni asked as the Energizer Bunny pounded his drum across the screen.

"He was sleeping in Jenna's room when I looked in on her," Cole responded absently, still absorbed in the report.

She crossed the plush green carpeting to a rock wall with a fireplace large enough to roast a side of beef. Surrounding it were pictures of a tall, extremely good-looking man posing casually with a variety of movie stars.

She turned back to Cole, who was chewing the inside of his lower lip in his concentration. "Complex computer game?" she asked, dropping onto the sofa again.

He looked up. "Excuse me?"

"That must be some game." She indicated the report.

"This?" he asked, lifting the heavy, bound material. "It's a prospectus on a radio station up for sale. There's a rap station in financial trouble. The price is right, so I'm considering it."

"I didn't know Ballinger Electronics was thinking of getting into radio."

He grinned. "It's not anymore. But I am."

"You?" she asked in disbelief.

Cole closed the report and reached for the white mug on the side table. "Now that's an interesting reaction." Some unfamiliar part of him wanted her approval, and for once he didn't question his motivation.

"I didn't mean you couldn't do it, but that kind of venture takes an awful lot of money." She pulled her legs up to her chest and rested her arms on her knees. With her hair damp from the shower and her face devoid of makeup, she looked about twenty. And far too appealing.

"True, it does," he said. "I've got a few investors in mind if I decide to go through with it."

"What about Ballinger Electronics?" she asked. "I don't think your father would want you to spend a lot of time on another business, as well."

Cole bristled at the mention of his father. "Ballinger Electronics has nothing to say about it. I intend to spend my time running my *own* business."

"But what about your dad?" she asked, her surprise evident in the widening of her deep brown eyes. "Do you really think he'll invest in something that will take you away from Ballinger Electronics?"

Cole tensed. Did she believe he needed his father's approval, or money? The thought irritated the hell out of him. "Don can take over for me," he answered coldly. "And I'll find my own funding."

Marni shook her head. "Carson's not going to be happy, Cole."

He shrugged. They'd discussed the radio station last week when Carson informed him the board of directors had decided against the purchase. But he didn't want to discuss his father, with her, or anyone. At least not right now, when the argument with his father still left a sour taste in his mouth. "It's getting late, and I promised Jenna we'd go riding in the morning. You staying up for a while?"

Marni unfolded her legs and reached for the mug she'd left on the table. "I want to see if there's any news on Kendell. The jury went into deliberation this morning and we still haven't heard anything. I guess the office would have beeped me, but maybe the networks have picked up on something."

"But the appellate court upheld the conviction," he said.

"Yes, but this is for the penalty phase," she explained. "We asked for the death penalty."

"And that bothers you, doesn't it," he said, setting the cup on the antique table beside him.

Marni sighed heavily. She hadn't thought much about what winning the case would really mean to her, other than the fact that she'd prevented a man from killing again. That she'd be responsible for sending a man to *his* death, regardless of how many murders he'd committed, did bother her. "I'm not supposed to care."

She glanced at the television again. April Burnell told of another drive-by shooting. "She," Marni said, with a quick inclination of her head toward the television, "asked me a similar question right after the guilty verdict was read. I told her then that I was doing the job the tax-payers were paying me to do."

Cole leaned forward in the chair, watching her intently. "But you don't believe that, do you?"

"Not really," she answered with a shake of her head. "My boss warned me that every prosecutor feels this way after their first penalty case. Still, there's a part of me that wonders if I'm any better than the killer I helped bring to justice."

He reached out and clasped her hand in his. "But you're not making that decision, Marni. The jury is."

She understood Cole was trying to ease her guilt, that there was nothing sensual at all in his touch, but the sparks shooting up her arm were another matter altogether. "They couldn't reach that decision if I hadn't presented my case well. James Kendell would be facing life imprisonment instead of death by lethal injection—if that's what the jury decides."

He gave her hand a reassuring squeeze. "Like you told the reporter, you're doing your job. If you really hate it this much, why not do something else?"

She pulled her hand out of his grasp and laughed. The attempt at levity sounded hollow even to her own ears. "I didn't say I hated it. I love the trials, I love being in the courtroom, and God help me, I love winning. I love the fact that what I'm doing proves the system works."

Cole stood and smiled down at her. "When the time comes, you'll know when it's time to move on. Trust me."

She returned his grin. "Civil litigation is looking better and better. I'm beginning to think representing little old ladies who slipped in a puddle of milk in the supermarket would be very satisfying."

He chuckled, a deep rumbling that caused her stomach to flutter. "I'll see you in the morning. Good night."

"Good night," she said, and watched him climb the stairs.

Finishing her coffee, she watched the end of the news. There'd only been a quick blurb that said the jury had been in deliberation until seven o'clock and was scheduled to return on Tuesday. Disappointed, she flipped off the television and lights, then climbed the stairs to check on Jenna.

After assuring herself that Jenna was sound asleep, she retreated to her own room. She turned down the bed, but sleep was the last thing on her mind. After a quick search of the room, she located her thick slippers, put them on and wandered out onto the balcony.

The night air was crisp, but the warmth of Cole's heavy sweatshirt and the knit leggings kept the cold at bay. The balcony was private, with thick walls jutting out from each end of the bedroom. She stepped toward the wrought-iron railing and braced her palms on the cold metal. Bending forward, she peered into the darkness.

"Hi."

She jumped at the sound of Cole's voice. She looked around her, but couldn't find him.

"Over here," he said.

Marni glanced to her left and saw him, his arms braced against a railing identical to the one she was leaning on. "Hi," she answered hesitantly. She hadn't realized they were sharing rooms so close to each other. "I couldn't sleep," she said, feeling inexplicably guilty at being caught outside this late at night.

"Neither could I," he answered.

"Too much to think about?" she asked.

"Yeah. Too much."

Neither spoke, and Marni wondered what was on his mind. The radio station? Her? She doubted that, although he had been doing his best to keep his part of their pact. It was a wonderful, if frightening, change in their relationship.

Since the day of the custody hearing, they'd steered clear of each other. She stayed late at the office to avoid running into him on his daily visits to Jenna. She'd known he'd been to the beach house, though. Every night when she walked through the door she'd felt his presence. His masculine scent, mingled with his cologne, evoked memories of the time she'd shared with him. Ever since she'd met him, she'd made wrong decisions where he was concerned. Despite their truce, she still needed to make him understand. Maybe now was as good a time as any.

She took a deep breath and bolstered her courage. "I hate to bring..." she began.

"I was thinking..." he started at the same time, then chuckled.

"You first," she said, smiling, the gentle sound of his laughter warming her.

"Ladies first," he prompted.

She spoke quietly into the night. "I just wanted to apologize for slapping you."

"Apology accepted." He lifted a hand to his jaw. "But you have a hell of a right hook, counselor."

Marni winced at the memory. She'd been so angry, she'd done and said a lot of things she regretted. And he'd said a few things that hadn't made sense to her at the time. That still didn't. "Can I ask you something?" she said.

"Sure."

"That night you'd said that Jenna was a means to an end. What did you mean?" There, she'd asked him. He could either answer her or walk away, but she'd taken the first step toward trying to understand his motives for turning their lives upside down.

"Marni, I don't think this is such a good idea. Let's just forget it, all right?"

"I can't, Cole."

He didn't say anything, and Marni wondered if he'd answer her. An owl screeched into the night from a perch not too far away. In the distance, the hectic yipping of coyotes could be heard.

"You used her to extort money from my father."

Marni shivered, and not from the cold air. The hardness in his voice turned her to ice. "That's not true," she retorted. "When Carson approached me, I didn't even know I was pregnant."

"What?" he snapped.

The darkness acted as a shield, preventing her from seeing Cole's expression, which she knew would be set in the hard planes of anger. She almost welcomed the wall separating them. The physical wall, anyway. "I said, I—"

"My father approached *you?*" he interrupted.

She nodded, then realized he couldn't see her. "Yes," she said softly.

Cole reeled from her statement. He didn't know what, or who, to believe any longer. She had to be lying. She was so good at it, he almost believed her. "*When* did he approach you?" he demanded, determined to find a flaw in her story.

"Two days before I left Elk Falls."

"But you told him you were pregnant on the Fourth of July." He had her now.

"That's ridiculous," she replied. "I didn't find out I was pregnant until mid-October."

She *had* to be lying. "That's impossible."

"Jenna's birthday is in *May*. Simple math, Cole," she argued heatedly. "You're a smart man. Figure it out." The slam of the door to her room was the last sound he heard from her side of the balcony.

Confusion gripped him. Everything Marni said made sense, but it contradicted what his father had told him.

Someone was lying, and he was determined to find out who.

He muttered a string of curses. He'd been doubting the wisdom of filing for custody for days. The thought that he'd done it for the wrong reasons made it a thousand times worse.

If Jenna wasn't born until May, that meant Marni hadn't even conceived until August. God, he felt like an idiot. Why hadn't he figured that out before? If he hadn't let anger cloud his judgment, he could have saved them all a lot of pain. And he was getting damn tired of the pain.

He stalked from the balcony and headed toward Marni's room.

MARNI WASN'T SURPRISED to hear a knock at her door ten minutes later. Cole entered her room without waiting for an invitation.

Weariness bracketed eyes that looked tortured and dull, and his hair was mussed as if he'd been running his hands through it. Just what *had* Carson told him? she wondered.

"I'm tired, Cole." She spoke the words with quiet but desperate firmness. Tired didn't begin to explain how she was feeling.

"So am I," he told her quietly, "but neither one of us is going to get any sleep until we resolve this once and for all."

"I'm not talking about sleep, Cole." And she wasn't. She didn't want to argue, and she sure as hell didn't want to hurt any longer. Would they ever stop hurting each other? "I'm tired of arguing with you. I'm tired of trying to explain and getting my heart trampled," she told him. "How much am I supposed to take?"

She moved to the bed, hoping he would take the hint and leave. Instead, he approached her. His strong hands gripped her shoulders and turned her around to face him. For once his guard was down. When she looked into his eyes, she saw a mixture of confusion and pain. Something told her the pain wasn't caused by her alone, that he was finally beginning to understand what his father had done to them.

"This is too important." His eyes searched her face as if he hoped to find the answers there.

She shrugged out of his grasp. "Leave it alone. We're only going to end up shouting at each other, and you promised me a truce. No fighting, remember?"

"Then sue me for breach of contract. I'm not leaving." The determination in his voice startled her slightly.

"Did you ask my father for money in exchange for leaving town and getting an abortion?" he asked.

Anger swelled inside her at his question. But her anger was directed at Carson. The question told her just how far he had gone to keep them apart. "No."

"Explain the canceled checks," he demanded, although she detected no heat in his words.

Marni walked to the window and peered into the darkness. She thought of the best way to tell him, but she decided not to mention her attempt to return the money. He'd never believe her, anyway. "He approached me," she said finally. "I've told you this before."

"I wasn't listening then. Now I am."

She wrapped her arms around her middle, hoping to quell the nervous fluttering in her stomach. "You'd gone upstairs to change for the barbecue your parents hosted every year. Carson asked to speak with me, so I followed him into the library." As she told him, she could see the day in her mind's eye. The weather had been warm, and they'd planned on making an early escape to go to the drive-in to see *Coal Miner's Daughter.*

"He told me that if I left town, he'd pay for my education and take care of my mother's medical bills." There, she'd said it. The truth was finally out.

"And you took it. Just like that?" He snapped his fingers.

"It wasn't just like that!" she returned with an irritated snap of her own fingers. "You have no idea what I went through." They were going to start shouting at each other again. She just knew it. They were destined never to hold a civil conversation.

"Then tell me, dammit."

Why was he doing this? How much more pain did they both have to suffer? Letting her irritation get the better of her, she said angrily, "Everything he said was true. I wasn't a part of your world. You weren't really in love with me. Two months after I left town, you married Elizabeth, so you see, he was right."

Cole clenched his jaw. A muscle in his cheek twitched, a sure sign of his anger. "You said you called when you found out about Jenna. Why?" he asked.

Marni stepped away from the door and approached him. She searched his face for any sign of softening and found none. What the hell, she thought. Why not lay all the cards on the table? He couldn't hurt her any more than he already had. "Because you deserved to know you were going to be a father. The money wasn't that important. If Carson's checks stopped coming in, Mama and I would have managed somehow."

Cole turned away from her. "What makes you think I would have done anything about it?" he asked.

Maybe it was the dejected slump of his shoulders, but the annoyance she'd been harboring slipped away. Marni approached him and placed a hand on his arm.

He looked down at her and the pain in his eyes tore at her heart. "No matter how angry you were with me for leaving, you never would have turned your back on your child."

He lifted his hand, brushing his knuckles gently along her cheek. "You would have given up your dreams? Just so I could know my daughter?"

Turning into his hand, she nodded. "I would have done anything for you." A stray tear rolled down her cheek, and he wiped it away with the pad of his thumb.

"I don't know what to believe anymore," he said, emotion choking his voice.

Neither one of them moved. Tension thrummed between them, until finally Cole slipped his hand along her throat, gently cupping her cheek in his large hand. She shivered at the tenderness of his touch. He lowered his head, his lips gently brushing against hers.

She sensed his struggle, his indecision, and she silently willed him not to turn away from her. Not to reject her again.

He didn't. His mouth slanted over hers, seeking and probing, demanding she respond to him.

Marni opened willingly to him, and he groaned deep in his throat, his hands sliding down her back. Encouraged, she pressed her body against his hard, firm length, needing his closeness and the comfort their bruised hearts could offer each other. She wound her arms around his neck, holding him close to her, kissing him back. She called herself ten times a fool, but right now, she didn't care. She needed Cole.

He dragged his lips from hers and brushed his mouth gently along her jaw until he reached that tender spot below her ear. She trembled in his arms.

"I'd better go," he said, his voice a hoarse whisper. He pulled her arms from around his neck and set her away from him, almost as if he feared her touch. He opened his mouth, then snapped it shut. Spinning on his heel, he left the room, leaving Marni feeling more alone than she had in thirteen years.

MARNI AWOKE to early-morning sunlight streaming through the windows. She needed coffee. Desperately. Flinging back the covers, she left the warmth of the feather bed and groped her way into the bathroom. Washing her face in ice-cold water did little to alleviate the sluggishness plaguing her mind and limbs. After pulling her hair into a ponytail, she left the bedroom in search of caffeine.

The kitchen was deserted, but someone had made coffee. Arlo lay under the oak table in the center of the spacious area, his tail thumping in greeting when she entered. "Where is everyone?" she asked the dog.

Arlo groaned in response and crawled out from under the table to the back door, where he sat on his haunches and glared at Marni over his shoulder. After letting him outside, she poured herself a cup of coffee. Caffeine. Straight up.

Sitting at the table, the house quiet, she let her thoughts wander. Nothing had been resolved, but she had a feeling her relationship with Cole had gone through another change. Until she saw him again, she could only wonder what the new phase would bring.

Sighing, she pushed her thoughts aside. She found the report Cole had reviewed the previous night. Curious, she flipped it open and began reading the prospectus.

She was already on her third cup of ambition when the sound of voices interrupted the solitude. Cole and Jenna came laughing through the back door.

"Morning, Mom!" Jenna chirped happily. "Happy birthday!"

"Thanks, sweetie," she mumbled, her voice still scratchy from sleep. "Where have you been so early?"

"Mom, it's after eleven." Jenna slipped out of her jacket and smiled devilishly at her father.

"Fine, but where were you?" Marni asked suspiciously.

"I took Jenna into town," Cole answered.

"Whatcha reading, Mom?" Jenna asked.

"A prospectus," she answered, too tired to want to play detective. To Cole she said, "You're right. This is a good investment. Rebecca's firm has an FCC specialist who could help you with the legalities."

"What's a prospectus?" Jenna asked, plopping into the oak chair closest to Marni.

Cole approached the table and stood behind Marni's chair, resting his hand on the oak. The hair on her nape tingled at his nearness and her heart ached. The simplicity of the family scene was making her wish for what would never be.

"A prospectus," he explained to their daughter, "is an outline or a plan."

"Oh. So what's the plan?" Jenna asked.

Cole moved to the counter and poured himself a cup of coffee. Coming back to the table, he sat in the chair opposite Marni. "I'm trying to decide whether or not I want to buy a radio station."

"Oh, too cool. Which one?"

"A rap station, of all things," Marni volunteered, and wrinkled her nose at Jenna.

"The first order of business—" he smiled, that devastatingly sexy grin that warmed her insides "—will be hiring a new program director."

"Sounds like you're really going to buy the station," Marni commented. "When did you decide?"

"Last night," he said, his gaze holding hers.

The look in his eyes said he'd made up his mind about a few things. She only wished he'd let her in on his decisions.

"But what about Car—"

"Let's not talk business," he said, cutting her off. "I promised Jenna a ride this morning. You coming?"

"Come with us, Mom. It'll be fun." Jenna pushed her chair back away from the table and stood. "I'll go put Arlo in my room so he won't follow us," she said, and disappeared out the door.

"You should be warned," Marni told Cole before draining her cup, "I haven't been on a horse since I was eighteen. And that was a long time ago."

The warmth of his smile echoed in his voice and the light suggestiveness of his tone. "It's like riding a bike...or making love. Some things just come back naturally."

Marni eyed him curiously, unsure exactly what he meant. Although she knew for certain he was talking about more than riding a horse.

COLE STOOD IN FRONT of the mirror, running a razor over the rough growth of beard, leaving streaks on his lathered face. He heard a knock on his bedroom door, and set the razor on the marbled counter to tie the sash of his robe.

"Come in," he called, then resumed shaving.

"Dad, you decent?" Jenna asked hesitantly.

"In here, kidlet," he said, carefully scraping the razor under his jaw.

Jenna stood in the doorway looking at him thoughtfully in the mirror. She looked a little too grown-up for his liking, dressed in a dark green velvet dress with a taffeta skirt in a lighter shade of emerald. She stepped farther into the large bathroom. He caught a glimpse of nylons on her skinny legs and shiny black Mary Janes on her feet.

"Is your mom dressed already?" he asked, wondering what had prompted Jenna's visit.

Jenna giggled, but the sound lacked its usual gaiety. "Naw, she takes forever. Especially when she's getting all dressed up. Wait'll ya see her." She leaned against the long vanity, her hands braced behind her, watching him with seeming fascination while he shaved.

"You laugh now. You'll take forever someday, too," he teased her.

He finished shaving, then rinsed the remnants of cream off his face before burying his face in a fluffy towel. He kept his gaze averted from Jenna's and waited for her to speak. Something was on her mind, if the way she kept tracing a pattern in the carpet with her shoe was any indication.

"I have something for you," she blurted out.

Turning to face her, he noted the indecision in her gaze. "What is it, Jen?"

She reached into a pocket on her dress and pulled out an envelope. Lifting her small hand, she held the yellowed paper out to him. "This came to the house yesterday."

Cole took the envelope from Jenna and stared at it. He'd seen this before, the day Marni's attorney handed it to the bailiff. He vividly remembered Judge Russo holding it in his wiry hands, proclaiming his lack of clairvoyance, then reading the damn thing without divulging the contents. It was now in his hands. "Does your mom know you've got this?"

Jenna shook her head. "Uh-huh."

"Why are you giving this to me?"

Jenna lifted her slim shoulders. "Because it's addressed to you," she answered him, worry knitting her brows.

He tossed the envelope on the counter. "I'll read it later," he said, hoping to ease Jenna's fears by not placing a great deal of importance on the missive. "I've got to get dressed, kidlet, or your mom's going to beat me downstairs."

Jenna nodded and turned to leave. She stopped at the door and looked at him over her shoulder. "I love you, Dad."

He smiled, and his chest filled with pride at the beautiful young girl who was his daughter. "I love you, too, kidlet. Now get out of here so I can get dressed."

She offered him a weak smile and went, leaving Cole alone with the letter written to him twelve years ago. The moment the door clicked, he retrieved the envelope and sat on the edge of the king-size bed. Hesitation, fear and curiosity all surged within him until he carefully opened the torn flap of the envelope with the words Refused— Return to Sender written across the front in what he now recognized as his father's handwriting.

CHAPTER THIRTEEN

Dear Cole,

I don't know where to begin, so much time has passed, so I'll just get to the point of this letter.

The beautiful baby girl you see in the photograph is your daughter, Cole. *Our* daughter. And because I believe she was conceived out of love, you deserve to know about Jenna Coleen's existence. She is a part of you as much as she is a part of me. She fills my heart with a joy I've never dreamed possible. Every time I look at her I think of you and the love we had. Every day of my life, I'll have a beautiful green-eyed reminder of what you'll always mean to me. For that, Cole, I thank you.

In the past year I've made a lot of difficult decisions, most of which I'm not proud of, but I don't want to regret not telling you about Jenna years down the road.

When I first learned I was pregnant with Jenna, I tried calling you. You were on your honeymoon with Elizabeth, and at the time I thought it best if I didn't interfere with your new life.

I hope you will find it in your heart to forgive me for not telling you about your daughter sooner. I did what I thought was best—for all of us.

I wish you all the happiness in the world, Cole.

Love,
Marni

COLE READ THE LETTER, yellowed with age, again. Finally he understood the pain Marni must have suffered because of his father. The thought left him reeling. His father's interference in their lives had hurt both of them, and their daughter. The realization of his father's manipulation, and just how far Carson Ballinger would go to get what he wanted, angered him beyond belief. Being a father might be new to Cole, but he would never forsake his daughter's happiness for his own selfish reasons. How could his own father have done this?

He carefully folded the letter and returned it to the envelope. He finally held the truth in his hands. A simple letter written by a terrified nineteen-year-old girl had told him what the woman he loved couldn't.

Yes, he admitted, despite everything, he loved her. He'd hoped that by denying his feelings for Marni, he could lessen his pain at what he'd believed to be her duplicity. Instead he'd hurt her.

When he thought of everything he'd put her through, his stomach churned. The hateful words, the accusations, the insinuations, all rushed back to taunt him. He'd thought he was a fool where Marni was concerned. How right he'd been, and how wrong. Now he needed to make amends.

He stood and shoved the letter into the pocket of his robe. He'd start now, tonight. Cole couldn't think of a better time to begin.

"HE'S WAITING DOWNSTAIRS," Jenna whispered, excitement sparkling in her eyes. "Aren't you glad you brought that dress? Dad's gonna love it."

"Jenna, quit. We're only going to dinner." No matter how many times Marni explained to her daughter this was not a *date,* Jenna continued to pretend otherwise.

Jenna crossed her arms over her chest and lifted her chin. "Then how come you're all dressed up?"

Marni blew out a frustrated sigh when the comb she'd slipped into her hair fell out again. "I've told you already. Your father is taking us to the Rusty Pelican. It's not exactly a place to wear faded jeans and battered sneakers." She pushed the rhinestone comb into her hair for the third time. It held. Satisfied, she repeated the process on the other side.

She fluffed her curly bangs and applied a spritz of hair spray. "Okay, earrings," she said, leaving the opulent dressing room.

"Wow! You look cool, Mom," Jenna said, retrieving Marni's black sequined evening bag and peeking inside.

Marni wouldn't exactly say she looked *cool*. Nervous, insecure, and confused, maybe. She knew her attempted indifference was weak at best. She felt anything but.

After her discussion with Cole last night, she didn't have a clue where she stood with him. He hadn't indicated whether he believed her or not, but she didn't want to break whatever spell he'd been under all day. He'd been friendly, if a touch pensive, and on more than one occasion she'd caught him staring at her. Not just looking at her, but staring. And other than the few times when she'd read desire in his eyes, she had no idea what he was thinking.

Oh, yes, she decided, confusion definitely ranked at the top of her list of emotions.

Marni put on a pair of dangly rhinestone earrings, then stood back to view the effect in the mirror. "Okay," she said, and took a deep, cleansing breath. "I'm ready."

"Wait!" Jenna called. "Let me go first. I want to see Dad's face when you come downstairs."

"Jenna, how many..."

Jenna disappeared through the door before Marni could finish the gentle upbraid. She really needed to talk to her daughter about the disasters of matchmaking. "That child is a hopeless romantic," she mumbled, picking up the evening bag Jenna had unceremoniously dropped back onto the bed.

Marni descended the stairs, her eyes searching the dimly lit room below. She could hear Cole's and Jenna's muted voices, but their words were unintelligible. As she reached the midpoint of the grand staircase, she saw him, seated on the end of the sofa in a relaxed pose with his ankle crossed over his knee, while Jenna prattled on excitedly about the movie stars in a grouping of photos above the fireplace.

"Oh, my gosh! That's Tom Cruise! He's such a hunk," Jenna said in a dreamy voice.

"What do you know about hunks?" Cole asked.

"Oh, Dad. Tom Cruise is to die for!" Jenna declared, coming up behind Cole and draping her arms around his neck.

Cole grumbled something Marni couldn't hear, but she could certainly imagine his retort. Poor Cole, Marni thought, enjoying the scene being played before her. He'd come into their lives at a time Jenna was discovering boys. He'd never had the chance to be Jenna's idol, the way most fathers are to little girls. Too bad things hadn't worked out differently for all of them. Perhaps they could even have had another child, another little girl just like Jenna, who would have known her father from the day she was born. Perhaps they could have had a chance to be a real family, a family that wasn't torn apart by dissension and visits relegated by court order.

Marni pushed her thoughts aside. This was her birthday, not a time for analysis and recriminations. She'd take one day at a time, one moment at a time, and try not to look too far into the future, because it hurt too much.

As she reached the bottom step, Cole glanced her way. Her gaze met his and her breath caught in her throat. Her heart pounded at the purely sexual light in his eyes. She'd have had to be blind not to notice. *Yes, Jenna, I am glad I brought this dress.*

Cole stood, momentarily speechless, staring at the beautiful woman he'd once called his own. The black dress reached just above her knees, shimmering in the light when she moved, enhancing her alluring curves. He wondered if she was wearing that skimpy, lacy black wisp of material under her dress. Maybe those black stockings with the lacy tops, as well. He smiled as he thought about unraveling those little mysteries for himself.

"I told you she looked great, Dad." Jenna's know-it-all tone broke through the spell he was under.

"I can see that," he said, never taking his eyes off Marni, wondering how the hell he was going to get through the next few hours without touching her. "You're stunning."

"You're late," Jenna added, heading toward the front door, "and I'm hungry. Can we go now?"

Cole chuckled. Leave it to the kid to ruin what could have been a beautiful moment. "Yes, Jenna," he told her patiently. "We can go now."

"Great! I'll race you to the car," she called, disappearing through the door.

Cole stepped around the sofa and approached Marni. Standing only inches from him, she had no choice but to look into his eyes. *Mistake,* she thought. *Big mistake.* His eyes darkened slightly. A shiver of apprehension shimmied down her spine. He was going to kiss her.

He leaned toward her but his lips brushed past her mouth and settled briefly against her neck. "You're beautiful," he said, his voice a low, throaty growl. Then, before she could react, he took her hand. "Come on," he said. "Our daughter's starving."

Too stunned by his last maneuver to protest, she wondered how she was going to get through the next few hours.

BY THE TIME THE DESSERT tray rolled around, Marni was more confused than she'd ever dreamed possible. Cole was attentive and humorous, and the deepening shade of his eyes told her exactly what was on his mind. And it was *not* the chocolate truffle.

Moreover, God help her, she found herself responding to him. All she needed was one word, and she'd be in his arms. Okay, she told herself, so maybe she was too old to believe in fairy tales. But she wasn't asking for a lifetime membership in the happily-ever-after club, only a short tour of the facilities. She settled for the truffle.

After dessert, they returned to the ranch house. It was a few minutes past eleven when they walked through the door.

"I'm going to bed." Jenna yawned loudly. "Happy birthday, Mom," she said again, and kissed Marni on the cheek.

"Good night, sweetie. I'll be up in a minute."

Marni waited for Jenna to climb the stairs, then turned to Cole. His back was to her as he locked up. "Thank you for dinner. I had a nice time tonight."

"Join me for a nightcap?" he asked as he turned to face her.

Marni's heart pounded. She doubted the wisdom of doing so, but knew she would, anyway. Without a doubt,

Cole Ballinger was her downfall. "Let me check on Jenna first," she heard herself saying. "I'll be right down."

Marni returned to the living room ten minutes later. A fire blazed in the hearth, and strains of soft jazz played on the elaborate sound system, filtering throughout the room. If she didn't know better, she'd swear Cole was trying to seduce her.

She searched the dimly lit room and found him standing before the large plate-glass window, staring into the night. If only she knew what he was thinking. If only he'd tell her he understood her reasons for leaving him all those years ago. If only he'd tell her the past was immaterial, that the future, *their* future, was all that mattered.

"Jenna's sound asleep," she said quietly. "I think she was out before her head hit the pillow."

Cole glanced over his shoulder, but he didn't say anything. He held out his hand to her, silently beckoning her to his side.

Hesitantly, Marni crossed the room. He'd shed his suit jacket and rolled back the sleeves of his crisp white shirt, exposing those wonderful forearms. A sudden thrill speared through her, systematically tearing down the barriers she'd tried to place around her heart.

"Have I told you how beautiful you are tonight?" he asked huskily, taking her hand in his when she reached his side.

Yes, she thought, *you have*. Before dinner, during dinner and after dinner. Now he was telling her again. He could tell her a dozen more times and she wouldn't grow tired of his admiration.

Moving to stand in front of him, she looked into his eyes and her heart beat in triple time. "Thank you," she whispered, thrilled by the blatant desire banked in his emerald gaze.

When he lifted her hand and brushed his lips gently across her knuckles, she should have turned tail and run. Run as far away as possible. But she knew she wouldn't, just as she knew she'd be in his bed before the night was over. She'd deal with the morning-after regrets in the harsh light of day. Maybe it was the magic of the moment or something deeper that continued to pull them both into a vortex of longing and need, but for now, tonight, she was going to be his.

"Wine?" he asked, breaking into her thoughts.

"Yes, thank you."

He stepped away and she took a steadying breath, hoping to quell the trembling in her limbs. Facing the window, she gazed at the moonlight and mentally pushed all her doubts and fears aside. She wanted nothing between them when they made love. No lies, no recriminations and no false hopes. Only two people, for whatever reasons they secretly harbored, needing each other in the night.

He returned with the wine and handed her a long-stemmed glass. His fingers brushed hers, and Marni marveled at the electricity of his touch. She didn't try to understand the feelings this man evoked in her, even after everything they'd been through.

The low, sultry saxophone of Kenny G filtered through the speakers. "Dance with me?" Cole asked.

Marni took a sip of wine, then handed the glass to him, which he set, along with his, on a nearby table. She slipped easily into his arms and he pulled her close, almost uncertainly, as if he expected her to bolt. *Oh, I'm not going anywhere tonight, Cole Ballinger.* Tonight she was his.

Cole breathed in her scent, a mixture of Passion and her own feminine fragrance. Her thighs came into contact with his as she easily matched his steps. When she laid her cheek against his chest, his heart pounded in a deep, throbbing rhythm. Desire coursed throughout his body, and he hadn't even kissed her yet. He wanted to go slow, to savor each moment and make it last forever. He wanted tonight to be special.

He brushed his lips against her hair and she raised her head, offering her sweet mouth. Cole drank in the honeyed warmth. Her tongue danced seductively with his, teasing him then boldly thrusting into his mouth. A groan rose from deep within him when she pressed her slim body closer. They fit perfectly, like two pieces of a puzzle. There was no doubt in his mind that he could never let this woman go again.

The music ended. He placed a light kiss on her lips and stepped away, retrieving their wine. When he handed the glass to her, he saw her hands tremble. Male satisfaction rose within him. Marni was just as affected as he was. He clasped her free hand in his own and led her to the sofa, pulling her down in his lap.

Marni shifted slightly and Cole groaned in frustration. "Do you know what you're doing to me?" he asked, his voice harsher than he'd intended.

She wriggled her backside against him. "Hmm, I think I do," she responded in a throaty purr.

"Do you want your birthday present now or later?" He couldn't take his eyes off her. Her mouth was parted slightly, and her eyes, damn, her eyes were driving him crazy. If he didn't have her soon he'd go mad.

"That depends on what you're giving me," she said.

Her voice was tinged with sex and sin, and Cole found himself trapped in the seductive web she so expertly wove around him. God, he felt ready to burst with wanting her.

"Dammit, woman, I was supposed to be seducing *you*."

She laughed and shifted her weight. Before he knew what was happening, she was straddling him, her dress pushed high, exposing her thighs and the lacy tops of those stockings he'd fantasized about earlier. She ground her hips against him. Cole squeezed his eyes shut, praying he wouldn't embarrass himself. "Marni," he warned, his throat tight with need.

He moaned when she kissed his chin, then his throat, before moving down to the open V of his shirt. Her hands brushed against his chest as she opened each button slowly, her lips following the path of his bared skin, lower and lower. She settled to her knees in front of him, her mouth and tongue continuing their carnal assault until she reached his belt buckle. He sucked in a sharp breath when her fingers fumbled with the buckle then the clasp of his slacks. He groaned audibly when she freed him from the confinement of his briefs. "Marni?"

"Shhh," she whispered. "Let me love you."

No man in his right mind could argue with that. When her tongue darted out and touched the tip of him, a fierce shudder ran though him. Her mouth closed over him and the heavy beating of his heart thundered in his ears. Only Marni existed, and the sweet torture of her lips and tongue caressing him in slow, heated strokes.

Unable to bear her erotic touch any longer, he drew her away from him before he lost control. She slid her body up his until their mouths were inches apart. Marni nipped his chin, then tugged on his lower lip. Enough was enough. He captured her mouth in a hard, possessive kiss while his hands glided over her back to cup her rounded bottom. She straddled him again and he rotated his hips against her. Pushing her dress higher, over her hips, his hands came into contact with lace. He knew without looking she wore the black teddy. He easily slipped a hand between their bodies, locating and unfastening the snap, then slid a finger into her moist heat. She was more than ready for him.

Marni moaned in protest when he stopped the delightful, erotic sensations he was creating with his fingers and mouth. Then his hands gripped her hips and lifted her, guiding her over him. In one quick movement, he was inside her, and she cried out at the sensations rocketing through her. With his hands clutching her hips, he moved her, slowly at first, then faster and deeper until Marni thought she'd scream from pleasure.

His breath came in short rasps, echoing her own, until he threw his head back against the sofa and issued a low growl of satisfaction. The throbbing, pulsating length of him exploded inside her, and Marni found herself pushed over the edge, her climax a jolt of sensation that screamed down her nerve endings.

In a state of mindless exhaustion, she collapsed against him, breathless from exertion. His hands gently roamed her back, and she shivered at his light touch. When her breathing returned to a semblance of normalcy and her heartbeat to a rhythm ensuring she wasn't on the verge of a medical emergency, she lifted her head to look at him.

"I can't move," he told her, his voice thick.

She grinned at him and shifted slightly. "That's too bad," she said, enjoying the knowledge she'd done this to him.

A low rumble of laughter shook him. "Woman, you're killing me."

"Only with pleasure," she returned saucily when she felt him begin to grow again inside her.

"Jenna..." he started, pulling her dress over her head.

"Is sleeping soundly," she finished for him, and began placing light kisses against his sweat-dampened chest.

Marni didn't think it was possible, but within seconds Cole had her beneath him on the sofa, his mouth hot and demanding, his body driving into her, pushing her closer and closer to another earth-shattering climax. He murmured her name and lifted her hips to meet his deep, insistent and urgent thrusts until she was awash with sensation. Her hands gripped his shoulders, her fingers tightening against the muscles tensing in his back. His mouth left hers and he buried his face in the side of her neck, his breath hot against her sensitized flesh.

"Cole!" she cried, reaching further into the sweet oblivion he was creating, trusting him to catch her when she fell. Cole inched her closer to the edge, then before she could prevent it, she exploded into a thousand tiny pieces of light. He swallowed her cry with his mouth as wave after wave of pleasure racked her body.

Marni's climax rippled through him seconds before the fire consumed him completely. He drove into her one last time before finding his own shattering release, then collapsed, exhausted, against her.

Bracing his arms on either side of her head, he lifted his body so as not to crush her with his weight. Her hair tumbled around her flushed face. Her eyes were distant and dreamy, and he smiled. He kissed her gently and she sighed, wrapping her arms around his neck. God, how he loved her.

Without a doubt, he knew he couldn't live without her. He wanted to wake up with her by his side every morning. Wanted to come home to her each night. He wanted the good times, the hard times, the happy moments and even the arguments he knew would ensue because they were both too damn stubborn for their own good.

"I love you, Marni," he said before he could stop himself, and he suddenly realized how much he'd *wanted* to say those words to her. He should have said them a long time ago. He should have trusted her, but like a fool, he hadn't. All he could hope for now was her forgiveness.

Marni stiffened. For too long she'd wanted to hear Cole tell her he loved her. Now, she knew it was too late. She tried to paste a smile on her face, hoping it wasn't a grimace of pain. "I realize I was good, Cole, but not that good."

He didn't laugh at her attempted humor. "I'm serious, sweetheart." He shifted his weight and kept her close to his side, his legs still entwined with hers.

So am I, she thought, holding on to him so she wouldn't slip off the sofa. "Cole, don't."

His brows drew together in a frown. "Why not?"

"Let's just have tonight," she whispered.

He didn't say anything, merely stared at her with that fierce frown marring his face. Did he think all the hurt would go away just because he'd said he loved her? Could his words force his father to accept their reconciliation? Not in her wildest dreams. "Cole, I—"

"Don't," he said shortly, then blew out a frustrated stream of breath, scattering her bangs across her forehead. "You're right. Let's have tonight and not worry about tomorrow."

"Thank you," she said, grateful he wasn't going to press the issue. He might tell her he loved her now, but how long would it be before he crushed her already-battered heart? History had repeated itself twice. She'd never survive having her dreams shattered a third time.

"Don't thank me yet, sweetheart."

She stole a glance at him. The shield concealing his emotions was back in place. While she hated that she'd done that to him, she knew it was necessary. But they still had tonight.... "I'll thank you in the morning," she purred.

Cole gaped at her. The woman was incredible. "Again?" he asked incredulously.

"Hmm," she murmured, sliding her leg between his thighs.

If all she was willing to give him was one night, then he planned to make the best of it. Tomorrow he would convince her otherwise. "You keep this up," he told her, "I won't be able to walk in the morning."

She giggled at the dark look he gave her. "Then we'll just have to stay in bed, won't we."

He placed a light kiss on her sweet, swollen lips. "Then I suggest we go there now," he said, reaching for their clothing strewn haphazardly on the floor. "I'd hate to embarrass Jenna when she comes downstairs in the morning and finds her parents doing things out of an X-rated movie."

MARNI LOVED WATCHING COLE sleep. The harsh planes of his face were softened, his full lower lip more relaxed. She lightly pushed aside a lock of hair that had fallen across his forehead, then brushed her lips gently against his.

"Hmm, good morning, sweetheart." Without opening his eyes, he pulled her against him.

"I have to go," she whispered against his lips, hating to leave the warmth of the bed and what she knew could be a very interesting morning. But the house was quiet and she didn't want Jenna to find them together. At least not like this. How could she explain to her daughter she'd spent the night with Cole but wasn't planning on spending the rest of her life with him? A contradiction to morality if ever one existed. No, it was better to slip out undetected and pretend last night never happened.

He frowned and opened his eyes. "It doesn't have to be like this."

Marni sighed. "Yes, Cole, it does."

He stared at her inscrutably. That damn barrier was back in place. Last night Marni had welcomed it, now she cursed its very existence. She'd give almost anything to know what he was thinking.

Perversely, she wanted to hear him say he loved her one last time. He didn't. Her heart sank and her eyes burned with unshed tears. She slipped away from him and reached for her silk robe. She pulled it over her nakedness, then tied the sash before standing.

"I need to get back to L.A. today," he said. "I thought we'd go to breakfast, then head back. There's a great pancake house overlooking the coast. Interested?"

"But I thought...weren't we staying through tomorrow?" Was he so anxious to get away from her he'd call their long weekend to a halt? *Oh, stop feeling sorry for yourself, Rodgers. This is the only way it can ever be between you.*

"Something came up," he said shortly, tossing back the covers, revealing the hard, lean length of his body. "I have a plane to catch tonight." He strode around the bed toward her.

Marni found herself a little flustered as she stared at his powerful, well-muscled body. Cole could have been a work of art, created by an ancient sculptor. Her breathing stopped when he reached around her to the chair she'd unconsciously backed into. He picked up a thick blue robe and slipped it over his broad shoulders, loosely tying the belt around his middle.

He eyed her curiously, then turned toward a tall bureau placed between twin windows. Opening the top drawer, he pulled out a small, square lavender velvet box. "I wanted to give this to you last night, but we...ah..."

"Were otherwise occupied," she finished for him, smiling at the memory of their lovemaking.

His mouth curved into a delicious grin. "I'm not complaining."

She returned his smile. "Neither am I," she whispered.

"Happy birthday, sweetheart," he said, and gently placed the box into her hand.

She hesitated for a moment, then opened it. Resting on soft lavender velvet were a pair of amethyst earrings. The delicate gold setting duplicated the small rose pin Jenna had given her at dinner, but in the center of each rosebud sat a perfect amethyst. "When did you..." She couldn't finish.

"Yesterday morning when Jenna and I went into town. I hope you like them."

"They're beautiful," she said. "Thank you, Cole." Snapping the box closed, she wrapped her arms around his waist. Standing on tiptoe, she placed a hesitant kiss on his lips.

The instant her lips touched his, he pulled her hard against him. His mouth slanted over hers, pushing her head back against his muscular arm. Marni grasped the fabric of his heavy robe, her knees weakening at the delicious onslaught of Cole's mouth. A sliver of hot need bloomed within her. She had to get away from him and now before it was too late. Before Jenna woke and came looking for them.

With effort, she tore her mouth from his and hid her face against his chest, trying to regulate her breathing. "I have to go," she said again, then stepped away from him on shaky legs. If she didn't leave right this second, she never would.

Dropping the earring box into the pocket of her wrapper, she turned to go. As she reached the door, Cole's voice stopped her.

"Marni?"

She couldn't look at him. She didn't want to see the questions burning in his eyes. Why couldn't he understand she couldn't stay with him now?

"I meant what I said last night."

She blanched, and tears sprang to her eyes at the tenderness in his voice. Her control slipped several notches, and in despair, she dropped her head against the heavy door. "I don't know what to say," she whispered in a strangled voice.

He was suddenly behind her, his hands on her shoulders. Resisting Cole was the hardest thing she'd ever done in her life. Leaving him in Elk Falls had been a snap compared to what she was going through now.

"Don't say anything, sweetheart." He brushed aside her wild curls and gently nuzzled the back of her neck. "You don't have to say anything."

"Damn you, Cole Ballinger," she said, then jerked open the door, slipping into the corridor before her resolve weakened completely.

"Hi, Mom!"

Marni stopped short at the sound of Jenna's cheery greeting. "Uh ... I was ... I ..."

A shy grin curved Jenna's lips. "It's okay, Mom. I understand."

"No, sweetie, you don't." Marni started toward her daughter. Somehow she had to make Jenna understand things were not as they appeared. Her parents had not reconciled, and from the gleeful expression lighting her daughter's face, Marni knew that was exactly what the girl was thinking.

"Morning, kidlet." The sound of Cole's deep voice rattled Marni's proverbial cage.

"Cole, I can handle this," she stated firmly. "Just go away."

"What is there to handle?" he asked, crossing his arms over his chest. "We didn't do anything to be ashamed of, Marni."

Jenna looked from Marni to Cole and back again, her smile widening. "It's okay, guys. You're not embarrassing me. I mean, what's the big deal? Denise's parents sleep together all the time."

Marni stared openmouthed at her daughter. Cole chuckled and she slanted a look in his direction, warning him to keep quiet. "Jenna, it's not . . . I mean . . . your father and I . . ."

Jenna giggled. "Gee, Mom. You're blushing."

"I am not," she said heatedly. Why were they even having this godforsaken conversation?

"Yes, you are," Cole told her, reaching out to pull her against his side. Obviously he wasn't the least bit upset.

She shrugged out of his grasp and glared at him before giving Jenna her full attention. "Sweetie, Dr. and Mrs. Lambert have been married for years."

"That's only a technicality," Jenna returned, sounding all too grown-up. "You and Dad could—"

"No," Marni stated firmly, divining Jenna's train of thought. "We couldn't."

"We could," Cole offered offhandedly.

Marni turned to stare at him in disbelief. He *had* lost his mind. Hadn't things been bad enough when *she* had dreams of happily-ever-after? How could he allow Jenna to harbor the same illusions? There was no chance of a future for the three of them as long as Carson Ballinger stood between them. "You've all lost your minds. I'm no longer a participant in this ridiculous conversation, and I strongly suggest we forget this incident ever occurred."

Marni squared her shoulders and marched purposefully down the hall to her bedroom, fully aware of the odd stares Cole and Jenna cast her way.

CHAPTER FOURTEEN

COLE PULLED THE RENTAL CAR into the semicircular drive of his parents' home in Elk Falls. Stopping beneath the barren branches of an ancient oak, he turned off the ignition, remaining inside the chocolate velour interior. A cursory survey of his surroundings mildly surprised him. Nothing had changed despite his lengthy absence.

His hand momentarily rested on the breast pocket of his sport coat, causing a crisp, crackling noise that sounded much too loud inside the interior of the rented Buick. After today, it might be some time before he returned home again. And when he did, it would be with Jenna, and Marni.

He stepped from the car and headed toward the massive brick structure. Funny, he thought, ringing the bell, how most of his childhood memories, at least the happier ones, were of his mother and their housekeeper, Gertie. He recalled his father as a stern disciplinarian and unbending authority figure. As far back as Cole could remember, his father had never once congratulated him on a job well done. Nothing less than perfection would suffice, simply because his name was Ballinger.

Cole pushed his thoughts aside as the large white door swung open. Gertie stood in the doorway, her chubby face beaming with happiness. "Ooooh, Cole, it's so good to see ya!" she squealed. Her eyes were moist when he stepped through the portal. "Now, you mind yer manners and give ol' Gertie a proper greetin'."

Cole chuckled and swept up the round little housekeeper in an affectionate hug. She smelled of baked bread and a splash of pine cleaner.

"Oh, let me go, you young devil," she demanded, wriggling out of his embrace. She patted his cheek as if he were still the small child she used to walk to the edge of the property to wait for the big yellow bus that took him to the local school.

Gertie tugged off his overcoat and hung it in the hall closet. "Come with me to the kitchen. I haven't seen y'all in years, and I'm dyin' to hear about that l'l angel yer mama's been goin' on and on about."

"I'd love to," he told her, his gaze searching the formal parlor to the left of the entry hall for any signs of life, "but I'm here to see my father. Is he in the study?"

At Gertie's reluctant nod, Cole crossed the foyer to his father's study. He didn't bother to knock.

Carson Ballinger stood with his back to the door, his hands thrust in his pockets. His shoulders slumped, he faced the long windows stretching from floor to ceiling overlooking what in a few months would be the rose garden, carefully tended by Miss Shaylene's loving hands.

His mother rose from one of the heavy ox-blood leather wing chairs in front of the antique mahogany desk. "It's good to see you again, dear," Miss Shaylene said gracefully, stepping toward him.

Cole kissed his mother's soft cheek. "I'd like to speak to him alone, please." His father hadn't bothered to acknowledge his presence. Cole supposed it was because he'd demanded this meeting when he'd called from Santa Barbara on Sunday morning. Carson must have an idea of what was coming.

"Whatever you have to say to your father, you can say in front of me." The sweet, lilting quality of her voice belied the hardness etching the contours of his mother's eyes. He wanted to spare her from the tension between the two Ballinger men, but if Miss Shaylene had made up her mind to stay, a bulldozer would have been hard-pressed to move her.

Carson glanced over his shoulder at Cole. "Sit down, son." His tone demanded compliance.

Cole faced his father squarely, vaguely aware of Miss Shaylene crossing the Aubusson carpet toward the liquor cabinet she claimed had been salvaged from the Yankees during the Civil War. "I'd rather not," he answered firmly.

Carson lifted his shoulders in what could have been a careless shrug. "Suit yourself." He strode from the windows to his desk, placing his hands on the back of the matching executive chair. "I'm glad you came today. The board of directors met over the weekend. We're transferring you to the Denver office."

"How convenient," Cole returned, sarcasm lacing his voice. He realized the move was a desperate maneuver for control on his father's part now that Carson's lies had been uncovered. Reaching into his sport coat, he retrieved the crisp white envelope and laid it on the polished mahogany desk.

Carson remained standing behind his desk. "What's this?" he asked, not bothering to pick up the envelope. His heavy brows drew together and he cast Cole a questioning glance.

Cole braced his hands on his hips. "My resignation," he stated flatly.

The sound of clinking glass shattered the heavy silence in the room. "Cole!" It was the first time he'd seen Miss Shaylene almost lose her poise.

Carson's frown deepened. "What the hell do you think you're doing?"

Miss Shaylene was instantly at Cole's side. "Explain yourself," she implored him gently, her composure firmly in place once again.

Carson's eyes darted from Cole to Miss Shaylene, a flash of irritation darkening his eyes. Obviously, he didn't appreciate his wife's interference. In fact, Cole couldn't remember his mother ever meddling in his father's business before. She had always been content to raise her children, tend her prize-winning roses and chair as many committees as she could fit into her schedule without depriving her family of her time. The perfect hostess, the perfect wife, the perfect mother.

Cole looked from his mother, then to his father. "I'm purchasing a radio station in Los Angeles," he told them. "I plan to run it."

"For chrissakes, why?" Carson thundered. "You've sued for custody of the child. Once the judge rules in your favor, you can take her anywhere. You're needed in Denver," he added with a note of finality.

"Not this time," Cole said quietly. "My daughter's home is in California. That's where I'm staying."

"Oh, dear," Miss Shaylene murmured, slipping into the wing chair again, pressing trembling fingers to her lips.

"Don't you ever learn?" Carson jeered. "She's using you, *again*. She knows you want the child and she's using the kid as bait."

His father's refusal to call either Marni or Jenna by name annoyed the hell out of Cole. "Jenna," he snapped. "My daughter's name is Jenna. And Marni. You remember Marni, don't you, Dad?'' In his growing anger, he didn't conceal his contempt.

"Very well," Carson conceded, "Marni. I knew she was trouble. That's why I finally gave her what she wanted."

Cole gaped at his father, momentarily stunned. Didn't he realize the jig was up? "What *she* wanted? You're confused, Dad. You got exactly what *you* wanted—Marni out of my life. Well, I've got a news flash for you. That wasn't your decision to make. It was mine."

Carson braced his palms on the edge of the desk and leaned forward. "Think about it, son," he said. "Marni made the decision. She came to me and used the child, *your child,* to get what she wanted."

"That's bullshit and you know it," Cole retorted, his tone rising dangerously. *"You—"* he pointed angrily toward Carson "—offered Marni money to get out of my life. What gave you that right? Dammit, we loved each other!"

Carson pushed away from the desk. "She loved the money I gave her," he roared.

"You lied to me," Cole accused. "Your own son." He turned away, no longer able to stomach the sight of his father. His prejudices had hurt too many people. Guilt surged through Cole with the reminder of how he'd blamed Marni when it had been his own father all along.

"Cole, please," Miss Shaylene pleaded softly.

"I'm sorry," he told her. "I never wanted to hurt you, but what he's done is inexcusable."

Cole looked around the room, and for the first time, he saw what Marni must have seen all those years ago. He imagined her fear at being summoned into this austere room. The rug alone had cost more than the trailer Marni lived in with her ailing mother. Nothing, not one object, offered warmth or compassion. The extravagant trappings Carson Ballinger surrounded himself with spoke volumes about the man.

"I did what I had to, to protect you," Carson defended himself. "That woman would have dragged you down to her level. She still will. She's no good, Cole. Why the hell can't you see that?"

He turned to face his father. "What I see is a scared, insecure eighteen-year-old girl who was bullied and manipulated. And despite what you did to her, she's still a warm and caring woman who has more love to give than anyone I know."

Carson emitted a rough sound like a grunt of denial and shook his head.

"She's a good person," Cole continued heatedly. "A wonderful woman and excellent mother. You could learn a few parenting techniques from Marni. Jenna's a great kid, and I have Marni to thank for that."

Carson sat in the swivel chair behind the desk but remained silent.

"It was my life, Dad. Mine and Marni's. Not yours. What do you have against her, anyway? That's the one thing I can't figure out." He paced the carpet, running a hand through his hair. "What is it about Marni Rodgers that scares you so much?"

"I can see she's gotten to you again," Carson said in disgust, looking at the dying embers in the ostentatious fireplace.

"What if she has? Are you going to pay her off again? How much are you willing to offer her this time?" The anger died away, replaced by sorrowful resignation. No matter what he said to his father, he knew the elder Ballinger would never accept Marni. The thought saddened him, but he couldn't allow that to prevent him from finally taking control of his life. If he didn't do so now, he'd never be able to live with himself.

"Cole, don't do this," Miss Shaylene whispered softly. "Don't walk away angry, dear."

He'd nearly forgotten his mother's presence. "No, Mother. What he did was unforgivable. Only this time, there's no Elizabeth to hold me hostage."

"Elizabeth was stupid," Carson snapped suddenly. "If she'd done as I'd told her, you'd still be married to her. She threw everything away because you couldn't get over your affair with Marni."

"Oh, my God," Miss Shaylene declared, her face paling. Leaning forward in the chair, her hazel eyes transfixed on her husband, she asked, "Carson, what have you done?"

"I knew he'd go running after the little tramp, so I took matters into my own hands to ensure that he didn't." He spoke as if Cole wasn't in the room. "Elizabeth was so much better suited to be a Ballinger. Even you have to admit that much, Miss Shaylene. She came from the right family, the right background, the right connections."

Cole stood transfixed, unable to believe the scene being played before him. Slowly, realization dawned. Elizabeth Wakefield had been better suited in Carson's mind because of what she had to offer Carson, not Cole.

"What Elizabeth had was Wakefield Computers," Miss Shaylene said, getting out of the chair, fire in her gaze. "You sacrificed my son's happiness for a company that Elizabeth would have inherited from her father."

Cole stared at his mother in astonishment. Her composure had more than slipped; it had vanished completely.

"He could have had everything," Carson countered, dismissing his wife with an imperious wave of his hand. "Hell, his children could have had everything."

Miss Shaylene glared at her husband. "You just don't get it, do you? You can't play with people's lives. You hurt my son, Carson, and I don't know if I can forgive you for that." She turned to Cole, her eyes bright with unshed tears. "I didn't know, Cole. I've failed you, and I am truly sorry."

He'd never doubted his mother's love, and instinct told him she spoke the truth. "You've never failed me, Mother."

She nodded, as if she didn't trust her voice enough to speak, and quietly left the room. Cole had never respected her more than he did right at that moment.

Turning to his father, he swallowed the scathing comment on his lips. The man who'd terrified him as a child, the man he'd gone out of his way to please all his life, sat quietly in the chair, staring at the spot his wife had vacated.

Turning away in disgust, Cole headed for the door. There was nothing left to be said.

"So this is it? You're leaving?" Carson asked, his tone laced with a mixture of disbelief and annoyance. "You're turning your back on your family for this woman?"

Cole hesitated for an instant, his hand resting on the brass door handle. "I'm not turning my back on anyone, Dad." He looked over his shoulder at his father. "You know where to find me. But unless you can accept Marni as my wife, don't bother."

Opening the door, he stepped through the portal. "If she'll have me," he grumbled to himself, closing the door on his father's astonished expression.

MARNI WAS BEGINNING to hate Fridays more than she did Mondays. After pulling her usual tour of duty in morning arraignments, she'd come back to the office to face one disaster after another. Three of the plea bargains she'd offered had been turned down, the defendants preferring to take their chances before a jury of their peers. Her boss was getting antsy about the Kendell jury still being in deliberation, and the trial of a woman accused of murdering her husband was scheduled to begin the following week. The merry widow managed to raise the exorbitant bail, despite the fact the prosecution was asking for the death penalty, and was now missing.

And to top off the glorious week, she hadn't heard a word from Cole since Santa Barbara. Jenna hadn't mentioned him all week, and Marni didn't even know if he'd returned from whatever business had taken him away from Los Angeles so abruptly. She'd felt like a teenager waiting for the phone to ring. Which was ridiculous, she thought, since she'd practically thrown his declaration of love back in his face.

Peg poked her head around the opened door. "Jury's in on Kendell," she said, her usual bright excitement replaced by an uncharacteristic somber demeanor.

Marni blew out a stream of breath, ruffling her bangs. "Any hint?" she asked, marveling at the jury's timing. Just in time to make the evening news. The networks couldn't have planned it better themselves.

"Nope. None," Peg answered quietly, then disappeared.

Marni sighed, then pushed away from the stack of probation reports she'd been reading. The jury had only been out for one week. The decision could go either way.

She slipped into the pearl jacket and adjusted the high collar of her scarlet blouse. Reaching into her purse for her cosmetic bag, she hastily refreshed her makeup, checked her hair and adjusted the red silk bow controlling her braided hair. Must look good for the cameras, she thought with mild irony, wanting this day to end so she could go home and drown her sorrows in a cappuccino. Maybe she'd even add a dollop of whipped cream for good measure. No sense wallowing in self-pity without the benefit of extra calories.

After slinging her purse over her shoulder and picking up her briefcase, she left her office. "Have you told Dorlan?" Marni asked Peg, leafing through a stack of mail.

"He knows," Peg answered, her gaze on the computer monitor. "Said to tell you to handle it."

Marni shrugged aside Peg's unusual behavior and concentrated on the task at hand. Still, she was about to receive a ruling on her first capital case. Couldn't her secretary at least show a little enthusiasm? "I'll call you when it's over." Hell, where was her own enthusiasm, for that matter?

Peg nodded absently and slipped on the earphones to the dictation machine. "Uh, Marni?"

When Marni remained silent, Peg said, "Good luck."

She gave her secretary a weak smile. "Thanks."

Marni left the office and walked the two blocks to the courthouse. She hesitated for a moment, then slowly mounted the concrete steps leading into the ancient building. Hard to believe, she thought, that two months ago her life had changed on these very steps. Until that day, she knew without a doubt the direction her life was taking. She owned her own home, she had a beautiful daughter, and her career had definitely been on the upswing with the conviction of Kendell. Or so she'd thought until she'd literally run into Cole.

Now, no constants remained in the life she'd built for Jenna and herself. She still had her daughter, but Cole had threatened that when he'd filed for joint custody, and sometime within the next few weeks, a judge could change her life forever.

Entering the courthouse that altered so many lives, she slowly walked toward the assigned room where in a matter of moments yet another person's fate would be decided. She wondered why she hadn't been met by a deluge of hungry reporters. Slipping through the old wooden door, she entered a deserted room. The wooden benches resembling pews were empty. The fourteen chairs in the jury box were unoccupied. Not a clerk, bailiff or court reporter in sight. Confused, she glanced at the judge's bench. Judge Gladstone's gold-tone nameplate resting atop the wooden rise assured her she was in the right place.

The shuffling of papers caught her attention, and she turned toward the noise. The defendant's table, her befuddled mind registered. Her mouth fell open in shock.

Cole.

And Jenna, still dressed in her school uniform.

"What're you doing here?" she asked when words could pass coherently through her lips.

Jenna spun around in the hard wooden chair, a pair of drugstore bifocals resting precariously low on the bridge of her nose. "My client deserves a fair trial," Jenna announced, her chin held high. The navy blue knee socks and black-and-white saddle shoes seriously detracted from the professional aura Jenna had attempted to project. As did the bun secured haphazardly atop her head.

Marni blinked several times. "Your what?" she asked cautiously, the sound echoing throughout the empty chamber.

"My client," Jenna repeated solemnly, pushing the clear plastic rims higher on her nose. They slid back down and Jenna sighed in frustration.

"Cole, what is going on here?" Marni asked, growing more confused with each passing minute.

Jenna huffily crossed her slender arms over her chest. "You must address my client through his counsel."

Marni was about to say something, but snapped her mouth shut. Uncertainty warred with curiosity. Just what were her daughter and Cole up to?

Her gaze traveled from Jenna to Cole. He sat looking forward, his features uncompromising, much like the last time Marni had been in a courtroom with him. The day of the custody hearing.

With a wariness she was becoming accustomed to, she pushed through the low swinging door and approached the pair, a little off-balance at the sight before her. She'd been summoned to the courtroom under false pretenses. Peg! she thought suddenly, finally understanding her secretary's peculiar lack of interest in the Kendell penalty. She'd been set up, and Peg had been enlisted in their cause. So much for loyalty.

"If you'll have a seat, please, we'd like to begin." Jenna turned her back on Marni, her attention on a stack of papers in front of her.

Marni deposited her briefcase on the prosecutor's table with an ominous thud. "Begin what?"

Exasperated, Jenna expelled a deep breath. "My client's trial."

Marni lifted a brow at her daughter. "I'm not sure what you're up to, but first of all, you can't have a trial without a judge." She risked another glance at Cole, wishing he would turn her way. If only he'd give her some sign, a reassuring grin, anything, to set her at ease.

Jenna frowned in sudden dismay, causing the dime-store glasses to slide farther down the slope of her nose. "I'll be the judge."

Marni smiled at Jenna's easy resolution but shook her head. "You can't be the judge," she told her, leaning against the table, her hands braced behind her. "You're playing the attorney."

"Well it's *our* trial and we'll do it *our* way," Jenna responded, undaunted by the slight obstacle.

Cole's jaw twitched as if he was trying to repress a smile. Marni's curiosity finally won out over her confusion, and she decided to play along for the moment, wondering just how far Jenna planned to go. "What about a court reporter?"

Her daughter frowned in concentration, then looked at Cole for guidance. "We don't need one," she finally answered when Cole offered no solution.

Marni crossed her arms over her chest. "Yes, you do." Jenna should have known that one, Marni thought, as many times as she'd reviewed court transcripts at home while preparing for a trial.

"Dad, do you want one?" the girl asked her father. Cole leaned close to Jenna and whispered in her ear. She nodded curtly, a smug grin on her pretty face. "My client wakes his..." Jenna paused and turned back to Cole for clarification. "*Waives,*" she emphasized with a snap of her fingers, "his right to a reporter. Any other objections, Mom?"

Cole cleared his throat, smothering a chuckle. The sign she'd hoped for had been issued. Amusement and relief took the edge off the trepidation she'd experienced upon entering the courtroom. "No. No further objections."

Jenna's eyes brightened with anticipation. "The defense calls its first witness. Ms. Marni Rodgers."

Marni straightened with alarm. The lighthearted atmosphere had taken a serious detour into dangerous territory. A detour she wasn't prepared to follow. "What?" She'd imagined Jenna calling Cole to the stand, but *her?* Hadn't she been through enough? After the night in Santa Barbara when Cole questioned her, she couldn't possibly offer any further defense of her actions. She'd told him everything. Well, almost everything, she amended.

Before she could protest further, Cole stood and faced her, the tender look in his eyes nearly unraveling her. A gentle smile canted the corners of his mouth. The jacket of his charcoal suit molded his wide shoulders, the crisp white of his shirt emphasized the brightness of his eyes. He looked entirely too handsome for her peace of mind. *What peace of mind?* She hadn't had a tranquil thought since he'd walked back into her life.

"I'm not taking the stand, Jenna. We're finished."

Jenna spun around, and a few of the pins holding her thick hair clattered to the table. The bun atop her head slid threateningly to the side. "We're not done!"

"Cakes are done," Marni corrected, reaching for her briefcase. "And we're finished." The ton of work piled high on her desk needed her attention. "I have to get back," she told Cole. "Will you take Jenna home?"

Jenna shot her a shrewd look. "You're a witness, Mom."

Marni's gaze darted between father and daughter. Cole casually hitched his hip against the low balustrade separating the forum and crossed his arms over his chest. The look in his eyes mirrored Jenna's. Marni had a sinking suspicion that if she bolted for the door, he'd attempt to block her path. Claustrophobic anxiety washed over her. "I won't do this," she said to him.

"Afraid?" he asked, lifting his brow. He appeared to be enjoying her struggle.

"I am *not* afraid," she returned hastily, ignoring his lopsided grin.

"Then take the stand," he challenged. The grin turned into a breathtaking smile.

"Please, Mom," Jenna begged. "You're gonna ruin everything."

Cole instantly recognized Marni's fear. The gold flecks in her eyes practically glowed as her gaze darted from him to Jenna. She turned away from him, her hand still gripping the handle of her briefcase, but then her shoulders slumped in defeat. She cast him a final glance, wariness flickering over her features, before she relented and took the stand.

Cole returned to the chair beside Jenna, praying Jenna's make-believe-trial theory would prove successful. He'd been hesitant at first, but when Jenna had presented *new evidence,* she'd been adamant, insisting her plan would work and Marni would be won over to their side. The fact that Jenna saw them on separate sides convinced him to go ahead with the ploy. Now all he could do was sit back and wait. And hope.

Jenna leaned forward at the table and jotted something down on the legal pad in front of her. "Why did you leave Elk Falls?" she asked as soon as Marni was seated.

Marni's brow creased. "We've been over this," she answered, her tone indicating her impatience with the interrogation. "I really don't think—"

"Mom, you're not cooperating," Jenna protested in agitation. "Why did you leave Elk Falls?"

Marni shifted in the chair, her gaze fixed on the empty jury box. "I was young and I believed your grandfather." The words escaped in a quiet rush.

Cole smiled. Jenna *had* been right. Marni was a lawyer, and the one thing a lawyer never did was lie to the court.

Jenna chewed on the eraser of her pencil as she consulted her notepad. "Did he lie to you?" she finally asked, strolling casually around the table toward the judge's bench.

A flicker of annoyance hovered in Marni's eyes. "I didn't think so then, but now I know differently," she answered, tugging on the sleeves of her jacket.

"Would you do it again?" Jenna stood on tiptoe and peered over the top of the bench, waiting for Marni's answer. "Well?" she prompted, moving on to the court reporter's transcription machine, testing one of the keys with a light touch of her finger.

Marni gave her a smile that lacked conviction. "Hindsight is twenty-twenty."

"Huh?" Jenna asked, obviously confused. She stepped away from the transcription machine and smoothed the kick pleats of her blue plaid skirt.

"I can't say, Jenna. Unfortunately, we can't rewrite history," Marni clarified, her gaze traveling restlessly around the empty courtroom.

Jenna pushed the glasses farther up her nose and strode determinedly back to the table. She winked at Cole and the glasses slid again. "Did you ever attempt to return the money to my grandfather?"

Marni finally looked at Cole, fear darkening her eyes. He waited with more patience than he'd ever dreamed he possessed. This little maneuver was a risk, but one he prayed would work in his favor. He'd apologize later, but he wanted *everything* out in the open. No more secrets. When Marni agreed to be his wife, he wanted her to be completely free of the deceptions of the past.

Jenna repeated the question, reaching across the table to the stack of papers she'd been shuffling earlier. Marni still didn't answer. Shock registered on her face when Jenna picked up a small blue book about the size of an index card from the pile. "What is this?" she asked.

"A passbook," Marni whispered.

"What's in it?" Jenna pressed, her eyes nervously darting to Cole.

He nodded his reassurance, willing Jenna to continue but hating himself for putting Marni though more pain. The knowledge that he was hurting her again almost made him stop Jenna. Almost.

"Money," Marni answered shortly. She lifted a trembling hand to her temple and massaged the area.

"Where did the money come from?" Jenna's voice caught, and Cole stood, ready to put an end to the game. Jenna had been enthusiastic when she'd cooked up this little scheme, but if his daughter was hurting as well as Marni, then he'd stop the charade now. At least Jenna's part in it. No way would he let Marni off the hook yet— they were too close.

"Jenna, don't." Marni's voice was shaky and her eyes bright with moisture.

Jenna darted to the witness box, placing her hands on the wooden platform. "Mom, you've got to tell him," she begged, tears choking her voice.

"Marni, answer the question," he said calmly, despite the churning in his stomach. The two most important women in his life were in pain but he couldn't stop. Jenna was right. Marni had to tell him everything. If they were going to have a future together, a secure future, then she had to trust him enough to tell him the truth.

Marni lifted her gaze to his. Tears welled in her eyes, blinding her. "What does it matter?" she asked, her throat tightening. "Why is this so important?"

He picked up something from the table and strode purposefully across the courtroom toward her. She wanted to run, but something kept her weighted to the chair.

Cole took the passbook from Jenna. "You okay, kidlet?" He slipped his arm around the girl and gave her a comforting squeeze.

Jenna nodded and took off the ridiculous glasses. "She has to tell you, Dad. She has to!" she cried, wiping the tears staining her face with the back of her hand.

The anguish in Cole's eyes ripped at Marni's heart with painfully sharp teeth. Why was he doing this? Hadn't they caused each other enough suffering to last a lifetime?

"I can tell you what it is." He closed the distance between them, coming to stand in front of her. "After you graduated from law school and landed the job with the D.A. as a clerk, you began making monthly payments to my father. You were repaying him."

"Where did you get that?" Marni demanded. Her gaze traveled to the young girl beside him. "Jenna?" Without a doubt, she knew her daughter was responsible for Cole learning about the money she'd tried to pay back to Carson. Every month, she wrote a check. Like clockwork, they were returned, so she'd put the money in a savings account in Jenna's name. She'd had no idea her daughter even knew about the money—until now.

"You should have told me, Marni. And you should have given me this," he said, producing a sheet of paper, yellowed with age.

Marni gasped, shock devastating her. *This* was the letter she'd written to him after Jenna was born. "You weren't supposed . . ." she whispered in disbelief, unable to finish her thought. Whatever happened to dying with dignity? she wondered absently.

"Then why did you write it?" he asked. "I think what's more important," he continued before she could respond, "is what this little note didn't say." The tenderness in his voice and the raw emotion shining in his eyes made her turn away.

Her gaze slipped to Jenna. She stood quietly near the defense table now, her Ballinger eyes bright with tears. She sniffed audibly, waiting for Marni's answer.

"What didn't you put in the letter, Marni?" Cole asked her again, his voice gentle and coaxing.

"I thought Jenna was the attorney," she countered, avoiding his question.

He moved closer, blocking her view of Jenna, demanding she give him her attention. "Tell me, sweetheart," he whispered huskily. "Tell me what you couldn't say thirteen years ago."

She released a deep, shuddering breath. For too long she'd dreamed and hoped. Too many times she'd had her dreams shattered either by her own actions or Cole's. She hesitated, torn by conflicting emotions. She wanted to tell him, to let him know how much she loved him, yet she continued to hold back. But what if . . .

Her life had been too full of what-ifs. What if she'd never taken the money from Carson? What if she'd attempted to contact Cole one last time after the letter came back? And now, what if she told him what he wanted to know?

Her emotions were out of control, but she was more tired of the struggle within her. She slowly lifted her gaze to his and instantly recognized the emotion softening his features. Love.

"I couldn't..." she started, but the words clogged in her throat. She didn't want to hurt him any longer, but she was afraid. More afraid than she'd ever been in her life.

"What couldn't you say, sweetheart?" he asked gently.

A sprig of hope planted itself within her and she fought to protect the hope from a heavy cloud of doubt. "I couldn't tell you how happy I was to have Jenna. That no matter what happened between us, no matter what I'd done, I'd always have a part of you. Every day of my life I'd have a wonderful, precious reminder of what we once had."

He reached over the platform separating them and grasped her trembling fingers in his warm hand. "What else?" he prompted, his eyes suspiciously moist.

Her tears flowed unchecked, escaping with the crumbling barrier surrounding her heart. The hope grew. "I couldn't tell you how hurt I was when you married Elizabeth. But no matter how much I hurt, I couldn't stop loving you. I've never stopped. I thought I had, but I was only lying to myself. Pretty pathetic, huh?" She laughed shakily and wiped away the tears with her free hand.

"Pretty damned wonderful, considering what an ass I've been." He gave her hand an affectionate squeeze. "I want to make it up to you, Marni. Let me love you. Trust me with your heart again."

Marni's heart slammed against her ribs. She loved him so much. "I'm scared, Cole," she admitted truthfully. "I won't survive another heartbreak."

He lifted her hand, gently brushing his lips over her knuckles. "Don't be afraid, sweetheart. Marry me."

Marni couldn't speak. Marry Cole? How could she? How could she not? Her gaze slipped past him to Jenna. She stood with her arms wrapped around her middle, worrying her lower lip with her teeth. Was this what Jenna wanted, too? Could they truly be happy together?

Jenna sighed in exasperation, her arms unfolding and slapping against her sides. "Mo-o-om, geez-oh-Pete."

So much for wondering what Jenna wanted.

"What about your father?" Marni asked Cole. She wasn't refusing his offer, but she wasn't exactly agreeing yet, either. Carson had come between them not once, but twice. How could they possibly have a future together if Cole's father continued to interfere in their lives?

The hopeful grin tugging at his lips caused her heartbeat to accelerate. "You're marrying me, not my father."

"Cole, I won't be the cause—"

"You're not." He stopped her, placing his fingers over her lips. "He has his own demons to deal with, and until he does . . ." Cole shrugged.

Marni understood. The matter was out of their hands.

"Marry me, Marni. I love you. I want you to be my wife. I want us to be a family."

Jenna clamped her hands on her hips. "Come on, Mom. Geez. Just say yes."

Marni stood and Cole released her hand. Slowly she stepped from the witness box and approached him. "Are you sure?" she asked, giving him one last chance to back out, to change his mind, all the time praying he wouldn't.

He grasped her hands in his, holding on to her with a fierceness that clearly told her he'd never let her go again. An abundance of love shone in those emerald eyes she'd always loved and knew she would until the day she died.

"I've never been more sure of anything in my life."

She smiled at him through her tears. "Yes, Cole. I'll marry you."

He pulled her into his arms, his gaze searching her face. "Are you sure?"

"She's never been more sure of anything in her life," Jenna answered for her, rolling her eyes heavenward as if asking for guidance in dealing with her stubborn parents.

EPILOGUE

"I ASK YOU, ladies and gentlemen," Marni addressed the jury, "is it Mrs. Hinkle's duty as a patron of Simpson's Market to be aware of a substance on the floor? No, it is not. The duty is required by the staff of the defendant."

She leaned against the plaintiff's table, crossing her ankles, one hand resting lovingly on her rounded tummy. As if in response to the slight pressure of her hand, the baby kicked, and Marni smiled contentedly.

"Because of the defendant's negligence," she continued, "my client was seriously injured when she slipped and fell in a puddle of milk. Her hip was broken in the fall and Mrs. Hinkle was therefore robbed of her daily pleasure of feeding the birds in the park across the street from her home. The plaintiff has suffered the agony and heartbreak of finding homes for her beloved cats. All fifteen of them. Cats that offered her comfort in her golden years."

Mrs. Hinkle dabbed at her eyes at the mention of the cats she'd been forced to give away because she could no longer care for them. Marni marveled at the woman's timing when one of the elderly jurors clutched her chest at the plaintiff's emotional display.

"When you commence deliberations, ladies and gentlemen, I ask you to consider how your own grandmother would feel being robbed of the simplest of pleasures, not to mention the pain and suffering of such a severe injury. The defendant has a duty to provide a safe and hazard-free environment for your grandmother to do her daily marketing. With that in mind, you can only issue a verdict in favor of the plaintiff.''

Marni returned to the table and slowly lowered herself into the hard wooden chair, supporting her weight with her arms behind her. Mrs. Hinkle patted her hand. ''Excellent job, dear. Simply excellent.''

The hairs on the back of her neck tingled, and she grinned again. Shifting so she could see the rear of the courtroom, she spotted Cole. Her heart flipped over in her chest and she marveled that after four years of marriage, he could still reduce her to delightful shudders whenever she saw him.

He gave her a lopsided grin and whispered something to the three-year-old girl on his lap, pointing at Marni. The blond imp craned her neck and waved wildly in Marni's direction. She returned the wave to her daughter, Shelby, then brought her attention back to the defendant's closing argument.

The defense attorney finished, and the judge adjourned until the following week for instructions to the jury prior to deliberation.

''Mommy,'' Shelby called, stretching her arms in Marni's direction.

She scooped the little one up in her arms. ''Mommy missed you today.'' Kissing Shelby's chubby cheek, she ignored Cole's frown. He treated her like porcelain no matter how many times she told him she was as healthy as a horse. And she could certainly hold her own child.

''I was on the radio, Mommy. Did you hear me?'' Shelby asked, playing with the bow of Marni's blouse.

''No, baby. Mommy missed it. What did you say?'' she asked.

"K-T-R-Y." Shelby sang the letters proudly, her Ballinger green eyes shining with happiness. "City's best." Her golden brows wrinkled in concentration. "Country," she finally finished.

"Did Daddy tape it?" she asked Cole, handing their daughter back to him. Her back had been aching all afternoon, but she'd never admit it to her overprotective husband. She had a Thanksgiving feast to prepare, and spending the night with her feet up was out of the question.

"Daddy taped it," he said, stealing a kiss in the process of maneuvering the overactive three-year-old into his arms.

Marni picked up her briefcase. "What time is Miss Shaylene's flight due?" she asked him, heading out of the nearly deserted courtroom.

Cole shifted Shelby onto his hip and took the briefcase from her. "She landed about twenty minutes ago. I've arranged for a car for her. Or rather, Liz arranged it."

"Where's Jenna? I thought she was coming with you."

Cole frowned, holding open the glass doors to the courthouse. "She went with Denise to the mall. I swear since that girl got her driver's license, she's never home."

Marni laughed. "I told you not to buy her a car."

"Don't remind me," he groused. Not only was Cole an overprotective husband, he was nearly impossible where Jenna and Shelby were concerned. At this rate, she mused, she'd have to sedate him when Jenna went to her junior prom in the spring.

The drive to Malibu was slow with the heavy holiday traffic. Marni settled back into the soft leather of the Jaguar and let the seductive music from Cole's radio station lull her into a state of relaxation. Her thoughts wandered, but she didn't stop them. The demons she'd once ought to keep at bay had finally been exorcised. Married to the man she'd always loved, with two beautiful daughters and another baby due in a matter of weeks, she didn't think her life could be any happier.

When Cole had purchased the station, as he'd promised, the first order of business had been a program change. Jenna hadn't been too pleased with her father's decision, but Cole wouldn't be swayed. And from the ratings they'd been racking up, Los Angeles *had* needed another country music station.

He reached across the console and grasped her hand, gently massaging the sensitive skin on her wrist. Sharp tingles of sensation skirted up her arms and settled in the pit of her stomach.

"I almost forgot." He smiled and glanced her way. "Peg called the house before I left. Your old boss phoned your office today. They've got an execution date for that Kendell guy you sent up. I guess Walter wanted you to know before the media plastered it all over the place."

Marni nodded. The day she'd received a ruling on Kendell's sentence, she'd handed in her resignation and accepted a position with Rebecca's firm in their litigation department. Suing grocery stores and inattentive drivers lacked the excitement of high-profile criminal cases, but it allowed her more time to spend with her family and didn't nag at her conscience.

He glanced in the rearview mirror. "She's asleep," he said with a quick jerk of his head toward the car seat strapped in the back.

"Her mommy's almost asleep, too," Marni said, setting her arm protectively over her tummy.

"You need to start taking it easy, sweetheart." His voice was low and husky, but no less concerned.

"I will. The baby's not due for another three weeks," she reminded him, shifting uncomfortably. Her sligh backache was picking up momentum. "As soon as th jury issues its verdict on Mrs. Hinkle, I'm going t leave."

By the time they pulled into the treelined drive of th Malibu Canyon home Cole had purchased, dusk had set tled over the beach community. A long black limousin was parked near the door, signaling the arrival of h mother-in-law.

The minute the car stopped, Shelby woke from h power nap, demanding to be sprung from the car sea Miss Shaylene was waiting at the door for them. "Nana! Shelby squealed, running into her grandmother's arm "Bring me surprise?"

Miss Shaylene smiled, catching the little girl as she flu herself into her grandmother's arms. "I have a big su prise for you, Miss Shelby. A very special surprise."

After customary hugs and kisses, they entered th house. The sprawling canyon home was warm and coz Someone had started a fire, and the scent of pine filled th open, spacious rooms on the lower level. Marni had falle in love with this house when she'd gone house huntin with Cole all those years ago, and she'd taken great pri and delight in decorating it herself. She'd kept the orig nal rustic air but added a few contemporary touches well, interweaving both of their tastes. The end result w comfortable elegance.

"Is Jenna home?" Cole asked his mother, frownin ferociously.

Marni felt sorry for him. Being the parent of a teena girl was not an easy job. She didn't think he'd find it a less difficult when Shelby reached Jenna's age. In fa he'd probably be even more protective, she thought wi

a wry grin, considering he'd actually had a hand in raising his younger daughter.

"She's in the kitchen shelling pecans for the pie,"
Shaylene answered, her attention on Shelby.

"Surprise, Nana?" Shelby asked.

"With your sister," she answered, setting Shelby down.

Cole headed toward the kitchen in search of Jenna.
Marni, Miss Shaylene and Shelby followed close behind.
He stopped in the doorway, his body tensing. A tingle of
alarm shot up Marni's spine, but she pushed the sensation away. Just more back twinges, she rationalized.

"Hello, son." Carson Ballinger's rich baritone drifted
across the room, and Marni froze.

Why now? she asked. Not once in the past four years
had Carson made any attempt to reconcile with his son.
Marni had occasionally prompted Cole to make the first
move, to bridge the gap with his father, but he'd stubbornly refused and she'd finally given up. She never knew
what the two men had said to each other that day so long
ago, but she had a suspicious feeling Cole had issued an
ultimatum to his father. Carson's presence in their home
apparently indicated he had finally agreed to whatever
terms Cole had lain down.

"Hi, Dad," Jenna said brightly, as if the thick tension
in the room were nonexistent. "Granddad's helping me
shell nuts for Nana Shaylene's famous pecan pie."

Marni stepped around Cole to his side. He stood stock-
still, staring at his father. His expression was unreadable.
The only sound in the room was the cracking of nuts.

Shelby pushed her way to the front, not one to be left
out of anything. Cole reached out and stopped her before she bolted across the kitchen. The girl eyed Carson
curiously. "Are you my surprise?" Shelby asked, wrinkling her pert nose.

Carson chuckled, but the sound carried an undertone of nervousness. "I think I'm everyone's surprise."

He looked older than Marni remembered, but no less imposing. His prejudices had caused them all so much pain that she'd expected to feel angry when she saw him. Instead, the only emotion she could summon was sadness.

Carson stepped away from the worktable and approached her. Cole stepped closer to Marni, but she placed her hand on his arm. She didn't fear Carson. She was no longer the frightened child he'd bullied and manipulated. She'd come a long way from Elk Falls and that dingy trailer on the outskirts of town. She was a junior partner in a prominent law firm, the mother of two, almost three, children and Cole's wife. But most important, she was her own person.

"What're you doing here?" Cole asked, his voice wary.

Jenna stopped shelling pecans, glancing nervously from Cole to Carson. She bit her bottom lip, a sure sign of her anxiety.

Carson smiled sheepishly. "Your daughter."

Cole frowned and he looked at Jenna. She answered with a weak semblance of a smile.

"Jenna wrote to me about a month ago. She said that I'd cheated her out of her father for twelve years and she didn't think it was fair that she and Shelby were being cheated out of knowing her entire family—" he gave Jenna a rueful look "—even though she referred to me as a mean old bastard."

Despite the gravity of the situation, Marni smiled and shook her head. Only Jenna, she thought.

Carson moved to stand in front of Marni, his gaze searching her face. "You've got a smart kid, Marni. And she's right. I am a mean old bastard and I don't blame you if you throw me out on my—"

"Carson," Miss Shaylene admonished, coming to stand beside her husband. "I hope you don't mind, Marni. Carson insisted on coming with me."

Shelby wriggled closer to her father, and Cole lifted her into his arms. She eyed the gray-haired man cautiously and laid her head against Cole's broad shoulder.

Jenna cleared her throat and crossed her arms over her chest. A determined glint lit her gaze. "Don't you have something to say, Granddad?"

Carson nodded and took a deep breath. "I owe you an apology." He looked at Marni. "I realize my son loves you. If you are what makes him happy, then . . ."

"Then what, Dad?" Cole prompted, his tone indicating he was unwilling to give so much as an inch.

"Then I have no choice but to accept her as your wife," he finished, not taking his eyes off Marni. "And because, as my granddaughter so eloquently put it, if I don't smarten up, I'll be a lonely old man nobody wants around."

Marni hesitated for a brief second. She'd imagined a scene similar to this a thousand times over the past few years, hoping that Cole and his father could reconcile their differences. She hated being the reason for their estrangement, but as Cole had once said, Carson had his own demons to put to rest. Apparently he had, with Jenna's prompting.

She took a deep breath and winced slightly at the sharp pain that shot down her back into her abdomen. Cole was right; she did need to start taking things easy.

"Are you all right?" Carson asked, concern creasing his brow.

Concern was the last emotion she'd ever expected to see on Carson Ballinger's face. "I'm fine," she answered with a hesitant smile, resting her hand over her tummy. "Your grandson's just trying to get comfortable."

"My grandson?" he asked in quiet amazement.

She nodded, and laughed at the expression on her father-in-law's face. "Miss Shaylene didn't tell you?"

"No." He smiled at his wife, and Marni was startled to realize how much he resembled Cole at that moment.

COLE AND MARNI STROLLED quietly, arm in arm, along the brick path leading to the gazebo near the end of the extensive grounds. The late afternoon air was chilly, but neither one paid any attention to the weather, enjoying a few moments alone after the Thanksgiving feast the Ballinger women had prepared. Cole led her up the steps to the ledge, where he propped against the lattice, pulling her to stand between his legs. She turned, her back to him, and rested her head against his shoulder. He wrapped his arms around her and the baby she carried.

"Are you sure Shelby's all right?" Marni asked, snuggling against Cole, enjoying the feel of his strong arms around her. When they were like this, she felt as if nothing could ever hurt them again.

He chuckled. "She's fine. It's Dad I'm worried about. He's read *Green Eggs and Ham* to her so many times he's beginning to recite it from memory." He pushed her hair off her shoulder. His hot breath caressed her neck and she shivered.

"Do you really think he's changed?" she asked. Her relationship with her father-in-law would never be a close one, but at least Carson had attempted to bridge the gap with his son.

"Hmm, we'll see," he answered absently, nuzzling her ear.

Marni sighed at the delicious sensations shooting through her. "Jenna has a date tomorrow," she told him.

"Like hell she does," he growled in response.

Marni pulled away and looked at him over her shoulder, not the least bit surprised to see the fierce frown marring his face. "Cole, Jenna's sixteen now."

"I was sixteen once, too. Remember?" He shook his head vehemently. "No way."

She turned in his arms to face him fully. "We need to talk about this. You can't—"

His mouth hovered near hers and the fight went out of her. His gaze darkened and he pulled her against him. "Be quiet, woman, so I can kiss you senseless."

"Yes, Cole," she said, slipping her arms around his neck. Her breath caught and her eyes widened. "Uh-oh. Cole?" she said against his mouth.

He lifted his head and sighed. "What now?" he asked.

"My water."

"Water?"

Marni laughed, and nodded. "Don't look now, but your shoes are getting soaked." When he still didn't catch on, she added, "We need to go to the hospital, coach."

Alarm, shock and sheer joy registered on her husband's features simultaneously. "My son has lousy timing," he said, slowly pushing away from the side of the gazebo. "Are you okay?" he asked.

"I'll be fine," Marni answered, walking carefully by Cole's side. "As long as you're with me."

With his arm possessively over her shoulder, he guided her with loving care toward the house. "Sweetheart, I'll be with you forever," he whispered huskily, tenderly kissing her temple. "You can count on it."

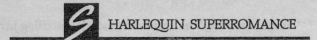

HARLEQUIN SUPERROMANCE

COMING NEXT MONTH

#666 AS YEARS GO BY • Margaret Chittenden
Showcase
The past: Englishwoman Bliss Turner falls in love with American
airman Paul Carmichael. But when the war intrudes, he leaves her,
unmarried and pregnant. She never sees him again. *The present:*
Simon Flynn is searching for "Bliss," the woman his grandfather
had loved during the war. He never dreamed he'd fall in love with
her granddaughter, Rebecca…or that he'd get caught up in the web
of deceit that had shaped the past—and threatened the future….

#667 FATHERS & OTHER STRANGERS • Evelyn A. Crowe
Family Man
Matt Bolt. A top homicide detective before he made one, almost
fatal, mistake and ended up with a bullet in his chest, another in his
leg. Then the final blow. His ex-wife dies, and his son—a child
he's seen only *twice*—is now in his care. Worse, the boy seems to
hate him. Enter Virginia Carney, a woman running from her past,
running for her life. And Bolt thought he had problems *before!*

#668 THE KEEPER • Margot Early
Reunited
Zachary Key married Grace Sutter for love—and for a Green Card.
When Grace found that out, she went home devastated. She
returned to Moab, Utah, to take over her father's Colorado River
outfitting company. Now, more than a year later, Zac reenters her
life. Something strange happened to him after she left—something
he doesn't remember. Grace is still in love with him, but does their
marriage stand a chance?

#669 A MOTHER'S LOVE • Janice Kaiser
Women Who Dare
Anne Leighton's ex-husband, an air force flyboy, has refused to
return her son after his "holiday" in England. His childless new
wife wants someone to mother. But not Anne's son! RAF Base
Commander Grant Sarver becomes an unlikely ally, yet it may
come down to a choice of loyalties—for both of them.

AVAILABLE NOW:

MILLION DOLLAR SWEEPSTAKES (III)

No purchase necessary. To enter, follow the directions published. Method of entry may vary. For eligibility, entries must be received no later than March 31, 1996. No liability is assumed for printing errors, lost, late or misdirected entries. Odds of winning are determined by the number of eligible entries distributed and received. Prizewinners will be determined no later than June 30, 1996.

Sweepstakes open to residents of the U.S. (except Puerto Rico), Canada, Europe and Taiwan who are 18 years of age or older. All applicable laws and regulations apply. Sweepstakes offer void wherever prohibited by law. Values of all prizes are in U.S. currency. This sweepstakes is presented by Torstar Corp., its subsidiaries and affiliates, in conjunction with book, merchandise and/or product offerings. For a copy of the Official Rules send a self-addressed, stamped envelope (WA residents need not affix return postage) to: MILLION DOLLAR SWEEPSTAKES (III) Rules, P.O. Box 4573, Blair, NE 68009, USA.

EXTRA BONUS PRIZE DRAWING

No purchase necessary. The Extra Bonus Prize will be awarded in a random drawing to be conducted no later than 5/30/96 from among all entries received. To qualify, entries must be received by 3/31/96 and comply with published directions. Drawing open to residents of the U.S. (except Puerto Rico), Canada, Europe and Taiwan who are 18 years of age or older. All applicable laws and regulations apply; offer void wherever prohibited by law. Odds of winning are dependent upon number of eligibile entries received. Prize is valued in U.S. currency. The offer is presented by Torstar Corp., its subsidiaries and affiliates in conjunction with book, merchandise and/or product offering. For a copy of the Official Rules governing this sweepstakes, send a self-addressed, stamped envelope (WA residents need not affix return postage) to: Extra Bonus Prize Drawing Rules, P.O. Box 4590, Blair, NE 68009, USA.

SWP-H1095

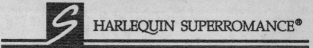

HARLEQUIN SUPERROMANCE®

A Superromance *Showcase* book.

As Years Go By
by
Margaret Chittenden

Cornwall 1943

Bombs fall. Gunfire echoes. The world is torn apart by war. But in the Cornish countryside, Bliss Turner meets and falls in love with wounded American airman Paul Carmichael. Then the war intrudes on their idyllic affair, and he leaves. They never see each other again.

Cornwall 1995

Simon Flynn is on a quest—to find "Bliss," the woman his grandfather Paul had fallen in love with during the war. Once in Cornwall, it isn't long before he finds her...and falls in love with her granddaughter, Rebecca. But Bliss has no memory of the past and an intense hatred of Americans. Simon must enlist Rebecca's aid in figuring out the puzzle. But as they unearth the past, old secrets are revealed—secrets that threaten their future together.

Watch for *As Years Go By* in November—the month of remembrance. Wherever Harlequin books are sold.

SHOW6

Become a Privileged Woman,
You'll be entitled to all these Free Benefits. And Free Gifts, too.

To thank you for buying our books, we've designed an exclusive FREE program called *PAGES & PRIVILEGES™*. You can enroll with just one Proof of Purchase, and get the kind of luxuries that, until now, you could only read about.

BIG HOTEL DISCOUNTS

A privileged woman stays in the finest hotels. And so can you—at up to 60% off! Imagine standing in a hotel check-in line and watching as the guest in front of you pays $150 for the same room that's only costing you $60. Your *Pages & Privileges* discounts are good at Sheraton, Marriott, Best Western, Hyatt and thousands of other fine hotels all over the U.S., Canada and Europe.

FREE DISCOUNT TRAVEL SERVICE

A privileged woman is always jetting to romantic places.

When <u>you</u> fly, just make one phone call for the lowest published airfare at time of booking— <u>or double the difference back!</u>

PLUS—you'll get a $25 voucher to use the first time you book a flight AND <u>5% cash back on every ticket you buy thereafter through the travel service!</u>